RAW NERVE

Also by Richard Greensted

Coming to Terms
Lost Cause
Parting Shot

RAW NERVE

Richard Greensted

HEADLINE

First published in 1998
by HEADLINE BOOK PUBLISHING

10 9 8 7 6 5 4 3 2 1

British Library Cataloguing in Publication Data

Greensted, Richard
Raw nerve
1. Thrillers
I. Title
823.9'14 [F]

ISBN 0-7472-1811-0

Typeset by
CBS, Felixstowe, Suffolk

Printed and bound in Great Britain by
Mackays of Chatham PLC, Chatham, Kent

HEADLINE BOOK PUBLISHING
A division of Hodder Headline PLC
338 Euston Road
London NW1 3BH

For Mum
Tireless supplier of warm cuddles and cold sausages

PROLOGUE

Strangely, there doesn't seem to be much blood. I mean, I don't know how much blood I was expecting, but I would have thought that there'd be more. Odd, that – disappointing, in a way. It would be somehow more satisfying if I were up to my ankles in it.

It's very quiet. Even with my ears still throbbing from the explosions, I know that. Three people in the same room and nobody's making a sound – mind you, you wouldn't expect much from those two, not now. But I can't hear any traffic, any signs of life coming from outside. When I'm feeling a bit stronger, a bit more certain of my legs, I'll probably get up and open a window. I'd like some fresh air, and I'd like to hear some noises, something normal like the rattle of a milk float or a postman's bicycle.

It won't be silent much longer, though. Someone will have raised the alarm, and they'll soon come crashing in. I'm looking forward to that, in an odd sort of way. Now it's done, and the whole thing's finished with, I need some company. I need to talk.

But maybe they won't just barge in. Perhaps they'll decide that it's dangerous, and they'll circle the house and try and talk me out with one of those loud hailers. I don't want that; I don't need that. They have no reason to be frightened of me. What I've done is all I'm going to do. Two shots and that's your lot. That's enough for anyone, isn't it?

It had to happen. I couldn't let it go on any more. I mean, I like to think of myself as a fairly reasonable human being, but what they did was totally unacceptable. Anyone in my position would have done the same, given the circumstances

1

and the opportunity. I hope they understand that.

I wish I had some mints with me. I've got a really nasty taste in my mouth, like I've been sucking pennies, and my stomach's a bit choppy. A Polo would be lovely. My mum always gave me Polos when I was feeling sick – if she couldn't put a plaster on, the next best remedy was a Polo. They're very comforting.

It's early still – six-fifty-four a.m. The time doesn't really matter, because I've got nothing else to do today. This was the only thing in my diary. I got here really quickly. There was no traffic, that time of the morning. It gave me some time to think, parked up outside the house. I thought of everything that had gone on, and whether I could have changed any of it, but it didn't change my mind. I knew it was going to happen.

I can smell them. There's a lot of different smells in this room, but I can definitely smell them. It's not particularly pleasant, but I can live with it. I won't be here much longer, in any case. I know they're going to come soon – if they don't, I'll have to ring them myself. I wonder what I'll say: 'Hello, there's been an accident and I need you to come as soon as possible'? That sounds a bit weak. 'Hallo, I've just shot two people dead. Please come round and sort it out'? Whatever – I've heard that if you call 999 they come round anyway, even if you put the phone down.

I really do need to open that window. If I could just get up, steady myself, I'm sure I'd feel a lot better. By rights, I shouldn't be feeling like this at all. I should be feeling much happier. Perhaps that'll come later, when I've had a chance to get things sorted out. A cup of tea, a nice chat with the police, a good long sleep – that should do it.

I wonder what they'll ask me about first. They'll need to get it all down on paper, and I don't want to forget anything. It's very important they have the whole story. It wouldn't make sense otherwise.

2

ONE

Michael grasped the slip of paper tightly, seemingly ready to scrumple it up, but Annie stopped him. 'Let me read it,' she said quietly. He relaxed his grip and she took the paper from him.

Hi—
Just wanted to let you know that it's extremely unwise to leave your Walkman's like that in the car. We should know – our car was broken into when our daughter left hers on the seat last week, and they took our camera as well!
Bon voyage.

'How kind of them,' Annie said, already knowing that Michael would not agree.

'Bloody Nosy Parkers,' he said, as if to confirm it. 'Typical Brits on holiday – they come to France and then all they want to do is talk to other Brits. Why can't they mind their own business? If I want to leave the Walkmans on the seat, I will! And they can't even write English – Walkmans doesn't have an apostrophe in it.'

'Perhaps it should be Walkmen,' Annie said. 'Anyway, I think it's very thoughtful to leave a note.' She said this without any intention of having a major disagreement over it; she knew precisely what Michael's reaction would be to this advice, which he saw as the worst kind of interference. Advice of any kind, however delivered, was difficult for him to accept. Every day he became more and more like his father: she loved them both in spite of their best efforts to annoy her.

3

They were standing in a little square in Bourdeilles. They had come to see the castle and then have lunch in the Hostellerie des Griffons, set on the bank of the River Dronne. The car was parked in the square, and Holly sat in the back as her parents debated the merits of the note. Aged four, Holly could already tell the difference between a proper argument and a mere difference of opinion, and she blithely ignored their discussion.

Annie, however, could see more in Michael's reaction than simply annoyance. For the first time ever, they had taken a three-week holiday: she had successfully argued that it took him a week to unwind and that she and Holly deserved to have him relaxed and happy for two whole weeks. To her great surprise he'd agreed; they had hired a *gîte* outside Bergerac and had taken three leisurely days to drive down from Calais. Michael did all the driving, even though Annie felt she was the better driver; she couldn't bear him as a passenger, and preferred to sit with her Walkman and listen to classical tapes as he shouted at 'bloody foreign drivers', his most vitriolic assaults directed, for no apparent reason, at Belgians.

Now, standing in the brilliant afternoon sunlight of the Perigord, she knew that he was ready to go back, anxious to return to work and discover his fate. He had appeared to keep his promise not to ring the office every day, although she suspected he made surreptitious calls when he went shopping, but as the holiday reached its conclusion he was becoming more tense, as if he were preparing himself for battle. She could read the signs so well, yet there was nothing she could do to ease his apprehension. She was sufficiently grateful that he'd given them as much time as he had; now he was leaving them, if only in spirit, and she had to accept it.

'Women,' he said dismissively as they got into the car. 'Only a woman could think like that.' He turned round to look at his daughter. 'Holly, you're to promise me you won't turn out like your mother. You'll never find a husband if you do.' Holly looked at him blankly, then smiled as if to humour him.

'Are we going home?' she asked.

'Yes,' Michael replied. 'And we'll have a swim and then, as a special treat, I'm going to barbecue.' Annie rolled her eyes theatrically and groaned. 'You don't have to eat it,' he continued with mock petulance.

'You know I love your cooking,' Annie replied, 'even when it's burnt.'

The drive back was uneventful. Annie took Michael's silence as further evidence of his preoccupation with what lay ahead, even though he often said nothing in the car. Superficially he was calm and content, looking tanned and fit, but Annie saw beyond that. In times of stress his face changed, skin stretched more tightly across bone, and he could lose all his colour in an instant. She longed to ask him if there was anything she could do to help, but knew better: Michael kept his fears to himself, determined to present himself as unflappable and phlegmatic, even to her.

Once back at the *gîte*, he opened a bottle of white wine and poured two glasses. Holly stripped off and retrieved her water wings, thrusting them into his stomach so that he had to attend to them. It was his turn for lifeguard duty: Annie eased into a garden chair on the patio and watched as they walked up the path to the pool. She sipped some wine and opened her book with little enthusiasm; she wanted to read but the book was dull, full of characters who talked and did little else. She needed, more than anything else, a night on her own with Michael. She wanted to look forward to dressing up, having a good meal with a nice bottle of claret, followed by warm sex. They had been married for eight years, and Annie thought they were getting pretty good at making love, even though they didn't get as much practice as she would have liked.

Holly saw to that – Holly and Michael's job. He worked for a financial news vendor – DataTrak International – as the sales director for Europe, the Middle East and Africa. He was constantly travelling, visiting banks and fund managers in his efforts to sell hundreds of computer terminals which they would install in their dealing rooms and stare at

5

all day. It was not, even by his own admission, an intellectual challenge, but the bonuses were phenomenal and he was a very good salesman. He used Annie when he thought it would help, and had taken her on several business trips. She would leave Holly with her mother, get some money to buy new clothes, and do a lot of sightseeing or sunbathing: in the evenings she would go to dinner with his clients and prospects, talking to bored and boring executives with big waistlines and dandruff. It was a small price to pay for living on expenses.

Michael had joined the company shortly after Holly was born, and was immediately sent to their head office in New York for what they described as 'orientation'. No sooner had he returned than he was making travel arrangements, too excited by the novelty to realise how lonely she felt and how desperately she needed him. Holly was not an especially difficult baby, but she didn't come with a manual and Annie struggled to cope: in the quiet times she would have appreciated Michael's presence to get her over the worst phase of her baby blues. But she never said a word. They had the rest of their lives to be together, and Michael was thriving, which counted for a great deal. Her time could come later.

A week before they were due to go on holiday, Michael got a call at home in the evening. It was Head Office; a man called Nick Zamboni, one of the top bananas according to Michael, told him that his immediate boss in London, Don Retzer, was leaving the company 'to pursue other opportunities'. The euphemism was well worn: pursuing other opportunities meant that Don had been fired. Michael was Don's protégé and they had become very close friends; he was shocked by the news and spent the rest of the evening shaking his head and saying that he couldn't understand it. Don was a quiet, thoughtful Canadian, a gentle man with genuine charisma. He ran the business well, as far as Michael could tell, and there was no good reason to get rid of him.

The shock soon wore off, to be replaced by uncertainty. With Don out of the picture, Michael had a chance to take his place. He was known as a producer, a man who regularly delivered his sales targets with the minimum fuss. He was respected, rather than liked, by the powers in New York: they failed to understand his humour and had their suspicions about his commitment as a team player. Michael worked, by and large, on his own, and rarely made any effort to cultivate allies at Head Office. That could count against him when they considered him as Don's replacement.

'Does it matter so much?' Annie had asked. 'Even if you don't get the job, so what? They'll look after you – they have to. You're too good to upset.'

'It doesn't work like that,' he'd told her. 'A new man in charge, he'll want his own people. It's almost *de rigueur* to fire everyone when you come into a new job. It shows you've got balls – you know, *pour encourager les autres.*'

'I think you're being a little pessimistic. Anyway, you'll get the job.'

They had left for the holiday without the situation being resolved. Zamboni had not called again, and Michael lacked the courage to call him, preferring to entertain increasingly fanciful notions about the final outcome. He had tried hard not to discuss it in France, but Annie could see the strain etched in his face.

She finished her wine more quickly than she'd planned. From behind the screen of pine trees which surrounded the pool, she could hear the sound of Holly's squeals and squeaks of delight as Michael played with her. He was probably naked; he often swam like that, and Annie would have liked to go up there and watch him. He had a good body, and the thought of this aroused her. In the dying afternoon heat, with the wine just beginning to reach her nerve ends, she was feeling very sexy. Her nipples tightened as she thought of what she wanted. Life was just so unfair: by the time she had an opportunity to do something about it, they'd both be too tired.

She fetched more wine from the fridge and paced restlessly around the patio before sitting down again. Michael's problem was inexorably becoming her problem; if he was

7

worried about work, then she should be too. She hated watching him suffer in silence, but felt that to confront him with it would only make matters worse. He didn't like to admit to doubt, another characteristic he'd inherited from his father. Michael's beliefs were black and white, and straight out of his father's locker: wives didn't work, men didn't complain, and all the rest was detail. He tried to live by a creed that was well past its sell-by date, a moral set which had no relevance in their complex lives. Secretly he might have acknowledged this to himself, but he would never tell her as much. He would rather let her make those decisions that contradicted his code than reach them himself in an explicit declaration of compromise.

Annie had learnt to live with this deception, condoning it by silence. Eventually, she reasoned, he would shed the pretence; he had already made concessions with the way he treated Holly, who had become a second love for him. His father would certainly not have approved of the way in which Holly was indulged and cosseted, her opinions sought and carefully considered. Michael was a modern dad, more liberal than Annie in many ways: she drew the lines, and Michael often rubbed them out. That inconsistency, that inability to hold a position, was one of the mysteries of men, she thought.

Holly and Michael appeared on the path, she running ahead in her little pink swimsuit, he ambling along as he rubbed his head with a towel. He was naked, just as she'd thought he would be, and she enjoyed watching him as he walked towards her.

'Mummy, Mummy,' Holly shouted as she approached. 'Daddy threw me in the pool and the water went up my nose.' She was neither concerned nor upset as she said this, and Annie stared over her head to follow Michael until he was standing right next to her.

'Put some trousers on,' she said quietly. 'You're making me horny.'

Michael made no effort to move away, his groin close to her face. 'Holly,' he said. 'Do you want a nice hot bath?' He looked down at Annie and smiled. 'It'll give us ten minutes.'

'That's more than enough time,' Annie replied. She grabbed Holly before she had time to disappear. 'Right, young lady, I'm going to run your bath.'

'Don't want a bath,' Holly said.

'Oh, yes you do,' Annie and Michael said in unison.

TWO

It was an unwritten rule that no one bothered to ask about anyone else's holiday. There were good reasons for this: no one cared, and no one had the time to tell or listen. The atmosphere in all of DataTrak's offices across the world was the same: one of pumped-up, hard-charging fervour where sales were everything and contracts had to flood into the building in an unceasing torrent. In response to these, the administrators generated reams of invoices which faithfully recorded every chargeable act of their clients. Small talk of any nature was superfluous, an unwanted obstruction in the scramble to produce revenue.

Michael nodded at a few people as he walked to his office. As the sales director he was senior enough to merit his own space, insulated by glass partitions from the thrumming backbeat of money being made. According to the strict criteria of the company, laid down in carefully written manuals produced by Human Resources, he could have a private office of certain dimensions with standard equipment – L-shaped desk, credenza, PC, DataTrak monitor, fax machine, executive chair, multifunction phone, two items from the corporate art collection (prints, not originals), two visitors' chairs. On the desk were his contact book, his diary and his in- and out-trays. The in-tray was neatly stacked with three weeks' worth of letters, memos, files, magazines, newspaper clippings, call reports, sales charts, budget plans and revenue analyses.

Senior as he was, Michael did not have his own secretary. Instead he had a sales assistant, Pam Shine. Pam was a short, dumpy woman of thirty who had joined DataTrak when it opened in London ten years ago: she had worked on every desk in the office and had a superficial knowledge of everything about the business. She had been assigned to Michael on his first day as sales director, and had guided him helpfully through convention, custom and practice. Nothing was too much trouble for Pam: she was one of those women on whom so many offices rely, hard-working without displaying any initiative and willing to undertake any task, much as she might privately grumble.

Michael hardly thought of Pam as anything other than a resource. Although she dressed well and was always neat, she had no obvious physical attractions, being far too heavy with a round, bland face, and he found it difficult to engage her in conversation about anything but work. He appreciated what she did, but that didn't make him any warmer towards her. He treated her almost as he treated his computer: it worked and it was useful, and he switched it on and off every day with the expectation that it would always perform as he wanted.

He dropped his briefcase on to the floor and stood behind his desk, relieved that it was still there and that his nameplate remained firmly fixed to the door. The pile of work which demanded his attention would have to wait; he knew that Nick Zamboni was camped in Don Retzer's office and would be looking for an immediate meeting. He could feel his skin tingle as he anticipated what lay ahead, a day of meetings and discussions which might ultimately seal his future.

Pam came in with a big grin on her face. 'Somebody caught the sun, then,' she said. He had not been looking forward to this initial chat with her: Pam was a little too interested in his personal life for his liking, sending Christmas cards to his home which were also addressed to Annie and Holly and never forgetting his birthday. He didn't want to talk about his holiday, a preference which everyone else understood but which Pam ignored.

'I managed to get a few hours working on my tan,' he replied, hoping this would be the end of it.

'Well, you certainly look fit and ready for action. I hope

11

you got a lot of rest – have you looked at your diary yet?'

'Haven't had a chance. What's the plan?'

'Nick wants to see you straight away, then you've got a sales team meeting at ten which he's going to sit in on. Lunch with those guys you can't stand from Morgan Stanley, conference call with New York to go through the budget at four, then a product development meeting at five-thirty. You're going to be a busy boy.' She grinned again and raised her immaculately plucked eyebrows.

'Do I need to take anything with me for Nick?'

'Not that he's said.'

'Have you heard anything?' One of Pam's strengths was her finely tuned antennae: if anyone knew what was likely to happen now Retzer was gone, it was Pam.

'Nothing. Nick's in charge and he hasn't said anything. He hasn't even said when he plans to go back.'

'OK. I'll try and catch up with you later. Wish me luck.'

'Hang on,' Pam said as he started out of the office. 'Your tie's not straight.' She moved towards him, obviously ready to sort it out for him, but he avoided her and continued to move away.

Nick Zamboni was a legend. Everyone who knew him feared him. He lived for nothing but work, regularly putting in fifteen-hour days and travelling almost constantly. He was fifty-six but looked fifteen years younger, his face barely lined and his body still taut. His tailored suits and starched white shirts accentuated the aura of fitness and vigour. The only blemish on his physique was a small scar across his right temple, apparently gained during an action in Vietnam for which he was awarded a Purple Heart. Zamboni, so office anecdote had it, would have preferred to pursue his military career but was considered too unstable. Michael could believe that.

When Michael stepped into the office Zamboni was hunched over his PC, typing laboriously with one finger. Michael guessed that he would be composing an illiterate e-mail to some unfortunate subordinate: Zamboni regularly fired off twenty or thirty electronic missiles every day, berating salesmen or flaying developers in his inimitable style which cared nothing for punctuation, spelling, grammar, syntax or even upper and lower case. An e-mail from Zamboni was always unwelcome.

Michael hovered uncertainly as Zamboni keyed in his flaming commentary. Then he hit the return button with venom and swung round on his chair to face Michael. 'Hi. Close the door.' Michael did as he was told and bravely sat down without instruction. 'Three weeks, huh? That's a hell of a long break, don't you think?'

Michael shrugged and managed a weak smile. 'I've got a good team, and August is always slow,' he said in justification. Zamboni frowned upon any time off, for whatever reason: when his own wife had died of cancer, he was reputed to have come into work straight after the funeral.

'You're right there. August is slow in this region. Your sales numbers are shot to shit. Doesn't happen anywhere else. Asia Pacific's up this month by ten per cent, and Latin America's already made budget for the year. What's the story?'

Privately Michael sighed. This was a battle he could never win. Zamboni cared nothing for cultural differences, and refused to believe that potential clients might want to go on holiday. 'Well, I can only say that we've tried everything we can to get the numbers up during the summer. We do special promotions, corporate hospitality, squeeze marketing, the whole nine yards. Nothing works. Buyers don't buy in July and August. But, if you have some new ideas, I'd love to hear them.'

'Michael, you're the sales director. We're paying you the big bucks to come up with ideas. Jesus, you're not even maintaining your call ratios. Twenty calls a month, that's all I ask for. Not one of your sales people has managed to hit the target for August. My opinion, that stinks.'

There was nothing to say, so Michael said nothing. Apologies were definitely out of order, an indication of weakness, and any attempt at justification would be futile. He would just have to ride out the storm.

13

'Retzer,' Zamboni continued, 'he didn't pay enough attention to this. I spent all weekend looking at the numbers, and he has left one hell of a mess. That puts you on the spot, buddy. People are looking at this region and wondering why we bother. It's dragging everything else down. You're the point man here, the guy we're relying on to turn it around. So what are you going to do about it?'

'We'll make budget, Nick. We always do.' This, at least, could not be disputed. Since Michael had joined DataTrak, he had always delivered his required numbers and, as sales director, he had made sure his team delivered theirs.

'Make budget. You know, that doesn't really excite me. I see the other regions and they always exceed budget. They're always ahead, never chasing the target. Do you know what you get for making budget? You get a pat on the back and nothing else. If you're some dumb sales jock, and you're not part of senior management, you expect a bonus for making budget. But you're a director, for Christ's sake. You're expected to do more. Making budget is what you're paid for – it's the minimum acceptable performance. Exceeding it is what we want out of you – consistently. Do you understand that?'

'Absolutely. And we have a number of initiatives planned for the rest of the year to help us achieve that goal. Do you want me to run through them?' Michael was staying calm in spite of his growing unease.

'Save it. We need a fresh approach. We need someone to come in and take a completely unbiased look at this region – someone who isn't carrying around all these preconceptions about what will and won't work here.'

Zamboni's cold stare, delivered through crystalline eyes, bored through Michael. The verdict had been announced: the corporation did not want Michael as the new regional director. There was no room for debate or compromise. Zamboni had decided and that was enough; no one would dare raise a challenge, least of all Michael. A bad word out of place now could see him losing even more, and he was not prepared to let that happen.

14

'Can I ask who that's going to be?' Michael replied, trying not to sound either disappointed or angry.

'Skip McMaster.' Zamboni held his stare, as if he could detect the slightest hint of dissent.

'Skip,' Michael said, frantically trying to put a face to the name. It meant something, but not enough.

Zamboni immediately picked up on his hesitation. 'He's running our office in Cleveland. Done a great job. Knows the products and sells them effectively. He's got to get a few things sorted out and then he'll come over.'

'That's great news. I'm sure Skip will be a valuable asset over here.' Michael tried to invest his remark with as much sincerity as he could muster, using the corporate language he had learnt to hide his true reaction.

'Yeah, well I'd get ready for some fireworks if I were you. Skip's got drive, and he'll make whatever changes he thinks are necessary. He's already given me some of his ideas and I like them.'

Michael struggled to rescue some lost ground, even as the world appeared to be disintegrating beneath him. 'Would it help if I called him, gave him some background on the state of play here?'

'That's your call, Michael.' Zamboni paused, letting the information sink in. 'Now, I need to do some things before our sales team meeting. We'll talk more later.' He turned back to his PC to signal that the meeting was over. Michael got up and left with what he hoped was deliberate and positive body language and, once out of sight, rushed straight back to the sanctuary of his own office.

Annie stood in the kitchen and looked at the small mountain of washing she had dumped on the floor. All morning she had waited for Michael's call; several times she had gone to the phone and started to dial his direct number but had stopped before being connected. She felt sick, her anguish much more to do with Michael's possible disappointment than her own. For herself she was not troubled by the prospect of Michael losing out: in many important ways she wanted him to remain where he was without adding to the pressures of his working life, but she realised that this was a selfish view and that Michael would be badly affected if he were not chosen to succeed Don Retzer. Balancing these conflicting desires, she found herself fretting for him and his aspirations.

Annie was, by her own criteria, a supportive wife. She recognised that Michael was ambitious and was prepared to encourage this without speaking of her own needs and fears. He was naturally insecure, feeding off praise and constant reaffirmation of his worth, a fact to which she had become inured. She stroked his fragile ego when necessary, consoled him when he felt he was receiving insufficient recognition, and hardened herself against the inevitable depression he suffered whenever his ambitions were thwarted. If he appreciated her sacrifices, he never said as much, but she reasoned that it was enough that he didn't actively complain. She could endure his silence on this matter, a small price to pay for the other things he gave her – comfort, laughter, love and, occasionally, real joy.

The laundry festered before her eyes but she did her best to ignore it, skirting around the pile as she prepared Holly's lunch. Why didn't he ring, just a quick call to tell her what had happened? Perhaps he was too busy, too elated, to get to the phone – but then, perhaps he was too crestfallen, too sad, too . . . ashamed? She didn't want to think about it, but nothing else mattered. Without knowing why, this had become for her a day like no other, when many matters would be resolved for better or worse. Instinctively she knew that much more than one wretched job, one stupid pay rise, depended on how it went today in the office, and her whole body tightened at the enormity of it all. Why didn't he ring?

THREE

Everyone said that Michael and Susannah Lensman were made for each other. Whilst other couples might grow apart until there was nothing left to keep them as a unit, Michael and Annie appeared to thrive only in each other's company, and it was certainly true that they were happiest when they were alone together. In the early days of their marriage they had been sociable, with a wide circle of acquaintances and plenty of dinner parties, but they had gradually culled these until they were left with just a few very close friends. Even these friendships were not conducted on conventional lines: weeks could pass without any contact, behaviour which didn't seem at all odd to them.

They had been married for eight years, moving after eighteen months from their first house in Raynes Park to a much grander, but very shabby, detached Edwardian house on the fringes of Wimbledon village. With every bonus they had undertaken some renovation, until they had refurbished all the main rooms and replaced plumbing, heating, wiring and the roof. Michael refused to do any work on the house beyond changing a light bulb or a plug, arguing that he was not an expert and his time was too valuable to waste when there were perfectly good workmen to do the job. Annie was, as usual, quietly complaint: after all, she had not married him for his DIY skills.

They were careful with their money without being mean. Their parents had taught them the values of patience and prudence, and they saved whenever they could. Annie had come from a poor but well-educated family, living in a draughty house in Purley where no room was ever warm, even in summer. Her father was a tax inspector with a great love of nineteenth-century French literature: amongst the papers in his briefcase one could always find a well-thumbed book by Zola or Balzac. Her mother used her days productively, making curtains, cushions and lampshades when she wasn't cooking pies and puddings. Annie had an older sister, Mary, who had married an Army officer and now lived in Germany with their three children.

Michael's background was similar, although his parents were slightly wealthier. His father had been a banker for a small City institution, working for them all his life until he died in his vegetable garden one cold Sunday – 'Just as he would have wanted,' his wife said. She remained in the family home after his death and lived on the generous benefits paid out by the bank. Peter, Michael's younger brother, hadn't progressed beyond his time at Exeter University and had never left home, doing a succession of petty local jobs and justifying this by telling anyone who would listen that his mother needed him. Her opinion was considered irrelevant, although Michael suspected she would have been quite happy to see Peter leave the nest.

At thirty-four, Annie was two years older than Michael. When they had met – at a party organised by a mutual friend – she had found him very young but interesting. He was just starting out on his professional life and was a little self-important, preferring to speak about himself more than anything else. But, despite his awkwardness, he left her in no doubt that he was keen on her and she found herself flattered. Their early dates were difficult, mainly because he seemed so inexperienced in the company of a woman, but this only served to strengthen her attraction to him. He was different, his youth completely natural and without the affectations that older men displayed when they were with her. With gentle coaxing and a lot of perseverance, she gradually got Michael to the stage where he knew he wanted to be with her for ever, and they were married in a quiet registry office ceremony.

Annie had always thought that she would have been happy

without children. She did not consider herself to be a natural mother and she had seen many of her friends wilt as they struggled to deal with motherhood. She saw their tired eyes, their weary limbs, their sagging spirits; she listened to them as they complained about the size of their hips and thighs and the sudden disappearance of their sex lives. With Michael she was content and secure and had, she believed, no need to threaten that with the introduction of children.

Michael was less sure. For him, starting a family was something that had to be done, even though he held no definitive timetable in mind. It was just a notion and, like many other things in their marriage, it would rely on Annie if it were ever to come to fruition. He had expressed his opinion, and the rest was up to her. Dutifully, but with much apprehension, she had come off the pill after one of their vague conversations and Holly arrived without much effort. It was a pregnancy which others could only dream of: Annie suffered little and the delivery was all over in three hours. Her excess pounds dropped off her in no time and Holly began to sleep through the night at four months. Knowing nothing else, Michael assumed this was normal and couldn't understand why others marvelled.

Holly was considered to be a good baby, a reasonable toddler and now, aged four, an extremely bright and likeable child. She was not beautiful, but probably would be in later years: she had her mother's dark eyes and pale skin, but her hair was still thin and wispy and refused to stay groomed. Michael, as was only natural, adored her and did his best to spoil her, but Annie tempered his indulgence with her own mild and inconsistent discipline. She was surprised by how easy it all seemed, but was wise enough to know that this was the exception and she had no desire to push her luck just yet. Another baby was going to have to wait: Annie wasn't ready to disrupt her life all over again, whatever Michael might have liked.

One of the most unexpected bonuses of Holly was the growth of Annie's breasts. She had always been slight – between a size eight and ten – and her chest was never a major feature. With the arrival of Holly, her bosoms blossomed and, even after she stopped breastfeeding, they remained magnificently plump. Michael was enthusiastic, in spite of earlier protestations that he was not a great fan of large breasts, and Annie was delighted. She carried her new *embonpoint* with pride and often checked them in the shower for signs of shrinkage. When they made love, Michael treated them with renewed vigour and passion, for which Annie was both grateful and inspired.

Michael and Annie were on their way: neither could have said where it would ultimately lead, but they both felt that they were heading in the right direction. They were comfortable on their journey and, most crucially, they were comfortable with each other.

Even when he was in a good mood, product development meetings were, in Michael's eyes, a waste of time. Michael had a very narrow – he would say focused – view of his role with DataTrak: he went out and sold the product. It was not his job to specify how it would look and feel; there was an army of developers and planners for that purpose.

Now, closeted in a stuffy conference room with three dreary, humourless young men, he could barely bring himself to any level of active participation. They talked about the Internet and bandwidth, they discussed new delivery mechanisms, and they debated the merits of various data warehousing techniques. For Michael this was more irrelevant than ever: a few hours earlier, as he had sat on the train that morning with his ambitions dancing seductively in his head, he could not have understood how trivial it would all seem by the end of the day. His fantasies lay shattered before him, his dreams of glory and power withered by Zamboni's arbitrary judgement. All day he had wanted to retire to a quiet corner and cry, and he felt his watery eyes and flushed cheeks must betray some of his disappointment. He sat hunched forward in his chair, his hands clasped over his nose and mouth to hide his boredom and frustration.

'Mike?' one of the men said. 'What do you think?'

Michael didn't change his position, but he pulled his hands down slowly from his face until they were curled under his chin. 'I think you're all doing a fantastic job,' he said without any conviction. 'The guys from Morgan Stanley were very impressed by what we had to say on our product plans. They might install two hundred of the new TrakPlus terminals if we get it right. You deliver, and we can sell it.'

The company was pinning all its hopes on TrakPlus, a new product which, as the draft promotional brochures put it, was 'functionally rich whilst retaining the user-friendly interface for which DataTrak has become so famous'. It was eighteen months behind schedule and the sales team had started to refer to it privately as TrakMinus. Michael took a small amount of enjoyment from reminding these people of their failure to get the product to the market on time, but it didn't compensate for his own loss. He was tired, and he was desolate. He wanted to scream.

The meeting broke up after ten more long minutes in which Michael's only contribution was to grunt occasionally. As he was walking into his office Pam slipped out of her seat and followed him. He slumped into his chair and stared at her as if he could think of no reason why she might be there.

'Do you want to tell me about it?' she asked quietly.

'Nothing to tell. The king is dead, long live the king. We'll go on pretty much as before, I'd imagine.'

'Do you know Skip?' She wanted to sit down but would never do so without him telling her.

'I may have met him at that sales conference in Palm Springs, but he can't have been very memorable.'

'We'll find out soon enough, I suppose,' she said, hoping to sound wise and consoling.

'That we will. So – have you got anything else for me tonight or can I go home?'

'I was going to suggest we went for a quick drink – my treat. You look as if you need one.'

'Pam, that's very kind, but I'm so tired I can hardly keep my eyes open as it is. One drink and I'll be on the floor.'

'Sounds interesting. OK – maybe another time.' Her tone

remained unchanged in spite of this rebuff.

'Sure. This' – he waved at the spread of papers across his desk – 'can all wait until tomorrow, can't it?'

'There's one thing I think you should deal with now,' she said. 'Nick mentioned to me that he'd sent you an e-mail, and he said you should read it as soon as you got back.'

'OK. Thanks, Pam. See you tomorrow.'

When she had left he logged on to the e-mail system: there were fourteen new messages for him, but only one from Zamboni, N. He double-clicked on it and the message popped up on the screen.

in view of our discussion today, i want you to focus all your efforts on the 7 key accounts in the uk. with immediate effect, your other regional responsibilities have been reassigned within the team and you are to concentrate solely on these names. skip will take on some additional sales dutys when he arrives. see his e/m attached for more details.

Michael shook his head to try and clear it; the message had fogged his thinking. It appeared that Zamboni was now stripping him of most of his powers, relegating him to the position of just another key account salesman. Stunned, he read the e-mail from Skip McMaster, which was addressed uniquely to Zamboni.

Nick

I'm very excited at the prospect of running the EMEA region. I can already see that the opportunities are immense, and there's a lot of potential waiting to be unleashed. It sounds like I'm inheriting a great team which, through no fault of its own, has slightly lost its direction. Be assured that I will bring a new vision and strong direction to the region. Give me thirty days and I'll submit a new strategic plan (including revised goals, key account structure, and resource redeployment schedule).

Onwards and upwards!
Truly

Skip

The words seeped from the glowing screen into Michael's consciousness. One phrase in particular resonated: resource redeployment schedule. There would be some firings, and no mistake. Skip had probably already been briefed on who should stay and who should go. Whichever way he considered it, Michael smelt trouble.

Holly had fallen asleep with the book still in her hand. Over the three weeks of their summer holiday she had become used to Daddy reading to her every night, and she saw no reason why this should change just because they were back home. Michael sat on the side of her bed and stroked her head gently, his tears now close to the surface. Annie hung back in the doorway, anxious and unsure of what to do or say.

Downstairs they sat in the breakfast room with a bottle of wine and she waited. He wasn't hungry, he said; he'd had a business lunch.

He sighed very deeply. 'Sometimes, just once even, I'd like things to go my way. I mean, for Christ's sake, what have I done wrong? I've played all their games, by their rules, and I'm still a loser. Sod them. First thing tomorrow I'm going to polish my CV and get on to some headhunters. Life's too short for all this crap.'

Now was not the time for dissent. Annie felt that sympathy was required, small nods of the head and expressions of mutual regret when appropriate. He needed to sleep it off before she could begin to rebuild his self-confidence. She would allow him some time to shrug aside his deflation, then she would start to inject some reason into the argument. There was no way he was going to leave DataTrak; that was too rash, too final, for her liking.

She gave him a sad little smile, a look that told him he was loved and that his pain was shared. Annie did hurt, but not for the same reason as him: she was wounded by what she saw in front of her, her husband brought low. It meant nothing to her that he would not be getting a consignment of corporate stationery with a fancy new title on it, that the car would remain the same, that the salary wouldn't change; these were achievements which left her cold, goals she didn't share. She wanted him, and she wanted him in one piece, not shattered by external forces.

But timing was everything with Michael. He was riding on the edge of his emotional barrier, just as liable to explode with rage as to dissolve with tears, and Annie had no desire to provoke him. She needed to tread very carefully: calm advice would not be well received, yet unchecked agreement would eventually be equally damaging. She'd had enough experience to know how to handle this, much as it distressed her to be so covert in her actions.

Annie refilled their glasses. 'So what exactly is the position now? I mean, what happens tomorrow?' she asked.

'I drag myself into work, totally disenchanted, and pretend that it doesn't make any difference. I don't have a tantrum, and I do what Zamboni says. I smile a lot and generally behave like a regular brown-nosing drudge.' He shrugged and swigged at his wine, replacing the glass carelessly on the table.

'When does this man Skip arrive?'

'The funny thing is, I had this immediate impression when Nick told me that Skip had to get a few things sorted out before he came over. I thought, he doesn't have a passport. That's why he hasn't arrived yet. He's a redneck from the middle of nowhere who probably thinks he needs a visa to go to California. He's spent his whole life in Ohio, probably married a cousin, and is frantically looking up England on the map. And hey presto! he's the guy who's going to tell us how to do business in our region.'

'That sounds a little harsh.'

'Probably. But it makes me feel better. He may turn out to be God's gift – Nick certainly thinks so – but I think I'll reserve judgement.'

'Is he married? Does he have a family?'

'Don't know. Why does that matter?'

'I'm not sure, though I've always thought that one of Zamboni's problems is that he doesn't have anything else to divert him. He lives for work. Every time I've met him he's been completely incapable of talking about anything else. If Skip has a family he might be . . . better rounded, more balanced, that's all.'

Michael made no effort to answer this, merely shaking his head wearily. 'You don't seem very upset,' he said.

She knew this would come. At some stage he would have to take it out on her, accuse her of failing to appreciate the depth of his feelings. In these dark moments he was always keen to protest that his darkness was the worst, that no one else suffered as he did. It was an inevitability for which she was prepared.

'Michael, I'm very upset. Of course I am. You had such high hopes and I hate to see them dashed like this.'

'But that's just the point, isn't it? I had high hopes – not you. You couldn't care less whether I get on or not. It's all some silly game as far as you're concerned. You have no idea of what it means for me, do you?' He was winding up for a fight and she had to avoid it.

'That's not entirely fair. You know I want you to do well, and I desperately want you to be happy at work. I know how important this was to you. I just can't bear to see you like this, and I don't want it to keep on happening. It isn't good for any of us.'

'So what you're saying is that I should stifle all my ambitions so that you'll be happy – is that it?'

'You know that's not what I'm saying. Perhaps I'm putting it badly. I'm simply very conscious of the fact that we have a good life now, we seem to be doing very well, and I don't want everything messed up by some small-minded Americans who don't realise how good you are. I think you're bigger than that. I think you can ride out this storm without it destroying everything we've got.' Against her better judgement, Annie was offering advice, an offer she

25

was pretty sure would fall on deaf ears.

She was right. 'And that's your proposal, is it – that I lie down and let them walk all over me like some doormat? That's going to do wonders for my self-esteem, isn't it? And I'll really command a lot of respect in the office – good old Michael, you can crap all over him and he'll come back for more. Brilliant.'

She leant across the table and put her hand over his. 'All I'm saying is that you should give it some time. You don't know what's going to happen. Maybe this Skip fellow will turn out to be fantastic and you'll get on really well with him. You can, you know that. When you want, you can be a real charmer. You'll just have to use your charms on him – you know, as if he was a client and you're selling yourself.'

His mood seemed to change immediately. 'You don't understand,' he said quietly. 'It's not as simple as that. I'm not even sure I want to do it. I'm completely demotivated.'

'Then we'll have to get you remotivated,' she replied brightly. 'We'll finish this wine and then we'll go to bed. Let's forget all about this tonight and see how we feel in the morning.'

Michael showed no emotion at this suggestion, and said little as they drank the rest of the bottle. Annie led him upstairs and, once in the bedroom, she undressed quickly and pressed herself against him. However he reacted, she would be ready for it.

FOUR

Teri McMaster was bored. By close of business she was due to complete a ten-thousand-word analysis of the proposed merger between two New England banks, and was still fifteen hundred words short with nothing more to say. She had considered writing about the personal life of one of the banks' chairmen, who was rumoured to treat his three secretaries as a private harem, but she felt this might have little bearing on the merits of the deal, interesting as it was. She scrolled back through the article on her PC, desperately seeking paragraphs that seemed light on information, but her search was fruitless. She had two hours to finish the report and hand it in to the editorial department. It would probably be the last thing she'd write for Bleacher Meadow, and she wanted it to be good. She owed that to her clients, and to the firm. But she could find no ready inspiration to tease the last few pages out of her, and she wondered if they could make up the shortfall with some fancy charts.

She stood up and looked out of her office window. From the twenty-sixth floor she had a wonderful view across Lake Erie towards Canada, a panorama she had taken for granted before the news. Teri had worked for Bleacher Meadow for three years, joining as an investment analyst and quickly working her way up to become head of research, a position she had held for the last thirteen months. Bleacher Meadow was the fourth largest investment manager in Ohio, looking after a variety of public and private pension plans as well as running some smaller mutual funds for high net worth individuals. Investment consultants liked the firm and it had been consistently ranked in the top quartile of performance

27

league tables. Teri's research was particularly well received by clients, who appreciated her concise and reasoned opinions.

She'd visited London just once, some twelve summers ago with her parents. They'd seen all the sights in a gruelling three-day tour as part of a two-week vacation in Europe. She'd liked London but remembered it as dirty and wet; she seemed to be wearing a cagoule in every photo. Skip had never been abroad, and was bursting with enthusiasm about the posting, flicking through her photo album and questioning her closely about what he should expect. He was like a kid at Christmas, she thought as he brought home tourist guides and maps. He had, of course, sought her full approval before agreeing to the assignment in the first place. He'd called her at the office to tell her, and they'd gone out for a meal straight from work, drinking a bottle of Chianti with their pasta. She'd asked a lot of questions and he'd promised to get answers before they made their decision, but Teri knew it was the right thing to do. They needed a change; they needed the stimulation whilst they were still young enough to enjoy it. There were no children to be considered, and all four parents were in good health and perfectly capable of coming to visit. It would be an adventure.

In reaching this decision, Teri spent little time in worrying about her own situation. Although she was considered a high-flyer in business – she fielded calls from headhunters on a regular basis – Teri had no particular ambitions. The work she did was not especially interesting and she wouldn't miss it. When she had told Bleacher Meadow about the move, they had kindly suggested that they could still use her as a consultant: they even floated the idea that, in time, she could set up an office for them in London. She smiled and was properly grateful for the offer, but warned them that she would need time to settle in and they shouldn't expect to hear from her straight away. If she got bored – which she doubted – she'd come back to them; if not, she'd let the proposals lapse in silence.

Her thoughts kept returning to London. What would the

house be like? How would they make new friends? Was there an American community, with American shops? Would they need a car? Skip had been briefed on the mechanics of the move, but there was little help available for the more practical questions that exercised her. The plan called for Skip to fly across in the next few days, introduce himself to the staff and spend a week or so acclimatising; then he'd return and they'd finish the packing before setting out together on their new life. She was excited, and wanted to get moving: there would be a million things to do, and Skip would be far too busy to help with most of them.

She rubbed her temples gently with her fingertips in an effort to get the blood flowing in her brain. The fortunes of two small banks seemed insignificant compared to what she was about to undertake. She turned back to her desk and forced herself to sit down and pull her chair back towards the computer. She kicked off her shoes and stretched her toes; in less than a month, she told herself, all this would seem to have happened in a different life. Fifteen hundred more words and she was finished here: grinning at the prospect, she began typing.

'You are, presumably, going to get rat-arsed tonight,' Brian said.

Brian Shale was the regional client service manager for DataTrak, a man whose job description was rather unkindly characterised in the office as 'custodian of the corporate screwdriver'. When clients had a problem, they called Brian.

He was slumped in a chair in Michael's office. At forty-seven, Brian was too old to be considered a threat by anyone, and he had lightly assumed the role of professional uncle: anyone who was miserable knew they could go and see Brian and he would cheer them up. He'd picked up the news about Skip on the grapevine, and realised how badly this would affect Michael.

'Tonight?' Michael asked. 'What's going on tonight?'

'Office piss-up, apropos of nothing. Everyone seems so bloody depressed, we thought it was time to go out and have some fun. You're coming, by the way.'

'I am?'

'You are. It'll do you good, let you know that you still have some friends around here.'

Michael liked Brian a lot. He was uncomplicated, never got involved in office politics, and was relentlessly optimistic. Head Office couldn't work him out at all, but recognised his value and left him alone. 'What's the plan?' Michael asked.

'Drink too much, fall over, throw up in a taxi and get grief from nearest and dearest. Very simple – even a salesman like you should be able to follow it.'

'To be honest, I don't know if I can make it. Annie won't be thrilled, and I've got a hell of a lot of work.' Michael had had enough experience of office drinking sessions to know that Brian's summary was extremely accurate, and he didn't fancy the inevitable consequences. He was not a big drinker and the prospect of six or seven hours in a dark and noisy Mexican bar, eating fajitas and drinking tequila slammers, did not greatly appeal. After the last party Michael had spent a large part of the following day in the lavatory and had drunk four litres of mineral water.

'You're being a wimp,' Brian said. 'That's not allowed.' Then he changed tone slightly. 'Does your reluctance have anything to do with the presence of our estimable leader, Mr Nicholas Iron Balls Zamboni?'

'Well, let's just say that Zamboni doesn't put me in the party mood, and his current visit isn't likely to change that.'

'If you'll allow me to be serious for one moment – which I admit is a severe breach of my duties here – I think you should come with us. You need to drink yourself silly and have some fun. Forget all the crap that's flying around. No one's happy about the situation, but we can't change it. Dear Skip will be with us soon enough, and he'll probably instigate a no-booze policy, so we've got to take our opportunities while we still can.'

'What do you know about him?'

'He is, by all accounts, one of the oiliest operators around. According to those who know, he's sickeningly good-looking, very well dressed, smooth as a billiard ball and totally in thrall to Zamboni. He's not the brightest guy ever to pass through the portals of DataTrak, but he's been a frighteningly successful salesman.'

'So he's Zamboni's grease monkey?'

'Absolutely. Zamboni will tell him what to do, and he'll do it with a winning smile on his face.' Brian paused, then added: 'Rather like you.'

Michael had to smile at that. 'Peas in a pod,' he said. 'We should get on like a house on fire.'

'There will certainly be a fire. The problem is, we don't know under whom he will light it.'

'I've already got some ideas about that,' Michael said more seriously. 'That's why I'm rewriting my CV.'

'Give him a chance, Michael. These crises often have a habit of turning out to be less catastrophic than we imagine.'

'You sound like my wife.'

'Yes, but she hasn't got my style, has she?'

'Why don't you push off and go and mend some terminals or something? I have work to do.'

'Do I take that to mean you will come to the ball?'

'We'll see.'

Brian pulled himself up and left. He had done a good job: Michael felt a shade brighter, even though he knew the effect would be temporary. He had spent most of the day avoiding Zamboni and fending off Pam's expressions of sympathy and support, diligently attending to his in-tray and editing the key account plans that were now his main responsibility. Annie had called him twice and was clearly determined to forestall any reckless action, gently prompting him to think twice before he did anything they might come to regret. No one could do it better, and he loved her for it. What would he do without her?

It was exactly as he'd feared. By the time he arrived, shortly after seven, the long table they had taken was already covered with glasses and bottles, the ashtrays overflowing. Brian was holding court, entertaining them with a ceaseless stream of anecdotes they'd heard before but which always amused them. Michael strolled over to the table and nodded at them all.

'Mr Lensman,' Brian said. 'A rare pleasure. Can I relieve you of a tenner for the whip?'

Michael pulled out a ten-pound note and handed it to Brian. He wasn't expecting much of a return on his investment: he had already promised himself that he'd stay for one, two maximum, and then go back to Annie and Holly. He was in no mood for this.

'I'll get you a drink,' Pam said as she leapt up from the table. 'What do you want?'

They walked to the bar together and Pam squeezed between two men to attract the barman's attention. 'I'll have a beer – Dos Equis will be fine,' he said. Pam ordered and paid for it. Handing him the bottle, she eased away from the bar but seemed reluctant to go back to the party. They stood at right angles to each other. It was noisy in the bar and Pam moved closer to him so that she could be heard.

'You kept a very low profile today,' she said.

'It's my new resolution,' Michael replied after taking a swig of the beer. 'I'm keeping my head well below the parapet – I don't fancy having it blown off.'

'We all feel like that. Zamboni's terrorising everybody. You shouldn't take it so personally.'

Michael couldn't decide how to respond. This was the first setback of his career, the first time when things hadn't gone according to plan, and he wasn't dealing with it very well. He didn't want to discuss his problems with Pam: she was insignificant, and she had no right to be giving him advice. He would have liked to have told her to mind her own business, but he knew that she was trying to be kind, and he did want to talk to someone.

'Oh, I wouldn't worry too much about me,' he said at last. 'These things have a habit of blowing themselves out after a while and everything gets back to normal. I'm just going to hang on and see how it all unfolds.'

'That holiday obviously did you some good,' Pam said

teasingly. 'I didn't think you'd take it as calmly as this.'

'Sure, it's been a bit of a shock, but I've thought it all through and it might not be as bad as we think. You never know, I might even get on with Skip.' He grinned as if to show that this was a remote possibility.

'What does Annie think?'

'She's been great, as always,' he replied. He took another drink from the bottle and looked across at the party in the corner. 'I think we'd better join them, otherwise there'll be hell to pay.'

'Michael,' Pam said, putting her hand on his forearm as he started to move. 'Take care, won't you?'

He looked at her in confusion, not understanding what she meant, then smiled to cover his bafflement. 'As always,' he replied, and they walked back to the long table.

FIVE

The fax from Morgan Stanley lay on the desk in front of Michael and he tried to focus on it through watery eyes. He had taken all the precautions possible, but he was still suffering from a senior hangover. He'd insisted on eating, but the raw onions were a mistake, repeating on him as they churned their way through his digestive system. He crunched his way through a packet of mints and rubbed his temples as he reread the message. Typically, they wasted no time on formalities.

Dear Mike

Whilst we like the concept of TrakPlus, our own needs appear to be some way ahead of your development plans. You'll appreciate that our traders simply cannot afford to wait for the new technology, and our IT steering group has therefore decided to progress with another vendor.

We will keep you informed of our project schedule, which will call for the removal of all DataTrak terminals by the end of this year.

Thank you for your support in the past. Good luck with TrakPlus.

Yours sincerely

Albert Stent
Trader Support & Business Services Director

That was all there was. Michael went over it again and again, but there was nothing to read between the lines. They had closed the door very firmly and had left no room for manoeuvre or counter-offer. He knew Al Stent well enough to see that this was not a bargaining ploy: what Al said, Al meant. Morgan Stanley was about to pull the plug, and the healthy revenue stream would stop by December. As a way to start off his new life in charge of key accounts, Michael could have envisaged several better scenarios.

Michael was the only person who knew of this decision, but it wouldn't be long before others within the company heard of it. Zamboni had taken a particular interest in the Morgan Stanley account; he wanted regular updates from Michael on where DataTrak stood and how the competition was doing. This one client delivered twenty per cent of revenues for the region, and its loss would have an inevitable and unpalatable impact.

His head throbbing unceasingly, Michael left his office and went across to Pam with the fax. She would scan it into her PC and then send it through the private data network to a number of destinations which he'd scribbled at the top of the letter. He'd have to take the original to Zamboni and talk his way out of it. Pam took the letter, glanced at it, then put it on the scanner.

'Is Nick around?' he asked her as they both watched the document.

'I'm afraid he is.'

'Now's as good a time as any, I suppose. Wish me luck.' She handed him the letter and winced.

Michael crossed the open-plan office, feeling that every pair of eyes was upon him and that they all knew the message he was carrying. Foolishly, he had talked up the prospects of Morgan Stanley becoming a beta site for TrakPlus, overstating their expressions of interest as promises of future business. Everyone was hopeful: to have such a well-known firm support the product, especially as a pilot, would make an immeasurable difference to its success. Now, as the account manager, he'd have to put his hand up and explain the reasons for their decision.

Zamboni was at his desk – Don's desk, as Michael still

thought of it – and he appeared to be waiting for something. He looked up when Michael came in. 'What?' he said impatiently, as if he was being interrupted.

'This just came through,' Michael said, holding up the fax. Zamboni put his hand out and flicked it. He snatched the letter from Michael's weak grasp and read quickly.

'This is it?'

'It appears so.'

'You've called Al?'

'He's at an offsite – won't be back until next week.'

Zamboni scratched beneath his left ear, then pinched his nose nervously. Michael's legs were collapsing but Zamboni left him standing in front of the desk. 'Called his boss?'

'Same story.'

Zamboni placed the fax very gently on the desk, holding his fingertips on the bottom of the paper as if worried that it might be blown away. He spoke quietly – too quietly for Michael's liking. 'This is critical, Mike, very critical. We cannot afford to lose this one. How has it got to this stage?'

'I think you know as well as I do. We've been promising TrakPlus for so long that they've got tired of waiting. They don't believe us any more. We've lost all credibility.'

'Mike, it's your job to sustain that credibility. If you can't do that, what's the point?'

'I can only go so far. If the product development guys don't deliver, I'm left selling vapourware. Morgan Stanley, understandably in my opinion, won't buy that. They want to touch and feel.'

Zamboni ran his top lip over his teeth. 'Who is the other vendor they're talking about?'

'I think it's Bloomberg. I didn't see anyone else in the frame for it.'

Now the explosion came. 'Bloomberg, for fuck's sake!' Zamboni shouted. 'Always fucking Bloomberg! Is that what we get beaten by? Jesus – how can they be so dumb?' There were a thousand smart answers, but Michael refrained from using any of them. Instead he waited. 'You can rescue this, Mike. Correction – you have to rescue this. Call their people

36

in New York, tell them what a major mistake they're making if they go with Bloomberg. Offer them price breaks, whatever it takes. You've got my full authority on this one. I don't care what it costs, but get them back, OK?'

With his head hurting as much as it could without bursting, Michael was struggling to take in all these orders, let alone contest them. 'I'll see what I can do,' was all he could manage.

'Not good enough. Let's set up a video conference call, you and me and their top guys. Let's show them we mean business. We're not going to be pissed on by Bloomberg, you hear?'

'I hear you, Nick. I'd just say that we've already pulled all the strings we can. If we're too aggressive it might alienate them even more.'

'That's a pretty negative attitude, wouldn't you say? Try and get with the programme, Mike. We need a result here, and it's all down to you either way.'

'I'll get on to it straight away and come back to you.' Michael didn't wait for further abuse; he went straight from the office to the lavatory and threw up.

Holly's afternoon naps were getting shorter and less frequent. She was due to start school in September and was ready for it – as was Annie. Holly was bored and Annie could no longer give her all the stimulation she needed; the three mornings a week at play school were helpful but insufficient for Holly's bright mind. Annie knew she should cherish these last days of having Holly all to herself, that she would hate it when the house was empty and there was no one to fuss over, but she also realised that Holly needed to move on and have a little piece of her life that was hers alone.

Annie sat with a cup of coffee and a magazine in the sitting room. Holly had reluctantly gone to bed – 'I won't go to sleep,' she'd said firmly – and was downstairs within ten minutes. Now she was playing, arranging a tea party of all her dolls and animals and trying to involve her mother. Annie would have preferred to read about decorating ideas, autumn fashions and erotic massages, but she was fighting a losing battle: when Holly demanded attention she got it. Annie dutifully held a plastic cup and saucer and drank the imaginary tea.

Ever since they'd got back from holiday, Michael had stopped calling her. Of course, she knew he'd be rushed off his feet and would have too much work to think about her during the day, but she felt the suspension of these calls, which she enjoyed so much, represented more. He was deeply unhappy; he no longer seemed to get the same joy from seeing Holly in the evening, nor did he display any interest in making love. He'd get into bed, look at a book for five minutes, then turn off his light and give her a desultory peck on her bare shoulder. She wanted to hug him, even if sex was not the end product, but he was too cold and distant for her to try.

To her, it felt as if a boil were growing and festering within their lives and that it needed to burst, however painful that might be. All that was going on at work was leading to some kind of explosion which would, she prayed, resolve everything. However it turned out, she wanted that resolution; she needed them to regain their former stability and forget about all these trivial problems. If Michael was unhappy, they had to confront it together and get him sorted out so that they could concentrate on what she considered to be most important in life. But, somewhere along the way, Annie had lost her touch: she couldn't connect with him as she had before, couldn't steer him in the preferred direction. He was slipping away from her whilst he fought his own battles at work.

The phone rang and she put down her cup and saucer quickly, hoping it might be Michael. 'Hallo?' she said, watching as Holly cut slices of non-existent cake for her guests.

'Annie? Hallo, this is Pam – from DataTrak.'

'Hi. What's up?'

'Sorry to bother you, but Michael asked me to call. He's really tied up and he just wanted you to know that he's going to be home very late – he's booked a conference call with

38

New York and it's not until seven o'clock.'

'Well, thanks for letting me know.' Annie slightly resented the fact that Pam knew more about Michael's movements than she did, but kept it well hidden. 'So how are you?'

'Oh, bearing up. Too much work, too little pay – the same as always.'

'How are things there?' Annie wanted to hear the story from someone else.

'Pretty desperate. Everyone's in panic mode, as I expect Michael's told you. Actually . . .' Pam dropped her voice for this word and Annie picked up on it.

'Yes?'

'Well, to tell you the truth, I'm very concerned about Michael. He just isn't his normal self – very moody and withdrawn. I think he's taking things quite badly.'

'I know what you mean, Pam. But I wouldn't worry too much about him. He can be very resilient, and I know he's going to bounce back.' Annie said this as much to convince herself as anything else.

'I'm sure you're right. And don't worry, I'll look after him here.'

Annie smiled to herself; she had long suspected that Pam carried a torch for Michael, and she felt rather flattered.

'OK. Send him my love, won't you?'

'I will. See you soon.'

In private – especially at dinner parties where everyone was an investment banker or corporate lawyer – Charles Turkwood liked to say that he had never done an honest day's work in his life. People would laugh nervously, not entirely sure what he meant, and then he'd explain that he was a management consultant and that, as everyone knows, consultants borrow your watch to tell you the time and charge you for the privilege. This was his defence mechanism: if he deprecated his own profession, it saved them the trouble.

But even Charles was hard-pressed to explain the circumstances in which he now found himself. He had carved out a useful niche in the technology sector, advising clients on what systems to buy and install, and now he was working on a project with Morgan Stanley. The deal was that he evaluate six different information vendors and come up with his recommendation as to which they should use; having won the contract, priced at £75,000 (plus VAT and out-of-pockets, naturally), he had worked his tail off and was close to presenting his report. The assignment had kept him busy for six months and would fund a new sports car. Life was looking good.

He was crawling along the M25 when the call came through on his car phone. 'Mr Turkwood?'

'The very same.'

'I wonder if you remember me – Michael Lensman from DataTrak?'

'Of course.' Charles had spent many hours in front of multicoloured screens as Michael had explained the finer points of TrakPlus; he knew all the vendors' sales people. Lensman was accomplished, not too pushy but politely insistent about his company's products. 'What can I do for you?'

'It's about the Morgan Stanley deal. I've received a letter from Al Stent, and he says they're not going to go with us. Were you aware of this decision?'

Charles had to think quickly. He had no intention of admitting that he knew nothing about it – that would diminish his influence in a flash – but what else could he say? 'Michael,' he began, then paused to give himself more time. 'I think it would be inappropriate to discuss this now. Why don't you let me speak to Al first and then I'll come back to you?'

'I'd appreciate that. You know how important this is to DataTrak. We're prepared to do whatever it takes to win your client's business. I hope we've demonstrated that already. But if there's anything else you think we should be doing . . .'

Michael left the thought hanging in the air. Charles believed he understood the suggestion: a little oiling of the wheels, perhaps, in the form of a small present or favour. He was routinely offered such private incentives, and only occasionally turned them down.

'I'll think about that, too,' he said. 'Look, Michael, thanks for the call. I'll deal with it, OK?'

'When do you think you can get back to me?'

'Today, I hope. Don't worry, we can get this straightened out, I'm sure. Talk to you later.'

Charles cancelled the call and smiled. In spite of the fact that Morgan Stanley had gone over his head, he was confident he could still get a result, a result that would be good for him and DataTrak. It was weird, but so what? That was his business, and he loved it.

SIX

Michael eschewed lie-ins. On weekend mornings he would be awake by six-thirty and would slip quietly from under the covers, creeping downstairs to make a cup of tea. Before Holly arrived Annie would not have heard him but, like every mother, her chemistry had changed so that now she rarely dropped below a light sleep, always ready for the first cry of her baby. She wasn't sure if Michael knew this, and she didn't ask; she merely longed for the time when she could rest more peacefully, undisturbed by the slightest sound.

This Saturday morning was no different from any other. Annie felt him leave the bed, heard him pull on his dressing-gown and pad away from the bedroom. She listened as he worked downstairs in the kitchen, rattling crockery as he set the cups and saucers. There was silence as he let the tea stand for a couple of minutes, and then he was on his way back upstairs. Eyes closed, Annie lay still under the duvet as he reached the bedroom and put the tray down on the chest of drawers. She wanted to surprise him, to catch him whilst he was off guard in the hope that he would succumb. He brought a cup round to her side and placed it quietly on her bedside table; he lingered there for a moment and she opened her eyes. She put her hand out and touched his bare thigh softly.

'Why don't you come back to bed?' she said, moving her hand up towards his crutch. Michael stayed where he was, giving no indication of what he intended to do. 'Come on. Do I have to beg?' Annie rolled over on her back and pushed the duvet aside to reveal her naked body. She raised her arms to him as he looked down at her, standing as if he still wasn't entirely sure what to do next.

'What about Holly?' he asked.

'We've got at least fifteen minutes,' she replied, trying to remain good-humoured. After a further moment of hesitation Michael took off his dressing-gown and lay on top of her as she spread her legs. Annie could feel that he was not yet aroused so she pushed him off until he was lying on his back; she straddled him and leant forward so that her breasts swayed across his face. She cupped one breast in her hand and held it to his mouth. Responding to this, Michael began to suck and kiss, tenderly at first and then more firmly as she felt him begin to stiffen. He switched attention between each bosom and moved his hands so that his fingers dug into the crease of her buttocks. Annie shifted to let him enter her and began to grind against him, keeping her breasts close to his face until she straightened her legs and pushed her hips down against him. He lay motionless beneath her, his hands now gripping her buttocks tightly as she moved more quickly; she knew he was ready and her actions came harder until he groaned and arched his back, driving himself into her as deeply as he could. She made one last thrust for herself, then held her position until their spasms had subsided.

'Better?' Michael said when she had rolled off him.

'Much. A perfect start to the weekend.'

'Except your tea will have gone cold.'

'You're so romantic. That's what I love about you.' She stroked his face and studied him: he was flushed but, behind the bloom, there remained a pallor which betrayed his true state of health. His body was not good at managing stress, and Annie found herself worrying for him in the same way as she might have fretted over Holly. The man she saw beside her was weak and vulnerable, not the Michael she had loved and married with his absolute sense of right and wrong and his fixed determination. A small incident – a slight in the office, a diminution of responsibility that mattered so little in the grand scheme of things – had brought him to this. She'd never realised just how much it meant to him, how important his status and position was and how his

43

professional life was the motor for everything else. She hadn't
been blind to his ambition, but she'd always believed that, in
a clinch, he would throw it all up for his family and personal
happiness. It shocked Annie to see him brought so low.

'Are you going to tell me about work?' she said after he'd
pulled the duvet over them.

'What's to tell? The Morgan Stanley deal is rapidly
disappearing down the toilet and my name is firmly nailed
to it. If I lose this one, we have a real problem.' He said this
without looking at her.

'We?'

'Yes, we. The bonus on that deal alone is probably worth
a hundred thousand. We could finish everything in the house,
even after tax. I really wanted it – for you, as much as for
me.'

This was clever and Annie knew it: to say that he was
doing it for her, that all his efforts were merely to satisfy her
aspirations, was a subtle ploy to shift some guilt. At another
time, in different circumstances, she might have leapt on it
and chastised him, but she took a calmer line.

'The house can wait,' she said mildly. 'There'll be other
deals. Losing this one doesn't make you a bad salesman,
does it?'

'It will look that way to Skip. It already does to Zamboni.'

'So what are you doing lying in bed?' Annie said teasingly.
'You're no use to me with a limp willy. You might as well go
out and sell something and prove them wrong.' But Michael
didn't want to see the joke. He simply stared at the ceiling
and put his forearm over his eyes. She rolled closer and
touched him on his shoulder. 'Come on, things can't be that
bad. You've got Holly and me, and we both love you. Doesn't
that count for something?'

'Don't be stupid,' he replied bitterly. 'It's nothing to do
with you and Holly. It's about . . . well, it's about me. There,
you've made me say it. It's all very selfish, and probably seems
utterly puerile to you. But it matters to me, and it hurts,
OK?'

Annie picked up the crack in his voice. 'I know it hurts,

44

and I want to make it better. Please let me help.'

'I don't think anyone can help me just now. I have to sort this out for myself.'

'But you don't have to. That's what I'm here for. For God's sake, what's the point otherwise?'

Michael turned on his side so that he was facing her. His eyes were watery and red. 'I don't know what the point is, all right? I haven't got all the answers, unlike you. Leave me alone and I'll get over it.'

'Oh Michael,' Annie said. A brief unpleasant thought crossed her mind: is this how men behave when they're having an affair?

At the last count, Pam Shine had forty-seven china cats in the front room. She had got a local joiner to build two glass-fronted cabinets in the alcoves each side of the chimney breast, and her cat collection was displayed in these. Strip lighting in the cabinets was connected to the main light switch and, even though she said it herself, the effect was really pretty. Every birthday and Christmas Cliff would buy her another cat – sometimes mail-order from the back pages of the *Radio Times*, more often from a lovely little shop in Chelmsford which specialised in such objets d'art. Cliff was good like that: he knew what she liked and had never once made a mistake like buying one she'd already got. That was what she liked about him: there were never any nasty surprises.

They'd been together for ever, she always said, forgotten when they first started going out it was so long ago. It was a fib, of course, but not a bad one. She remembered every date, celebrated every significant anniversary, if only by herself. Cliff wasn't like that, didn't spend time thinking about the past, but she didn't mind so much; after all, they were together and happy and she faithfully recorded all the major and minor events of their life. She kept the photo albums up to date, recording and indexing each snap so that they'd never forget, even when they were old and grey and toothless; she booked the table at the Italian restaurant for their wedding anniversary; and she put the date in his diary at the start of every year, with a big reminder in underlined capital letters a week before. He never said anything about that, but she knew he appreciated it.

They couldn't have real cats. Cliff had an allergy to them, sneezed and came up in an enormous rash whenever he was close to one. Pam loved them, would have had forty-seven real ones if she could, but she knew that wasn't going to happen. She swallowed her disappointment and settled for the next best thing. Every Saturday morning she took them all out of the cabinets and dusted them whilst Cliff worked on the car: he'd bought an old 5 Series BMW and spent every spare moment renovating it. As a hobby, Pam would have wished for something slightly less grubby, and the mess he made in the drive made her feel slightly ashamed. They lived in a nice neighbourhood where everyone had a good car and a neat front garden, and Pam didn't want to upset that balance. Of course, they had the Mondeo as well, but she couldn't help feeling that the sight of Cliff in his oily overalls was bound to lower the tone a bit. Still, it kept him amused and that was what was really important.

They had a nice little routine at the weekend. After she'd finished the dusting she'd pop down to the supermarket in the Mondeo and do the week's shopping. She'd get something special for his lunch, something to set him up for the afternoon when he'd be off fishing with his mates whilst she sorted out the house. There wasn't much to sort out, in truth: with no children, and both of them working all week, the house never really got dirty or muddled. But Pam liked to keep it spotless; you never knew when someone might drop in unexpectedly and she wasn't going to be caught with an untidy front room and a kitchen littered with washing-up.

Saturday nights were special. Often they'd get a takeaway and a video and curl up in front of the television, Cliff with some lagers and Pam with a bottle of Liebfraumilch. It was nice, this time alone together, although Pam wouldn't have minded at all if they'd had one or two kids to complete the picture. They'd seen the doctor, had the tests, but nothing

46

was happening on that front, and she suspected that Cliff wasn't quite as anxious as she was. Pam dreamt of a little girl, then a boy. Well, it would happen if it was meant to, she reasoned with herself, and tried not to fret too much over it.

Sundays they'd go round to see his parents, have a nice roast dinner with all the trimmings; Pam would help his mum in the kitchen and Cliff would go to the pub with his dad for a couple of pints. Pam liked the way they'd taken her on almost as a daughter: her father was dead and her mother lived with her aunt in Torquay. Sometimes she needed someone to talk to: for all his good points, Cliff could be a bit lacking in that department, his face dropping whenever she suggested they should talk about this, that or the other. Cliff's mum made up for that in a way, although it wasn't ideal.

Cliff was a landscape gardener. He had a van and all the equipment – mowers, trimmers, chainsaws and an arsenal of spades, forks, shears, scythes, hoes and secateurs – bought in a job lot off a mate of a mate who'd gone broke. He had a box advertisement in Yellow Pages but picked up most of his work from nosy neighbours who hung over garden fences as he worked and asked if he might be able to do something for them, too. Pam handled all his paperwork and ran his diary, sent out invoices and managed the money; he didn't earn a fortune but, with her salary, they had a pretty good standard of living. They had the new car, a nice house, a holiday in Spain or Tenerife every summer, and Pam watched the pennies very carefully: there was a pension plan, a savings account, a few shares from privatisations. They were well set up.

As much as anyone could be, Pam was happy with her lot. There were things she might have liked – children, of course – but she didn't waste energy striving for them. Cliff was good to her, and she knew how lucky she was with that. There were plenty of women who regularly had the daylights beaten out of them by drunken husbands, women who did disgusting jobs to subsidise their partner's indolence, women who could never speak their mind for fear it might provoke a storm. Pam was not one of those: she lived in a different world, a world with few surprises and where everyone adhered to a reasonable moral code. She liked that. She was glad to be safe.

Teri McMaster was on her own in the house and she didn't like it. Having left Bleacher Meadow on Friday – an affair that involved lots of hugs, promises of unceasing correspondence, a few tears and some rather nasty semi-sweet sparkling wine in the office whilst a short eulogy was given by the senior partner – she was now a lady of leisure. She spent Saturday with Skip as he prepared to fly to London; he was nervous and excited, unsure of what clothes to take and planning his wardrobe with enormous care. They went out for dinner on Saturday night and he talked of how big the challenge was, how much he wanted to do well and make a success of it. She smiled as she listened to him; he was so enthusiastic that it was impossible not to be dazzled by his glowing optimism, just as she had been when they'd first met and he was about to embark on his business career with IBM.

Throughout his working life Skip had lost none of his zest, managing to retain a childish belief that all would turn out for the best in the end. Driven by a deep religious conviction, he truly felt that people were intrinsically good and that, given the right circumstances, goodness would prevail. Sometimes this clarity, this absolute certainty, frightened Teri a little; although she shared his religious faith, she was much less convinced of man's propensity towards righteousness. Her commercial experiences had taught her a very different lesson, and she worried for Skip, concerned that his vulnerability would eventually expose him to serious harm.

Teri delivered him to the airport early on Sunday morning, then drove back to their neat town-house condominium. When she opened a kitchen cupboard to get a glass, she found a message stuck to the inside of the door:

HI! I LOVE YOU AND I ALWAYS WILL. MISSING YOU ALREADY.

Further messages were secreted about the house; Skip must have got up in the night to set them all up, and she couldn't help shaking her head and grinning at the thought of him padding from room to room with his Scotch tape and scissors. He was a lovely man, a very special guy who genuinely thought more about others than he did about himself.

And, now she found herself alone, Teri realised how much she had come to rely on their partnership. Even though she regarded herself as independent, strong-willed and single-minded, she could no longer imagine life without Skip. He was as much a part of her as her skin; he was a vital organ without which she would cease to function. As she sat and sipped her coffee she tried to work out when this transformation had occurred, when he had become an irrevocable component of her metabolism, but it wasn't as simple as that. There was no defining moment, merely a process of accretion over their years together. Without him, even for this short time, she was incomplete, and it came as quite a shock. She was dependent after all.

The coffee tasted foul, and it made her stomach churn so much that she had to rush to the bathroom to retch. Stooped in front of the lavatory bowl, her eyes watering and saliva filling her mouth, Teri had no idea of the strange biological symmetry forming within her.

SEVEN

Crisp – that was the only way to describe him. As he stood in front of them they took in all the details of his appearance, the women with mouths slightly open and the men with a hint of a sneer. He was wearing a plain navy suit, immaculately cut and newly pressed, with a fresh, white cotton button-down shirt and a burgundy woven silk tie. His black loafers shone beneath the turn-ups of his trousers. His light brown hair was perfectly styled and combed, and his blue eyes sparkled with health and vigour. When he smiled – which was often – Skip McMaster's perfect teeth were on display. He stood well with his weight on both legs, but he didn't seem stiff – just crisp.

Monday morning, ten a.m.: Zamboni had convened a staff meeting, attendance compulsory, in the large conference room. Brian had quickly spread the word that the meeting was to be for them 'to witness the second coming', and had made all manner of tasteless jokes about looking for signs of the stigmata on Skip's hands. Brian had popped his head round the door of Michael's office and given him a big wink, hoping for a positive reaction but merely getting a V-sign in response. Michael was still smarting from a bad weekend and the prospect of meeting Skip McMaster was almost too much to stomach.

The staff duly assembled, clutching mugs of coffee and chattering nervously before being silenced by the arrival of Nick Zamboni, with Skip in tow. 'OK guys,' Zamboni growled. 'Let's get things moving.' He turned to look at Skip, who was hovering behind him with his arms folded across his chest, and gave him a knowing smile. 'I called you in this

50

morning because I want you all to meet your new boss, Skip McMaster. Skip's been running our business in the Midwest, and he's one of our most successful salesmen. He's going to be relying on you folks to bring him up to speed on how things work around here. There's a lot to be done, and Skip's the man to do it. Support him and you'll have a great future here.'

Zamboni looked around the room, as if searching for someone, anyone, who might not want to support Skip. Appearing satisfied that he could find no such person, he started to speak again. 'It's no secret that this region has underperformed, and we need to fix that. There are going to be some changes around here, not all of them very comfortable. But I guarantee that there'll always be a job for guys who are hard-working, loyal and team players. We're a client-focused organisation, and we need every one of you pulling for our clients. Skip's going to be teaching you how that should be done.' Zamboni pulled one ear, and this seemed to be a signal for Skip to step forward. 'Skip. You want to say a few words?'

'Thanks, Nick. Well, good morning everyone. I'm Skip.' His face broke into a huge smile as he looked at the audience. There was a chorus of 'good mornings', then silence. 'I don't have a lot to say right now. In fact, I guess I won't be saying a lot for some time yet. My first job is to listen. I really need to understand how you operate, what motivates you, how we can make things better. That'll take time, and I want to ask for your patience. I'm also going to ask for your trust, but I don't expect that from day one. We're new to each other and I have to earn your respect, I understand that. But let me just say that I am confident we can upgrade our performance significantly in this region – and, by doing that, we can make sure we don't see this guy quite as often.' He smiled as he jerked a thumb at Zamboni and there was a small murmur of laughter in the room. Zamboni, however, did not smile.

'Seriously,' Skip went on, 'this is a huge challenge for all of us. We're going to be working real hard, but I hope we have some time for fun too. I'm looking forward to it. That's really all I wanted to say for now. Thank you.'

Nobody knew what to do next – should they clap? Some did and immediately felt very foolish. Others sat and waited for the two men to leave; a few got to their feet and looked sheepish, not sure whether they were allowed to go first. Zamboni and Skip looked as if they were deep in conversation at the end of the room, oblivious to everyone else, so the bravest staff simply wandered off back to their desks. They were careful not to share their thoughts until well out of earshot. The women, on the whole, were overcome by Skip's boyish good looks and easy charm. The men, on the other hand, wondered how much he was being paid to afford to dress like that, and doubted the sincerity of his smile.

Michael had a plan. His natural inclination was to sulk, but he knew this would be counter-productive. Instead, he forced himself to approach the two men and introduce himself to Skip. He timed his arrival so that he was the only person near to them – he didn't want to stand in a queue, like waiting to kiss the Pope's ring – and caught Zamboni's eye.

'Hey Michael, you know Skip?' Zamboni asked. Skip turned to face Michael and immediately turned on the smile.

'I think we might have met in Palm Springs at that sales conference,' Michael said.

'Sure, I remember,' Skip said, quite untruthfully. 'Great to see you. I've heard a lot about you.'

'I hope you won't hold that against me,' Michael replied.

'Certainly not. You've been doing a great job. Tell me, how's the Morgan Stanley situation? Can we salvage something there?'

'Nick and I have been working on it. I have some new ideas I'd like to discuss with you.'

'Look forward to it. I'll catch up with you later, OK?' The audience was clearly over and Michael was dismissed. It hadn't gone too badly, after all. Perhaps there was some hope.

Michael spent the entire day waiting for Skip to catch up

with him, but he never did. Whatever had been planned for him, it did not include a visit to Michael's office. People came and went, asking Michael what he thought and giving him the benefit of their own opinions, but the man himself was locked away somewhere – presumably with Zamboni – and did not appear until after six-thirty that evening.

When Michael finally saw him he still looked freshly pressed and immaculate, as if both he and his clothes were made of some crease-resistant fabric. The grin was just as dazzling as it had been that morning and the eyes sparkled no less clearly. Skip was walking across the office with Zamboni, entirely relaxed and easy as he listened to what his boss was saying. They were approaching Michael's office and he hurriedly called up a file on his PC to give the appearance of hard work, even though he had wasted most of his day wondering how, and if, he would ever recover his former status in the organisation. He had called Charles Turkwood three times about the Morgan Stanley deal, but his messages had gone unanswered, and this had sufficiently deflated him so that he was unable to concentrate on anything else.

'We're going for a beer and a bite to eat and we were hoping you could join us,' Skip said as the two of them reached Michael's door.

He knew he couldn't refuse, even though he wanted to delay this moment. 'That's fine,' he replied. 'I'll just call my wife and let her know.'

'OK. See you in five at reception.' Skip flashed a smile at Michael and retreated; Zamboni never even looked at him. Michael tried and failed to read the body language. Annie would have picked up the signals in a second, he thought. Perhaps they ought to hire her instead.

He called Annie and explained the situation. She asked him how he felt. 'As sick as I've ever been,' he answered honestly. 'The thought of spending the evening with them isn't my idea of a good time.'

'Just relax and be charming,' she advised. 'You'll do brilliantly. You always do.'

He liked the way she stroked him but it wasn't enough. 'We'll see. I have this awful feeling about it all. Skip is so far up Zamboni's backside he needs Vaseline. He'll do whatever Zamboni says.'

'Stop being so silly,' Annie said gently. 'You're very valuable to them, and you simply have to make them see that. Now, go and get on with it.'

He rang off, got up from the desk and put his jacket on. His body throbbed in nervous anticipation and his mouth went dry. He had this one chance to stake his claim, to make them realise that he was delivering the goods and would continue to do so, but the confidence he usually carried so well seemed to have drained from him. He stood completely still and practised breathing deeply, pushing out all the stale air from his lungs and pulling in fresh oxygen until his fingertips tingled. Then he moved out towards reception.

The bar was light and airy, a far cry from the gloomy wine vaults and cellars that had been so popular in the City in the eighties; it had been converted from an old bank branch, and the huge windows let in the last of the day's autumnal sunshine. There were long scrubbed tables and huge blackboards advertising exotic sandwiches and trendy salads, with not a Cumberland sausage in sight. The bottled beers they sold were all foreign and had fancy labels, and the wines were mainly New World. It was an environment that had been designed to suggest healthiness and good living, fresh and supposedly in tune with the new aspirations of the nineties. City boys and girls stood around clutching their beers and discussing the incompetence of their bosses; only a few brave souls smoked. They would still get just as drunk as their predecessors had in those dingy wine bars, but they'd feel better about it.

Michael preferred to stand, but Skip moved them to a table as soon as they'd bought their beers. The three of them sat around one end, Zamboni taking the chairman's seat. They all sipped modestly from the bottles and Skip grinned. 'Wow, that certainly hit the spot,' he said after his first tiny

54

swig. 'I never thought English beer would taste this good.'

'It's Australian, actually,' Michael corrected him.

Skip studied the label. 'Really? Well, it still tastes pretty good.' Zamboni observed the exchange impassively, unwilling to make a contribution.

Michael turned the bottle round in his hand, anxious not to outpace his partners even though he would have liked to gulp the beer down in one. 'So, how was day one?' he asked.

'Truth to tell, I'm totally confused,' Skip said. 'I've taken in so much information it'll take a few days for it all to sink in. I'm kind of slow in that department.' Again the teeth flashed as he smiled.

'A little different from the Midwest, I'd imagine,' Michael said.

'Yes and no. Clients are pretty much the same the world over, I guess. They're demanding and they want everything yesterday. The accents may change, and the culture may be different, but they all want great service, and that's what we've got to focus on.'

Michael shot a glance at Zamboni. His expression gave nothing away; he seemed to be content to let Skip do the talking. 'Well,' Michael said, 'I hope you'll find that our service levels here are in pretty good shape. Certainly all the research we've done suggests that they like the way we look after them.'

'That's my gut feel,' Skip replied. 'Obviously I need to get out there and talk to them, but I'm pretty relaxed about the service aspect.' He put the bottle to his lips and took another minuscule sip. Michael did the same. 'My instinct is that I'm going to be spending most of my time on sales development. Right now that's the top priority.'

'That's great news, Skip. We're very conscious of the need to upgrade our sales skills, and your expertise is going to be vital.' Michael could hardly believe he was saying this: it sounded so false, so insincere, yet it was what he felt they wanted to hear. He was a good corporate man, a team player on whom they could rely. He would swim with the tide, roll with the punches, go with the flow: this was the new Michael Lensman and Annie would be proud of him.

Zamboni's intervention caught him by surprise. 'On that subject,' he said, 'we need to have a discussion about your future role within DataTrak.'

The statement was so blunt that Michael missed a beat. 'Fine,' he said when he'd recovered. 'Should that happen now?'

'Now's as good a time as any,' Zamboni said. 'Skip, why don't you get us another round of beers?' Skip dutifully went to the bar and Zamboni shifted in his chair so that he could look directly at Michael. 'Something's come up and I'm disturbed by it. I was hoping you could explain.'

'I don't understand,' Michael said honestly.

'The Morgan Stanley deal. I got a call from a guy named Charles Turkwood. Ring any bells?'

'Of course. He's the consultant working with Morgan Stanley on the deal.'

'Right. He claims you tried to bribe him.'

'He what?' Michael exclaimed. 'This is a joke, isn't it?'

Zamboni's tone remained flat. 'Apparently not. He says you told him that you'd do whatever it took to get the deal. He interpreted that as an illicit inducement. What's your reading on that?'

Michael could feel his face flushing and he took a swig of beer in the hope that it might cool him down. 'Nick, this is preposterous. Yes, I did say that, but I didn't mean it the way he thinks. What I meant was that we'd be prepared to lower our prices, offer additional services, whatever. It was a normal pitch, for God's sake. We say it all the time in these situations – you know, "What do I need to do to win the business?" It was nothing more than that. He knows that.'

'Obviously not. He was pretty bent out of shape. I guess he's going to raise it with the folks at Morgan Stanley. It puts us in an impossible position, Mike.'

Skip returned with the beers, his smile intact. He sat down and looked at Zamboni, who now spoke to him. 'I was just bringing Mike up to speed on the Morgan Stanley affair.'

Skip nodded thoughtfully, then looked at Michael. 'What do you propose we do?' he asked.

'Off the top of my head, I have no idea. It's so ludicrous that I can't really focus on it. You realise that, don't you?'

Skip and Zamboni exchanged a meaningful glance. 'Mike, it's not quite that simple,' Zamboni said. 'What we think isn't the issue here. The problem is one of perception. Rightly or wrongly, the image of DataTrak has been tarnished by what you said to Turkwood. He may be an asshole, but he's an important asshole and we need him on our side. We have to show him, through our actions, that we are whiter than white. We need to send that signal very clearly. You know how these things get around town, blown out of all proportion, so that before you know it everyone who matters thinks we're a bunch of shysters. We simply cannot afford to let that happen.'

'Then we've got to go to Morgan Stanley and explain it all,' Michael said, keen to offer a good defence.

'Skip's already working on that. But we have a more immediate problem.'

'Which is?'

'You, Mike. You've been hurt by this whole deal. And there's collateral damage to DataTrak as a result. Bottom line, we need to review the whole thing, see where it went wrong, make sure there are no weak points in the system, nothing we couldn't have done better. I'm sure you appreciate that.'

Michael guzzled the remaining beer from his bottle, no longer caring if he was keeping pace with them. 'I do, Nick, and I'll be happy to cooperate in any way I can.' He heard himself sounding slightly desperate but could do nothing to temper it.

'I'm glad you said that. We'll be needing your help, I'm sure. In the meantime, Skip and I feel it would be appropriate for you to stay away from the office. Spend a few days at home with the family and get your thoughts in order.'

'What are you saying, Nick? Am I suspended?'

Zamboni turned his head towards Skip, passing responsibility to him. 'It's a tough call,' Skip said, 'but it's better for everyone if we do this. The guys from Human

57

Resources will be in touch, and we'll work something out. We have to play by the rules here. Do you have your security pass on you?'

Michael froze as the full horror of the situation dawned on him. He had been set up, of that he was sure, but as his mind swam he couldn't see any avenue out of the crisis. He reached into his trouser pocket and pulled out his pass. 'Here,' he said, sliding it across the table to Skip.

'Thanks. One word of advice, if you'll take it. We want to be honourable, to do the right thing. We have no desire to treat you badly. You've been a very valuable employee and DataTrak will acknowledge that. Play ball and we can sort all this out amicably, I'm sure.'

Michael was suddenly very angry, and he made no effort to disguise it. 'You're firing me over some trumped-up charge that has no validity, and you want me to play ball? I can't believe you've said that. You have no grounds for dismissal whatsoever, and you know it. If you're hoping I'll go quietly then you're much mistaken.'

Now Skip seemed oleaginous, the smoothness sickening. 'That's your choice, Mike. I hope we can conduct this on an entirely professional level. It's not personal. Don't think it is. It's simply a commercial decision. You'll come to see that eventually.'

'Like hell I will.' Michael got up from the table. 'I hope you'll excuse me if I don't join you for dinner, but all of a sudden I don't feel hungry and I have a very unpleasant taste in my mouth. Was there anything else?' He glared at both of them in turn.

'We'll be in touch.'

As Michael turned his back he could feel them watching him as he stormed out of the bar. The feeling burnt his skin and it was all he could do to prevent himself from issuing a primal scream.

EIGHT

'It's classic management practice. If you're going to fire someone, do it on a Monday. That way, so the theory goes, you have the whole week to recover.' Michael shook his head in disbelief, keeping his eyes fixed on his mug of coffee.

'Listen,' Annie replied, 'we both know this is completely unfair and irrational, but we can't let it ruin our lives. We just have to get on with things and do the best we can. In a few months' time we'll probably look back at this and say it was the best thing that ever happened to us.'

'I wish I could believe that,' Michael said. 'The problem is, my perspective is pretty screwed up at the moment.'

It was Wednesday morning. Tuesday had been one of the toughest days Annie had ever known: after the shock of the news on Monday night – with Michael incandescent and more aggressive than she'd ever seen him – they had had little useful rest and had spent the whole of the next day working on strategy and tactics. Michael had made long phone calls to a solicitor who specialised in employment, Robin Stone, during which he was told that it sounded like a clear case of constructive dismissal and that, although it would be expensive to fight it, he had good cause to do so. The three calls he had made to DataTrak – Skip, Zamboni and the head of Human Resources – had all gone unanswered. This didn't surprise him: he could well imagine that a corporate command had already filtered through the ranks, advising the troops that all contact with him was strictly forbidden. In a matter of hours Michael Lensman had become a pariah, no longer touchable by his former peers and colleagues. They would be talking about him, wondering what could possibly have happened to precipitate this crisis, and Brian would probably be oiling the rumour mill.

Annie observed his behaviour closely, and was quietly proud of him. The anger was entirely understandable and, to her mind, completely justified. He had been a loyal servant of the company, a rainmaker who had brought in excellent clients and a lot of revenue, and now he was being ditched in a cynical political manoeuvre. She was just as angry, but that ire was different, less violent and overt; to her, such raw emotion merely fogged reason and logic, and it was she who would have to focus him so that he got whatever result it was that they both wanted.

The problem for Annie was that she wasn't quite sure what she wanted from all this. For Michael it was easy: he needed revenge, and he needed to defend his reputation against the charges. A substantial wedge of cash would be the primary measurement of his success in achieving this, as well as a good reference and other signs of goodwill. While he would continue to maintain his innocence, and fight hard on that front, he had already accepted the fact that he would not be reinstated: it had gone too far for that, and he knew the rules of the game. Mud sticks, as he well understood.

But Annie had a different agenda. Even knowing how badly wounded he was, she could see that this was a situation which might have some eventual benefit for the family, that the very thing which caused him so much pain would ultimately make him stronger and wiser. She would gladly have throttled Skip McMaster and Nick Zamboni if she'd thought it would do any good, but she doubted the validity of such action: the dish of vengeance, if it had to be eaten, could wait a while yet, she reasoned. Uppermost in her mind was a desire to see Michael recover from this and for the damage to be limited and quick to repair. A protracted battle with the mighty forces of DataTrak would be debilitating and counter-productive; how much better if Michael could retreat gracefully, honour intact, and move on to the next challenge.

She knew – at least, she thought she knew – what would be coming in the days ahead. The fury would dissipate, turning to despair as Michael's confidence evaporated and he struggled to reconcile himself to reality. He would become frustrated, edgy, scratchy, and they would all suffer; but how precisely he would seek refuge from this turmoil she couldn't yet say. Her task was to manage him through the process, to buttress his defences so that he sustained no permanent harm. However he reacted, Annie needed to be behind him, beside him, with him.

What she did know was that he was, in these early days, ready to lash out at anything or anyone which strayed too close to him without good cause. He had snapped at Holly for nothing, berated secretaries for their unwillingness to connect him to the right person, and had accused her of many perceived slights. It hurt her only when she saw him short with Holly – the rest she could abide, in the hope that it would soon fade – but their daughter was blameless, an innocent bystander who could not possibly comprehend the motives behind Daddy's rage. Annie had arranged for her to go to a friend's house after play school on the Tuesday, but she could not be protected indefinitely, and she needed to know that their love was still unconditional. With her usual soft approach, Annie confronted Michael on the subject.

'I know exactly how you must feel, and I don't blame you one little bit,' she said, 'but we must try not to let it affect Holly. She doesn't know what's going on, and we've got to insulate her from all of it.'

His reaction was what she had expected. 'You're always so perfect when it comes to dealing with her, aren't you? I'm not allowed to lose my temper – and, of course, you never do. Well, I'm very sorry I can't live up to your expectations, but the whole of my world's falling to pieces, in case you haven't noticed, and I'm quite upset about it.'

Annie could see his face start to tighten as he prepared himself for a row, but she refused to rise to it. 'I'm talking about us. I'm just as upset as you are, and I know how annoying she can be, so I'm equally likely to have a go at her. It's an observation, not a condemnation. Under normal circumstances you're so good, and so patient, with her –

61

much better than me – but we're neither of us under normal circumstances.'

'Fine – I'll bear it in mind.' He had lost interest in a fight, much to Annie's relief. He still wouldn't look at her directly, as if fearful that he might see some trace of weakness – or, worse still, reproach – in her face. As he finished his coffee the phone rang and he sprang up to answer it.

'Michael Lensman,' he said, his tone laced with defiance.

'Michael, it's Mary Strutter.' Mary was the personnel manager, although her business card said Director of Human Resources. She didn't wait for a greeting. 'We need you to come in tomorrow morning at ten-thirty. Can you do that?'

'What's the purpose of the meeting, and who will be there?'

'We want to present our proposals for a settlement. I'll be there, with Skip.'

'I see. I'll have to check whether my lawyer can make it.' He waited to see what effect this would have.

'Off the record, it wouldn't be too smart to bring a lawyer. It's better if you come on your own.'

'Thanks for the advice, Mary,' Michael said curtly. 'On the record, I'll be the judge of that.'

'It's up to you. But we want to be fair, and we don't want any unpleasantness. If we can avoid a confrontational situation, it'll be better for everyone.'

'I get the message. I'll see you tomorrow. Thanks for the call.' Michael put the phone down without giving Mary the chance to say anything else. He looked across at Annie and raised his eyebrows. 'Judgement day,' he said.

When Michael was eight, he was sent to board at a small preparatory school on the Sussex coast. It had a steady, if unremarkable, record of getting the boys into their first choice of public school, with a headmaster who seemed entirely indifferent to the well-being or development of his charges. Having been a commander in the Navy, he treated the boys like ratings and the school like a ship, with all the teachers – referred to as masters – as officers of varying seniority. It was not an unkind environment, simply one devoid of any true care: there were no cold showers, no early morning cross-country runs, no unusually cruel punishments, but neither were there any concessions to the normal fears and uncertainties of boys who had been separated from their families unnaturally early in their little lives. There were two exeats each term, with a short half-term break, and parents were allowed, but not encouraged, to visit on school match days.

Michael's parents deposited him into the school and, having paid the fees, expected him to be nurtured by the staff. In moments when she was in the kitchen, making a cake or a pudding with Peter by her side, Michael's mother felt sad and wished she could see more of him, but it was a feeling she kept well hidden from his father. The decision to send him away was hardly a conscious one: like father, like son. It was what parents did if they could afford it, like the instincts of birds when pushing their fledgelings out of the nest for the first time. Michael was never consulted, and his views on life as a boarder were never solicited.

In spite of this, he flourished. He was a talented sportsman and a good scholar. He received his fair share of black marks for bad behaviour but always avoided the ultimate punishment, which was six of the best from the headmaster. He wrote happy letters to his parents in which he related the minutiae of his life, and he rarely complained about his lot. The masters generally tolerated him without ever encouraging him to excel, so that he was left to make the best of things for himself. He studied hard and asked intelligent questions; he became captain of most of the teams in which he played; and he won a place at his father's choice of public school, a second division institution which was even further away from home in Somerset.

His promise declined as soon as he changed school. From being a big fish in a small pond, he was suddenly surrounded by boys who were bigger, stronger, fitter and cleverer, and he reacted badly to the challenge: instead of rising to it, he gave up. It was easier to survive as someone unexceptional, someone to whom no high hopes were ascribed, and he spent little time trying to compete, preferring to keep the company of others like himself who were merely concerned with staying the course and moving on. Any ambitions he had had as an innocent twelve-year-old were washed away by indifference and lassitude so that, by the time he was sixteen and had finished O-levels, he had no idea of what he wanted to do. He chose History, Economics and English as his A-levels, subjects he felt were soft and therefore easier to pass, something he did without too much effort. Armed with two Bs and a C, he went to university without taking a year off and became a serious and introverted undergraduate.

Through all of this his parents offered minimal support. They loved him and were kind to him, but they were ill-equipped to give him anything more. His adolescence was not especially painful, and he didn't rebel in any noticeable way, so they never saw the need for additional help or advice. They took it for granted that he would get a sound degree and go on to a comfortable job; they never expected anything different, and he did not disappoint them. They did not see the missed potential, the slow erosion of ambition as he learnt to settle for something slightly less than might have been gained, the loss of opportunity and motivation as he swam with the tide to lessen the burden of expectation. For them, Michael was what he was: they did not harbour unrealistic hopes of what he might become, let alone provide him with any impetus to achieve more.

Michael took this well, having known nothing different, and he remained a good son. Up to the day his father died their relationship was cordial but remote: they had nothing in common other than blood, and the subject of their conversations never strayed into personal territory. His father could not give him any special insight into life and its tribulations, and Michael did not seek it. Instead, they talked of cricket and, just occasionally, politics – but only in a vague and abstract way, as if there were some unseen mechanism that prevented them from divulging any true feelings or beliefs. Michael mourned his passing but showed little sadness and soon recovered from the temporary feeling of lost opportunities.

Michael's mother had lived for so long in her husband's shadow that she hardly seemed to have a personality of her own, and Michael would not have dreamt to have asked her questions that he felt he couldn't ask his father. They had an easy, loving relationship that tested neither of them and was based on her role as provider of early cuddles, hot meals and clean laundry. From that experience, she was a resource he valued.

The dynamics of his relationship with Peter were altogether more complicated. There was a gap of five years between them, but the gulf was not predicated on age: Peter was treated differently by his parents, sent to different schools and allowed a leeway in his behaviour that Michael noticed, even if he didn't resent it. It was not until much later, when he talked about Peter with Annie, that he began to wonder whether Peter's character was formed by his parents and their attitude towards him, rather than by the complexities of genetic chemistry and chance. Would he have been more like Michael if he had been treated the same, or would he still have turned out as the rather wet and whingeing individual Michael now perceived him to be? He would certainly not have chosen him as a younger brother and, as a result, he spent little time thinking about him or trying to understand what made him tick. He was just there, something to be endured and possibly even pitied.

Once armed with his degree, Michael was anxious to get on with his life, not because he wanted to leave home but more because he realised that he needed to work very hard to keep up with all those competitors he had avoided during his education. He knew that life beyond school and university would not allow him to duck these challenges any longer, and his backbone stiffened the minute he moved into the real world. What he chose to ignore as a boy he would face up to as a man; he was ready in a way he had not been when there were so many convenient hiding places during his time as a student.

Although his plan for life was not fully formed, Michael had little trouble in adapting to his new circumstances. He got himself a job – at a rival of DataTrak – and worked diligently for promotion and the approbation that came mainly through pay rises. He met Annie and let her shine a light on his existence, turning it from something small and unexciting into an altogether more satisfactory state of affairs. From the moment he realised that they would get married, it was as if he shrugged off the last doubts of youth and could begin to think and act exclusively like a man. She unburdened him of that part of his soul which could not let go of his immaturity, and he moved on with a new poise and purpose. Almost unknowingly, he had found the support that had been so deficient when he was a boy and this, more than anything else perhaps, was why he loved Annie so much.

Michael was preparing himself for the challenge of his meeting – making notes as he read and reread his employment contract – when the phone rang. He expected it to be Robin Stone, his lawyer, and was surprised when it wasn't.

'Hiya,' a woman's voice said. 'It's Pam.'

'Oh,' he replied falteringly, not knowing how to react.

'I'm not disturbing you, am I?'

'Er, no, not really. How are you?'

'More to the point, how are you?'

'Look, Pam, I don't mean to be rude, but should you be calling me? I'd assumed there was an embargo on speaking to me.'

'There is, silly, but you're a friend and I just wanted to find out how you're bearing up. I'm calling from home and I don't think Zamboni's tapped my phone – although I wouldn't put it past him.' She giggled nervously at this breach of discipline.

'Well, I appreciate the call. I suppose I'm all right, considering everything that's happened. I'm coming in tomorrow for a meeting, so things will be much clearer after that.'

'Yes, I heard about that. They've been locked in meetings all day. It's all very hush-hush.'

'What else is going on there? What's the reaction been?'

'Everybody's terrified. They reckon that if they're prepared to do this to you, no one's safe. I expect I'll be out before too long.'

'I think that's pretty unlikely, Pam. If they let you go the whole place will collapse.'

'Oh right,' she said mockingly. 'But listen, if you want to meet up for a drink or anything, let me know, OK?'

'That's great, and as soon as I've got everything sorted out I'll do that.'

'Annie and Holly all right?'

'Fine. We'll get through this, don't worry.'

'Best of luck tomorrow, then. Wear your blue suit – it looks really good on you.'

'Thanks, Pam.'

When Michael returned to his paperwork Annie came over and rubbed his back. 'I can't quite put my finger on it,' she said, 'but there's something not quite right about Pam. I know she's very sweet and kind, but something doesn't ring true and I find her very annoying.'

'I don't know what you're talking about,' he said, only half-listening to her.

'No. It's probably just my devious mind.' Annie nodded slowly and tried to dispel the thought, but it didn't budge as easily as she would have liked.

NINE

Skip had no time to be tired. In any event, he wasn't the sort of person who complained of exhaustion: he had a constitution which adjusted itself to meet the demands put on it, giving sleep if time was available and pumping fresh energy into the system whenever required. Skip didn't get ill, either. He awoke every morning feeling exactly the same, his body ready to snap into action and his mind clear and clean. He took it for granted, this general well-being, and wasn't quite able to understand those who weren't so robust: his was a world of health and efficiency, where spare time was always used productively and there were no excuses for wasting it.

He'd been up late on Wednesday night, sitting with Nick Zamboni and Mary Strutter in his hotel room as they went over and over the details of the deal. They'd ordered pizzas and soda and Skip had felt comfortable as he chewed on a slice of American Hot and guzzled Diet Coke: this was how he'd imagined it, dropped into the thick of the action and having to make tough decisions from day one. He worked hard to sound thoughtful, anxious to let Nick know that he could handle this – and anything else that was thrown at him. He was very conscious of the need to prove himself, to demonstrate his management skills and justify Nick's faith in him; he wanted to succeed and, more importantly, to be perceived as a success, and this was an early test that he must not fail.

Once back in his room he'd called Teri and briefed her on the day's events. She was a good listener, occasionally asking intelligent questions and getting him to clarify certain points, but waiting until he had finished before voicing her own opinions. There had never been a time when Skip did not seek her advice and guidance: on all major issues he turned to her for help, and she had become his mentor. Teri didn't see this as a weakness in him, didn't even notice that it happened this way, and her contributions were made without condescension. She liked to be involved, but didn't demand it; he would not have had it any other way.

In their phone conversation Teri gently reminded him that Michael's family must be taken into account, that this was not simply a case of shedding someone whose sell-by date had expired, and that he must factor that into the package. If the wife was satisfied, she reasoned, it tended to lessen the blow. Doubtless he would be tempted to say to himself: 'Don't let personal feelings cloud your judgement', but Teri told him to think about what it would do to him if he faced the same situation as Michael. He took this on board and undertook to apply sensitivity; when he finally got to sleep, his thoughts were still affected by what she had said.

On Thursday morning his routine was unaffected by the foreign surroundings and the shortage of sleep. After he'd finished his stretching exercises, he showered and shaved, rubbed a special moisturising cream on to his face, then attended to his hair with the blow-drier. Having already put out his clothes the night before, he checked each item carefully before dressing in front of the mirror. Skip placed a high value on presentation – 'Look good, feel good,' as he said – and he worked hard at achieving just the right look. Gold tie, white shirt, blue suit, black loafers: this was the uniform of power and authority. He buttoned his jacket and shot the sleeves before he was fully satisfied, then gave himself a salute in the mirror and retrieved his briefcase. A big day lay ahead, but Skip was ready for it.

They sat in a private meeting room on the third floor, away from the business units and prying eyes and ears. Zamboni, Mary Strutter and Skip convened early and had spent a few minutes on the final details of stage management – who would lead the meeting, what would be said and when – and now they shuffled their papers as Michael came in and sat down. He looked serious and determined, pulling out a large manila folder from his briefcase and placing it on the table in front of him.

'Thanks for coming in at such short notice,' Mary said.

'I can't think of anything that takes priority over this,' Michael replied. 'After all, we're about to discuss the future direction of my whole life.'

'I wouldn't put it quite as starkly as that,' Mary said with a little smile.

'Probably not – but then, this isn't happening to you, is it?' He smiled back.

'OK,' Skip intervened, keen to end hostilities. 'Let's get started. Mary?'

Mary moved some of her papers, more to give herself time to settle than to find anything specific. 'Michael, as you know, certain allegations have been made regarding your conduct during negotiations for the Morgan Stanley business. These allegations are serious enough to warrant immediate dismissal without compensation if they are found to be true.'

'Which they patently are not,' Michael said.

Mary held up a hand so that the palm faced him. 'Please – let me finish. DataTrak has no wish to pursue that particular line. We see no value, for you or us, in going down that route, as I'm sure you'll appreciate. What we want to do this morning is to reach a mutual and binding agreement on the best way forward. We have some recommendations, which have been approved by Head Office, and which we hope can settle this affair amicably. That's why we're here.'

Michael rubbed a finger across his mouth. 'Before we get started, you'll understand that I can't agree to anything without consulting my advisers. Whatever you're proposing will have to be approved by them.'

'Yes, we know that, but the timing is critical here. We want this resolved quickly, and I'm sure you do too.'

'So how long do I have?'

'We'll need a definitive response from you by close of

business on Monday. That'll give you the weekend to think it over. But I must warn you that the offer is non-negotiable – it's take it or leave it, and we won't consider any counter-offers.' Michael made no effort to acknowledge this, just as he'd been advised. 'Skip is going to give you all the details.'

Skip had a yellow legal pad in front of him, and he referred to this as he spoke. 'As Mary said, your professional conduct has been called into question following allegations made by Charles Turkwood. We also feel that you are exerting a bad influence in the office and that your continued presence will have a damaging effect on morale. Certain employees have made complaints regarding your attitude, and we have taken these into account. We therefore feel that it's in everyone's best interests if you leave DataTrak.'

Michael was writing all this down and Skip paused to let him catch up. 'What we propose is that you resign from the company with immediate effect. Your notice period will be waived. In return for your voluntary resignation, DataTrak will undertake not to pursue any disciplinary action against you, now or in the future. We will provide excellent references for potential employers and this agreement will not be disclosed to any third party, either by you or us. Additionally, we will pay you a one-off fee equivalent to two years' gross salary, and will allow you to keep your company car until the end of its lease. Finally, we will announce your retention as a consultant to DataTrak for a period of six months from the date of your resignation. This will mean that you will be available to us for consultation and advice as and when we deem it necessary, for which we will pay you a monthly retainer of three thousand pounds. In practical terms, we do not see this as an onerous requirement on your part.'

Michael continued to write even though his eyes were watering and his hand shook. He realised that Skip had learnt this by heart and didn't need his notes: it was a mechanical recital of a document they'd dreamt up between them, and Skip was merely the mouthpiece for it.

When he had finished writing, Skip wrapped it up. 'That's the deal, Michael. No negotiation. It's up to you.'

71

Michael looked up from his pad. 'And if I say no?'

'Then we'll formally suspend you and instigate a full investigation which may lead to disciplinary proceedings and, possibly, legal action against you.' Skip's voice was steady and firm; he'd been well coached.

'Was there anything else?' Michael asked.

Skip looked at Zamboni and Mary for confirmation, and they both shook their heads. 'Nope,' he replied, 'that's it.'

Michael put the top back on his pen. 'To whom should I give my response?'

'Me,' Mary said. 'I'll be in all day Monday.'

Michael wanted to say so many things, to protest his innocence once again and put them straight on the real story, but resisted the impulse. He got to his feet and packed his folder in his briefcase. 'I'll be in touch,' he said before leaving the room, knowing already that he would never return.

Even though it was a Thursday, there was little resistance to Brian's suggestion that they all went out for a drink after work. The office was buzzing with rumours and Brian wanted to flush them out with alcohol; whatever was going on with Michael had to be known about by someone, as nothing ever remained a secret for too long. He even managed to persuade Sharon, one of the less discreet secretaries in Human Resources, to join them.

Once they were all settled and the effect of the beers started to kick in, there was little discussion of anything other than Michael. Everyone had an opinion, or a snippet of information – except Pam. Whilst she was quite happy to come along, she kept her own counsel and merely listened to what was being said. Brian noticed this and tried several times to draw her into the conversation, but without success. She shrugged, she smiled, but she didn't crack. Sharon was more amenable.

'They've done a deal,' she announced confidently, and everyone's attention turned to her.

'We know that, my little beauty,' Brian said, 'but give us the dirt. Come on, we need facts and figures.'

Sharon was enjoying her moment of glory and wouldn't give it up lightly. 'It's confidential. I can't tell you any more.'

'Get this lady another drink,' Brian commanded. 'If that doesn't work we'll have to use the thumbscrews.'

'Brian!' Sharon squealed. 'I'm not going to tell you so you can just forget it.'

'Yes you are, sweetie.' He leant across the table and clutched her hand in his. 'You know it makes sense.'

Sharon thought for a moment, then looked at Brian and drew her finger across her throat. 'He's out. History. They've shafted him good and proper. We won't be seeing Mr Lensman again.'

'How? What have they done? More to the point, what's he done?'

All eyes and ears were now on Sharon. 'I don't know what he's done, honest. Mary's been really secretive about that, typing all her own stuff and everything. But I did happen to see a memo on her desk and I managed to read a bit of it. They're going to pay him off and he's going to resign so that it doesn't look like he's been sacked. They told him this morning. He came in for a meeting and they made the deal.'

'And he's accepted that?' Brian asked.

'Don't know. And whatever he did is going to be hushed up too. I've heard that it's got something to do with one of his customers. Someone told me he might have been having an affair with a client.'

There was general agreement around the table that this was highly unlikely; Michael was known to be a devoted husband and father and infidelity was considered too far-fetched. Then, without warning, Pam spoke.

'He's not like that,' she said. 'He'd never do that.'

'What makes you so sure?' Brian asked.

'Because I know him. I've worked for him and I'd know if something had been going on. Michael's an honourable man. He doesn't cheat on Annie.' It was a definitive rebuttal and the conversation soon moved on to other speculation, but Brian remained struck by the quiet force with which Pam had spoken. She knew things that others did not, and she was bloody good at keeping them hidden. This annoyed him, but he had to admire her for it.

It went like that all evening: as the beer flowed the theories became ever more fanciful until they reached the stage where they would all have been quite happy to believe anything that was suggested. Sharon had quickly exhausted her supply of hard facts but continued to chip in; Pam listened and only occasionally said anything; and Brian egged them all on, enjoying his role as convenor and stirrer. By the time they all reeled back to catch their trains, Michael Lensman was already becoming a blip on the DataTrak history chart.

Teri didn't want to tell him on the phone. He was too busy, and she wanted to look him in the eye when she broke the news. It had finally happened, not without some considerable effort, and she felt that they needed to be sitting together when she announced her pregnancy. She could well imagine the shock, and the elation, that would engulf him once he knew: Skip was a sucker for children, and the prospect of having one of his own would be the greatest thing he could hope for. Teri was as excited about telling him as she had been when she'd gone to her doctor for confirmation of her home test.

Conceiving was not a straightforward matter. Skip apparently had a low sperm count, but that was not the real issue. There was a bigger problem for Teri to deal with, and that was Skip's lack of drive. Sex was the one area where they did not seem to be in step: Teri liked it a lot, but Skip regarded it as little more than a duty. For him there was no spontaneity, no sudden pumping desire that had to be fulfilled, whilst Teri frequently ached for rough, urgent sex without the frills. He always needed to be coaxed, to have the right ambience and circumstances, and rarely made the first move.

He was also too courteous, almost too respectful of Teri so that nothing ever descended to the level of baser instincts, appearing to be shocked if she tried to initiate sex without

74

warning or a long seduction period. He had put sex into a box that needed careful unlocking: for him, it was not the ultimate demonstration of their love for each other, and he did not treat it as a glorious gift to be used whenever they liked. She was frustrated by this but was well able to deal with it; it seemed churlish to complain when everything else in their lives was so good. She had to be grateful that, when they'd reached agreement on starting a family, he'd uncomplainingly complied with the schedule she'd drawn up. They changed their diet and kept themselves fit, checking her temperature before religiously performing on alternate nights as advised. He'd played his part without demur, though she knew how much it pained him.

Now they had their reward, and Teri glowed with anticipation. He'd be home soon and they'd celebrate, tell their parents and start planning this next phase of their lives. There was a lot to be discussed, and many questions to be answered, but that didn't frighten her. She was ready for this, and she was sure that Skip would be as well.

TEN

It was not how Annie had expected it to be. She was anticipating a dreadful time, a day filled with Michael's bitterness and recrimination, but instead she got something different, something almost more difficult to deal with: he was calm and restrained, telling her the details of their offer in a flat, disinterested manner, as if he were recounting the news of someone he didn't know very well and cared for even less. He had written it all down and read each item to her without comment as they sat in the kitchen, the background noise of the dishwasher filling the gaps between his sentences. He seemed peaceful, yet she knew that this could not be so: he had suffered so much turmoil, so much misery and anger, that she felt he must be functioning through some unrecognised instinct of self-preservation, unwilling to let it all burst out in case they were both helplessly caught in the torrent.

'What do you think?' he asked her when he had finished reciting his notes, his tone suggesting that he didn't mind one way or the other.

'I don't know. It seems very fair, if you can describe the way they've treated you as fair. But it doesn't matter what I think, does it? It's really up to you.'

'No, I don't think so. This affects you and Holly just as much as me. Remember that you're going to be the ones to suffer if I can't get another job.'

She didn't understand him, couldn't make out his angle or whether he was merely so shocked that he wasn't functioning normally. 'Have you spoken to Robin Stone?' she asked.

'I will do, but I guess he'll say that it's up to me – to us. He can only advise, after all. He gets paid whatever the outcome.'

Was he defeated? she wondered silently. He gave the impression of a man who had finally met his match and who was now doing his best to come to terms with it without cracking up. Annie thought she knew him better than that; in other tough situations he had always put up a fight, especially in business, and she couldn't reconcile this with what she was now witnessing. Was there something he wasn't telling her? Had some terrible incident occurred to make him behave like this? Although it was unpalatable, she couldn't help thinking that there was something more behind this façade of reason and submission, but she didn't want to know – not yet, at least. That could come later.

'I drew up a list on the train,' he continued. 'You know, a T-square of advantages and disadvantages. The main minus is that I lose my job, obviously. But there are plenty of positive things that come out of this. It gives me time to think about what I really want to do. I've never had that before. The money buys us that time. There's a lot to be said for it.'

'Are you saying you don't want to start looking for a job straight away?' Annie asked, hardly able to comprehend what he was suggesting.

'The jobs will come to me. I'm not worried about that. I'm well enough known in the market for the news to get around to the headhunters before too long. But I'm not going to jump at the first thing that comes along, no. I want to be sure that it's right, and that may take some time. Is that wrong?'

'No, it sounds sensible,' she replied, trying to hide any doubt in her voice. It was as if she weren't talking to the Michael she knew, the man who was driven by deals and bonuses and promotions and targets. One short meeting appeared to have changed him completely. 'But . . . you're sure about this? I mean, it would be quite an adjustment – for all of us, but especially you.'

'I'm not going to have an early mid-life crisis, if that's

what you're worried about,' he said, almost cheerfully. 'I simply need some time to reflect – you know, to grieve. I'm losing something that's been such a major part of my life, and I have to have time to get over that.'

Whilst she might have agreed with the sentiment, Annie could not figure out how he had reached this state of cold logic so quickly. In his shoes, she would have been furious, wanting to lash out at Zamboni and Skip and make their lives a total misery, but he was already beyond that stage and wasn't looking back. It was bizarre and it made her uncomfortable; perhaps, she thought, he was still in shock and this was his defence mechanism.

'You know we'll support you whatever you decide to do,' she said. 'For what it's worth, I think you should accept the deal. They're never going to give you your job back, so you might as well take them for as much as you can get.'

'That's pretty much the conclusion I'd reached. I'll speak to Robin, but I don't think he'll come up with anything new. Let's get it out of the way and concentrate on the rest of our lives.'

And then Michael did something that was so unexpected, so totally alien, that Annie was completely confused. He smiled. It was a big smile, genuine and warm, coming from within his soul and illuminating his whole face. It was the first time she'd seen him smile like that for . . . well, she couldn't remember it was so long. He looked serene, as if in the grip of some epiphanic moment, and her heartbeat accelerated in response.

She couldn't think of anything profound to say. 'You're relieved, aren't you?' was all she could manage.

'Funnily enough, I think I am. I don't think I realised how much stress I was under. Now I do. I don't want this feeling to end, the sense that an enormous weight just fell off my shoulders. It's so good, Annie. It's as if I've been released.'

All her doubts fell away in that moment, in the glow of his smile and his piercing honesty. She could see that he was genuine, that this was not some elaborate charade designed to protect them from further wounds. It was an awesome display of his inner strength, and one that she needed more than anything else at this time in their lives. If he felt good about himself, that would reflect on to her and Holly and they would all be the better for it; her hopes raised, she couldn't help returning his smile.

'Good for you,' she said. 'So you'll call them today?'

'I'm not feeling that generous,' he replied. 'Let's make them sweat a bit over the weekend. Anyway, I've got other things to do today.'

'Such as?'

'Well, first we're going to go upstairs and go to bed. I haven't felt this horny for ages.'

'I see.' Annie got up and walked round to him. 'Why upstairs? We have everything we need right here.'

'In the kitchen?'

'Why not?' Annie undid her blouse and threw it on to the floor, then unfastened her bra and slipped it off her shoulders. 'Come on, you randy sod. Make the most of it.' And he did.

Charles Turkwood was not a happy man. Granted, he had the final payment from Morgan Stanley in the bank, but he was disturbed by the arbitrary way in which the contract had come to an end: he wanted to be a player, not some insignificant pawn used in the convoluted mind games that buyers and sellers used to try and gain an advantage over each other. To him, the whole deal smelt bad and he might suffer as a result; his business depended on good references and, more importantly, what was said about him in various wine bars and restaurants around the City. He couldn't bear the thought that they would be laughing about him and how he had been sidelined in one of the biggest deals of the year.

His temper was not improved by the prospect of lunch paid for by someone else. Skip McMaster – God, these bloody Yanks had some incredible names – wanted to introduce himself and to update Charles on the latest developments within DataTrak. Normally Charles would have had no problem with a free lunch, especially from a systems vendor, but he was still smarting and he felt, however irrationally, that DataTrak had something to do with the unseemly manner in which he had been released from the Morgan Stanley contract. Whoever this McMaster was would have to do some pretty fine dancing to rescue the situation.

Skip had redeemed himself a little by booking a table at Rules, one of Charles's favourite spots. The food was reliable, if uninspired, and they had a passable wine list – but what if Skip didn't drink? So many Americans were purer than the driven snow nowadays, sipping poxy glasses of mineral water with a pathetic twist of lime floating about. Charles was a claret man himself, with a dry sherry to start and a port to round things off. He could only hope that, as the guest, he would be asked to do the ordering.

Charles arrived late, as was his custom. He had come straight from a meeting in Bishopsgate and the taxi got snarled in lunchtime traffic, but tardiness had its advantages: it showed that he was busy and in demand, and also meant that he didn't have to wait for his host, whom he wouldn't know from Adam. Skip was already seated and Charles was escorted to his table. Skip leapt up to greet him.

'Hi, Charles. Skip McMaster. Good to meet you.' His handshake was firm – too firm for Charles's taste, who suspected that strong handshakes compensated for something weak within – and the grin was a little too brilliant. Charles sat down and immediately noticed a glass of Coke in front of Skip; he sighed internally. 'You'd like a drink, I expect,' Skip offered as a waiter hovered next to their table.

'Please. A chilled Tio Pepe would be lovely.' Skip made a face which suggested he'd never heard of this, but the waiter nodded and moved away briskly. 'Sherry,' Charles said with just a hint of condescension.

'Not a lot of demand for that where I come from,' Skip replied, the grin intact.

'So – you're over here on a visit?'

'At the moment. I'm going to be moving here permanently next month.'

'Oh well, congratulations are in order. To do what, exactly?'

The sherry arrived and Charles admired the colour of it before taking a small sip.

'I'm going to be running the sales function for Europe, the Middle East and Africa – or EMEA, as we call it.' Skip was clearly proud of his appointment.

'Yes. So how does that tie in with Mr Lensman? Will he be working for you?'

'That's one of the reasons I wanted to get together with you – to tell you about the changes at DataTrak. I may be new in town but I know you're one of the top consultants here so I figured I'd better introduce myself and put a face to a name. You're very highly regarded by everyone at DataTrak.'

He was good, Charles had to admit: it was naked flattery but none the worse for that. 'Thank you. I try to do the best for my clients.'

The smile evaporating, Skip's face suddenly turned very serious. 'Look, let's cut to the chase, shall we? As you can imagine, we were very disappointed not to win the Morgan Stanley account. They've been a very good client of ours for a number of years, and we're desperately sorry to see them go. But, hey! that's history, and we have to move on. There'll be other deals and other opportunities. What's important is that we continue to have a good relationship with you, one that's built on trust and mutual respect.'

'I couldn't agree more.'

'I'll be totally frank with you. I'm concerned that we didn't conduct ourselves very professionally during the bidding process for Morgan Stanley.'

'I wouldn't say that. In fact, I think quite the reverse is true. We were all very impressed with your presentations. Al Stent was particularly taken with your ideas for TrakPlus. But somebody has to lose, don't they? This time it was you. Next time, who knows?'

Skip seemed perplexed by this. 'Forgive me, but are you saying that you were completely satisfied with the way we ran the bid?'

'From my perspective, yes indeed. You gave us all the

information we needed, when we needed it, and Michael couldn't have been more helpful. Is that a problem?'

Skip was at a loss for words. He had no wish to dig any further, but his whole reason for the meeting was to repair the damage supposedly done by Michael when he had offered an inducement to Turkwood. He couldn't understand it: was Turkwood playing a game? Was this the way British consultants did business, with nods and winks and funny handshakes? Nick had not found time to brief him fully – 'Just schmooze the guy,' he'd said – but Skip was certain he'd been sent on a specific mission. Now Turkwood was affecting no understanding of Skip's drift.

'I must have missed something,' Skip said after some reflection. 'I was under the impression that you had expressed some concerns about our behaviour. I must have been wrong.'

Charles finished his sherry and picked up the menu. 'Well, I'm sorry to disappoint you,' he said with heavy irony, 'but your people were first class. Now, shall we order? I can recommend the venison.'

The menu swam in front of Skip's eyes. The two possibilities for his confusion were both grim: Turkwood was a two-faced double-dealer, or Nick had not told him the whole story. Either way, Skip was in a weak position. 'Tell you what, why don't you order for both of us?' he said, his mind on other matters. 'I'm happy to be guided by you.'

'If that's all right with you. I can promise you won't go hungry. The servings are very generous.'

Skip hardly heard Charles order the meal and the wine, and the rest of lunch was taken in a haze as Charles talked about himself and his business. Skip nodded at appropriate moments and made a few comments, but Charles seemed happy to talk and Skip was in no mood to deliver his standard sales patter. He was hurting, though he tried not to let it show. He would have liked to call Zamboni there and then, to get clarification on what was really going on, and only his manners prevented him from leaving the table.

When Charles had finished his port, and the bill was paid, they walked together to the door. 'Look, about what you said earlier,' Charles said. His face was flushed from the bottle of wine, three-quarters of which he had drunk. 'I am known as a tough operator, and I have a reputation amongst suppliers for squeezing them very hard. But we're all professionals and we all have a job to do. I think DataTrak is a very fine organisation, and I have a lot of regard for your products and your people. I hope I haven't given any other impression.'

'No, fine, I understand. I'm not thinking straight, I guess.'

'Jet lag, I expect.'

'Yeah, you're probably right.'

'Incidentally, you never did say about Michael.'

'Didn't I? Oh well, it's not important now. I really just wanted us to touch base.'

'And I'm glad we have. Send him my regards, won't you?'

'Sure thing.' They left the restaurant and Skip let Charles get the first available taxi. He needed to walk, to clear his head and come up with a strategy. Something was very badly wrong and he had to resolve it.

ELEVEN

'It's watertight – I mean, there's no way back for him?' Zamboni already knew the answer, but he wanted to be sure.

Mary Strutter nodded. 'Absolutely. We've run it past Legal Affairs and they're happy. It's a done deal.' She disliked Zamboni – an abrasive, humourless personification of all that was bad about Americans, with no saving graces – and had found this particular transaction more distressing than most. Michael Lensman was a popular and decent individual, a hard worker with no obvious flaws, and she disliked the way in which they'd contrived the current situation. Mary felt true compassion for him: he didn't deserve this fate, and would surely suffer from it. She promised herself that, when the dust had settled, she'd call Michael and see how he was getting on.

'Good job,' Zamboni said. 'You'll deal with all the paperwork, right?'

'It's already in hand. He's sending us a resignation letter. As soon as we get it, we'll pay the money into his account and set up the standing order for his consultancy fee. He knows the agreement is confidential and, if he breaches that confidentiality, the deal is off.' Zamboni moved as if to leave her office, but Mary put her hand up. 'There is one other thing.'

'What?' he said impatiently.

'We have to deal with the internal communication of all this. The staff need to hear what's going on. They'll be talking about it, coming up with all manner of outrageous stories about Michael. It's important we knock that on the head.'

'What do you suggest?'

'I think you should send a memo to all staff. We can write it for you, if you'd like. You know the kind of thing – very sorry to see him go, tremendous contribution, best wishes for the future – something which demonstrates that we're a caring employer and sends a very clear message that he resigned. We can't let them think that he was fired. It would be very damaging for staff morale.'

'Sure,' he said unenthusiastically. 'Send me a draft, OK?'

'I'll prepare it today. We need to move quickly.'

'Whatever.' Now Zamboni did get up. 'Tell you what,' he added as he reached the door. 'Let Skip handle it. It's good training for him.'

As he walked away from her office, Mary shook her head in frustration. Skip was being shafted, and he didn't even know it. The poor guy was so green, and so beholden to Zamboni, that he couldn't see what was happening to him. She spent several moments considering this before she turned to her PC to get started on the memo.

It had been the best weekend Annie could remember. Michael was mellow – she had actually used that word to him – and he gave her and Holly all his attention. On Saturday they had driven down to West Wittering, on the Sussex coast: Michael had gone to Marks & Spencer early and bought everything they needed for a picnic. He left Annie to read a book whilst he played endless games with Holly and took her for a long walk along the beach. It was a mild September day and everything went perfectly.

Sunday was just as good. They had lunch in a pub on the river outside Kingston, and Michael spent the afternoon in the garden, pruning and trimming and planning new flower-beds as Holly followed him and tried to help. He was full of energy and patience, and Annie glowed inside: he was riding the storm as if nothing had happened.

As she sat in the garden and watched them, Annie recalled how she had once feared that she was losing Michael. It was three years ago, when Holly was still a baby but was trying to walk and make comprehensible sounds. Annie was permanently tired; the demands on her, both physically and mentally, drained her of all vitality and she ached for Michael to come home at a reasonable time and relieve her from the dutiful vigilance required to deal with Holly. But he didn't return early. He was always working late, always ringing with a perfectly good reason for not coming back. Annie was so confused, so uncertain of everything, that she cracked and accused him of not caring for them.

They had let their row fester until the weekend but, as usual, it was Annie who had to make the first move towards reconciliation. Once this was done, he had promised to organise himself better at work and take on more of the strain at home. It became, like many domestic arguments, something neither wanted to talk about or revisit, and its significance diminished.

She had believed that he was ready to walk out on them, that if she pushed too hard he might actually do it without a backward glance, and she therefore gritted her teeth and kept her anguish to herself. She had no wish to push him away, and no stomach for further useless confrontations; she was smart enough to realise that she was submitting to his will, but that was how life turned out sometimes in the cause of peace and harmony. She wasn't bitter, but she thought less of herself for it.

And, in the garden that Sunday, with Michael so carefree and loose, Annie congratulated herself. She had waited and it had all come back to her, something she had hoped for but never truly expected. They would pick up where they had left off, and would not make the same mistakes again.

'Welcome to the real world.' Skip thought he saw a trace of a smile on Nick Zamboni's lips, but he couldn't be sure.

'So it was all . . . fabricated? You're saying it never happened?'

'What I'm saying is that we needed to get Lensman out of the organisation. His face didn't fit, and he was going to cause you a lot of problems. That's now taken care of.'

'But Nick, there are rules, conventions for this kind of

stuff. We can't just go firing people for no good reason.'

'We didn't fire him, remember? I have his letter of resignation right here. He could have disputed the deal, but he didn't. That makes him guilty in my book.'

'We know better than that.' Skip surprised himself by the way in which he was confronting Nick. 'Surely you see how totally unethical this is.'

Zamboni took the criticism in his stride. 'Skip, you're a fine man and I rate you very highly. I've invested a lot of time and energy in you and, frankly, I've taken a bit of a gamble putting you into this slot. Don't go fucking it all up by introducing alien concepts like ethics or morals into the equation. We're not here to make those kinds of judgements. We're here to make a lot of money – for us and for DataTrak. If you can't focus on that, you're going to fail.'

'Don't misunderstand me,' Skip said, frantically backtracking to save face. 'I'm incredibly grateful for all the support you've given me, and I'm determined to repay the faith you've shown in me. It's just . . . well, I guess I'm having problems coming to terms with the way we've handled this one.'

'Then learn from it. If you do, you'll be all the stronger for it. And believe me, you'll have to make much worse decisions than this. Hey, no one enjoys being the executioner, but someone has to do it. Show that you can, and you'll go places.'

'Don't worry, I won't let you down. I just wish you'd told me before I saw Turkwood. That could have been embarrassing.'

'But you handled it, right? No harm done. Now it's history, so move on. And on that point, I'm going to get out of your hair. I'm flying back to New York tonight and I don't expect to be in London again for at least a month. The show's all yours from now on.'

'That's great news. Got any final thoughts for me?'

'Focus on sales, revenue, exceeding budget. Nothing else matters.'

'Like a laser beam. There is one minor point, though. I

was planning to go back home and help Teri pack up.'

'She's all grown-up, isn't she? I'm sure she can handle that by herself. No, you need to be here. You're my eyes and ears. We'll pick up the tab for the move and everything, so you just stay on the ground and don't take your eye off the ball. The next ninety days are going to be critical.'

Skip thought of Teri, and how disappointed she'd be, but he knew she'd understand. 'No problem,' he said.

TWELVE

'So they got you in the end,' Don said with a wistful smile.

'I suppose my only consolation is that it cost them an arm and a leg,' Michael replied.

'I'll drink to that.' Don raised his glass and saluted Michael with it. They were sitting in a wine bar in the City, Michael dressed casually in chinos and a polo shirt, Don in a grey suit and tie. Don was short and slightly overweight, his thinning hair brushed carefully to try to conceal his bald patch – the Bobby Charlton look, as they'd referred to it in the office. His face was permanently sad, as if he carried some secret grief; even when he smiled, it was only with his mouth, his eyes betraying the misery beneath.

Don Retzer had been an odd choice to run DataTrak's London office. He had no direct experience in their business and could be painfully shy, seemingly totally unqualified to take on such a senior, high-profile position, especially working for Nick Zamboni. But logic appeared to play a minor part in many of Zamboni's staffing decisions, and Retzer was drafted in from a management consultancy on a huge compensation package. Zamboni tired of Don almost from the moment he was on board, undermining his decisions and failing to keep him advised of Head Office policy. His staff knew that he was a lame duck and treated him with courtesy rather than respect; he was a noble, gentle man who didn't deserve the indignities heaped upon him by Zamboni, but he endured them without explicit complaint and, to those who watched him and worked with him, he seemed resigned to his fate.

It was therefore no surprise when Zamboni's patience

finally expired and Don was unceremoniously dumped. Michael had meant to call him a dozen times, but had been too preoccupied with his own problems, for which he now felt guilty: this lunch was intended to be an apology for his selfishness.

'So you're going to stay in the UK?' Michael asked. 'No plans to go back to Vancouver?'

'It's always an option,' Don said. 'I guess I could find a job there, but we've got used to it here. The boys are settled in school, and it would be a hell of a wrench to leave now.'

'So what are you doing with yourself?'

'Some consulting work, small assignments here and there. Funnily enough, Charles Turkwood gave me a project I'm working on at the moment, but I'm only doing the boring bits he's too lazy to handle. He's hell to work for, but it keeps me out of trouble, and a full-time position looks out of the question right now. I'm too old, and too many people know about my inglorious spell at DataTrak.'

'But you did a great job there. What's the problem?'

'That's very kind of you to say so, but there's more to it than that. Chinese whispers, you know the kind of thing. They promised they'd give me good references, but they never promised they wouldn't bad-mouth me. One headhunter I saw even implied that it would be very difficult for me to get a job whilst there was so much uncertainty about my past. I asked him what he meant precisely, but he just smiled and shrugged it off. I'm damaged goods in this market.'

'I'm truly sorry to hear that. I loved working for you and you were always fair. I'm quite prepared to put that in writing, if you think it will help.'

'I may take you up on that.' Don finished his glass of wine and sighed. 'There's another problem, though.'

'What's that?' Michael asked as he poured more wine.

'My wife, Jean. This whole thing's really screwed her head up. She never liked Zamboni, of course, but when he sacked me she went ballistic. She took it really badly, got incredibly worked up and said how she was going to get revenge, even if I didn't care. I tell you, it frightened me. I've never seen her like that before, and I didn't know how to deal with it. She's calmed down a little since then, but I still can't mention DataTrak or Zamboni without getting her agitated. I haven't told her about Skip – or you, come to that – I think she'd go completely haywire if she knew.'

'I had no idea.'

'You never know how people are going to react to adversity, even people you're really close to. I figured, well, I've been paid off, we're pretty comfortable, the school fees are taken care of, so what's the point of letting it eat away at your guts? Worse things happen in life. Jean, she saw it differently. She took it personally, convinced that we'd been singled out by Zamboni and victimised. She won't let go, you know? It's . . . well, it's corrosive, that's the only way to describe it, and as long as she's like that, it's hard to do anything else. It's not exactly a conducive environment for job-hunting.'

'But that's exactly what you've got to do. You have to get another job and bring some stability and order back into your lives. Jean will soon forget about Zamboni once that happens, won't she?'

'Yeah, I guess. It's tough at the moment, that's for sure, and I need to get things sorted out on the home front. Even the boys have been affected by it. It's impossible to shield them from what's been going on. They see what Jean's going through.' Michael vaguely knew Don's sons – Oliver and Daniel – who, he thought, must both be teenagers. He could only imagine how difficult life must be with them.

Don assumed a pale smile and cocked his head. 'Anyway, enough of my problems. How are you doing?'

'Not so bad, surprisingly. I thought it would take a long time to recover, but I'm in pretty good shape. Funnily enough, I haven't lost much sleep worrying about DataTrak. What they did was wrong, and I've accepted that, but there's no point standing still and brooding on it. I'm actually quite excited, planning what I'm going to do next.' Michael felt that he was saying this as much to reassure Don as to state his own feelings; he didn't want Don to suffer any more than he had to, and he needed to believe that he would recover quickly. Setting an example seemed to be a good way of achieving this.

'And what will that be?'

'I haven't got a clue. Annie agrees that I shouldn't rush into anything else, and the money buys us some breathing space. This is the first time in my life where I've had the opportunity to work out what it is I really want to do. It's a bit intimidating, but at the same time it's exhilarating.'

'I'm pleased for you, Michael. You're a good guy and Annie's a super wife. I want things to work out for you.'

'Thanks. And I'm sure they will – for you and me.' Michael caught the slight look of doubt in Don's eyes, and wondered just how deep it ran. He did not want to see his friend destroyed, but there was only so much he could do to help.

Pam didn't often get depressed. She had Cliff, she had her house and her china cats in a nice cabinet – what was there to be depressed about? But today, sitting outside Skip's office and being made to feel as if she had some highly infectious disease, she was coming close to being a little blue. She missed Michael desperately and wanted to have things as they were before; Skip wasn't nasty, but it wasn't the same. He was a little too stiff for her taste, a little distant in spite of that big grin and his impeccable manners. Each time he asked her to do anything – and that hadn't happened too often – it was as if they had only just been introduced and he wasn't quite sure how she'd react to the request. She didn't like that.

She didn't like his writing, either. He used funny brown ink and all his words were a jumble of upper- and lower-case letters. He liked to scribble on every piece of paper that went across his desk, just, she supposed, to prove that he'd looked at all of them. But that wasn't her major gripe. That morning he'd come up to her and smiled broadly. 'Pam,' he'd said, 'there's a policy we have in all our offices in the States that I'd like to introduce here.'

'Oh yes?' she'd replied, trying to sound interested even

though she couldn't give a toss about what they did in the States.

'Clear desk,' he'd said firmly.

'Clear desk,' she'd repeated, without the faintest idea of what he was talking about.

'Yup. At the end of each day we file away everything that's on our desks – all the files, paperwork, everything that isn't nailed down.'

'Why?'

'It helps to promote efficiency. If you come into work every morning with a clear desk, it looks good and it makes you think about priorities. It's a very good way of keeping you focused on the job in hand. It also means that you tend not to keep things on your desk that really live somewhere else, so everyone benefits. I want to implement that policy here. What do you think?'

Pam thought the idea stank, but she had no intention of saying this. 'Have you seen the desks around here?' she'd replied.

'I have, and that's why I'm so keen to get the clear desk policy into operation. Without it, we're going to be inefficient.'

'We can but try,' she said bravely. 'But it'll be a bit of a shock. I think it may take some time before it's fully accepted.'

'Let's go for it and see what happens, shall we? Can you draft a memo along the lines I've just described, then I'll sign it?'

'Fine.' Satisfied, Skip returned to his office and closed the door, something Michael never did.

Pam tried hard not to giggle about this incident. Here was the hotshot American parachuted in to rescue the business, and he spent his day worrying about whether everyone had a tidy desk. Michael would never have wasted his time like that: he had more important things to do.

But, once Pam started thinking about Michael again, her moment of amusement was brief. He had, she well knew, been treated appallingly. She had pieced together the full story from a number of sources and was convinced that Skip was a master of disguise, that the thin veneer of affability hid

93

a darker, more sinister soul within: he was an evil man, casting Michael aside without reason simply to further his own career. Pam suffered from equal pains of anger and sadness as she thought about Michael and, more immediately, his absence from her life. Suddenly, their relationship had been brutally severed and she felt the loss as much as if he had died unexpectedly.

Cliff, naturally enough, would have understood none of this. He had no interest in what Pam did at work, and no concept of how much she had enjoyed working for Michael. He liked the money she brought in, but that was it, and Pam would no more have considered discussing her agony with him than she would with a total stranger. She didn't resent this, though: it was perfectly acceptable in her eyes that he concentrated on his work without paying any attention to hers. She had no illusions about Cliff.

Michael was in an altogether different league, however. He was educated, well mannered, thoughtful, good-looking too. He represented a class to which Pam knew she would never belong, but she was content just to be near it. Losing him was a blow for which she was unprepared, and it hurt badly. As her fingers skipped across the keyboard of her computer, typing the inane memo on clear desks, Pam tried to ignore that pain.

When she was finally able to kick off her shoes and stretch her toes, Teri felt much better. She had been on the go all day, running final errands, organising the packers and trying to bring some order to the chaos that moving was already causing. Friends and relatives had all been contacted and she'd arranged a party at a smart restaurant for their final night; the realtors were on stand-by, poised to unleash a stream of potential tenants for the house as soon as Skip and Teri closed their front door for the last time; and she had consulted with her obstetrician on when she should fly back from London so that the baby could be born in the States. That baby was wasting no time in making its energy-sapping presence felt.

She sipped her herbal tea and closed her eyes, not for sleep but to try to block out all the turmoil. She'd underestimated the amount of work involved in closing down this chapter of their lives, the tedious detail which was so wearing, but Teri, in spite of her slight build, was in good physical condition and had reserves of strength to call on in times of crisis. She could rest later; for now, she needed to keep on going, supporting Skip by insulating him from all this administration. She knew he would be working all the hours he could, making the right impression and submerging himself in the job. He knew no other way; he never took his foot off the pedal.

As if he could read her thoughts – even from three thousand miles – the phone rang as she lay on the sofa. 'Hi, babe,' he said softly, almost apologetically. 'How's it going?'

'Well, the consolation must be that one day it'll all be behind us. I didn't realise how complicated our lives had become.'

'You sound tired. You bearing up?'

'I'm just fine, Skip. So, how's life as a heavy jelly?'

'I don't know about that,' Skip replied. 'Sometimes it feels as if the whole world's gone crazy. But I'm hanging in there – just.'

'I'd expect nothing less. Is Nick still there?'

'Gone. I'm all on my own. It's kind of scary.'

'You'll deal with it. What about your problem with Michael?'

'All taken care of. Everyone seems to be very happy with the result, so I don't expect to hear anything more about it. That's a weight off my mind.'

'So when are you coming home? I'm missing you.'

'That's why I'm calling. I hate to do this to you, but Nick is insistent that I stay here. I tried to tell him that you needed me there, but he wouldn't listen. He says I have to be visible, close to the action. He doesn't want me to lose the momentum, and I guess I can understand where he's coming from.'

Teri said nothing. She didn't want to be angry with Skip,

but she was devastated by this news, overwhelmed by what it would mean. She needed him with her, especially now she was carrying his child. Suddenly she felt very inadequate, incapable of managing without him.

'Baby? You OK?'

'I suppose. I was hoping you'd come back and help out, but I guess I can handle it on my own.'

'You don't sound so sure. Perhaps I should call my dad, tell him to come over and give you a hand.'

'No, Skip, don't do that. I'll get through it.' She liked his father, but anyone other than Skip would be an additional aggravation.

'I'm truly sorry about this, and I'll make it up to you, I promise.'

'You don't have to make it up. It's not your fault. It's life, and it happens. So when do you want me to come over?'

'The sooner the better. There's no point you staying there getting miserable. Pack your bags and get going.'

'I wish it was that simple,' Teri said. 'There's still a ton of things to get done, and I really can't leave until they're all settled. I might be able to get there by next week, earliest.'

'I'm not sure I can wait that long.'

'You've got plenty to keep you occupied in the meantime. Look, don't worry about any of this. I'll manage somehow. You just get on with your work and stay healthy. The time will fly by, you'll see.'

'I hope so. I'm thinking about you all the time.'

'And me too.'

'OK. I have to run. Got a dinner with clients. Call me, OK?'

'I will, Skip. Be good. I love you.'

'And I love you, and I always will.'

Teri replaced the handset and tried very hard not to weep.

THIRTEEN

Annie found the note on his pillow.

Gone for a walk. See you later.

She looked at the alarm clock: six-thirty-three in the morning. He must have slipped out very quietly, unless she had been woken by the front door closing without realising it. Annie sighed and rolled over back to her side of the bed. She didn't like being on her own: even though he had only spent a few days at home, she had already become used to him there, enjoying their time in bed after he had made tea and he climbed back in with her – 'Well, there's no point getting up just yet, is there?' as he'd said when he did it for the first time. She didn't need to get up for another hour, and yet she was now wide awake.

Annie lay on her back and stared at the ceiling. Michael had always been a little enigmatic, she thought as she studied the paintwork and discovered a small patch that the decorator had missed with his second coat. She was never quite sure how he'd react to any given circumstances. He bristled at the suggestion that he was moody, and yet that was how Annie thought of him: some days he'd be in the most equable mood imaginable, unshakeably happy, whilst others would find him sullen and liable to explode at the most minor irritation. Michael didn't notice – or wouldn't admit – how much his temper could swing, but Annie and Holly had plenty of experience.

Going out for a walk was something he'd never done before, at least not on his own. He might drive them up to

Wimbledon Common on a Sunday afternoon and wander around the golf course with them, but he was not enthusiastic about walking for the sake of it. He remained fit despite the fact that he rarely took much exercise, a fact which annoyed Annie to distraction as she struggled through her aerobics classes twice a week. He played golf only when clients expected it, and refused to throw away his rusting Wilson T2000 metal tennis racquet which he'd had since school. 'It's a good racquet,' he'd say every time Annie tried to give it to the local Oxfam shop, 'and you never know when it might come in handy.' He had not played tennis since his brother challenged him to a match and beat him 6-0, 6-0.

Annie decided there was little point trying to work out why he might have gone for a walk. He was, after all, going through an extremely difficult time, well as he had disguised that with his show of relentless optimism and general cheerfulness. If anything, he had rather overdone this, to the extent that Annie now felt he would eventually come down to earth with a bigger bang than if he'd been deflated in the first place. It was in her nature to worry about him – he told her so often enough – and she was almost physically braced for the moment when it all came crashing down around their ears. He would have to have some negative reaction eventually; it was only natural.

For now, however, she was much more ambiguous than he was about the whole affair. It was she who carried the greater anger, the keener pain, and it was she who would have supported him wholeheartedly if he'd taken a machete up to the City and cut Zamboni and McMaster into fine ribbons – she'd even have cleaned up after him. But he wasn't displaying any such emotions, and Annie began to revise her immediate interpretation of his calm acceptance. When she'd suggested he was relieved, and he'd agreed so readily, she'd taken that at face value and was grateful for it. With hindsight, she began to wonder how he could possibly have worked it all out so rationally; he'd said that he needed to grieve, but there was scant evidence of him doing that. Perhaps, like the loss of a close friend, he was merely building walls to protect himself. That would make more sense.

Michael's report of his lunch with Don was no less puzzling. He told Annie of how deeply he felt for Don and Jean, and how their world seemed to have fallen apart; he expressed a desire to help Don, to try to set him up with something so that they could start to recover from the terrible blow. All the time Annie was thinking: 'But what about us? What about you? Isn't that more important than Don and Jean?' She couldn't understand how he was thinking, what was driving him to take such an odd route when, right on his own doorstep, there were problems piling up. Was he just going to ignore it all and hope it would go away?

She was still lying there, her hands gripping the bedstead behind her, when she heard the front door open and close very softly. She listened as he pottered in the kitchen and made tea, then heard him come up the stairs. He appeared in the doorway with two mugs and routinely set one down on her bedside table.

'Where have you been?' she asked a little desperately.

'It's come,' he said brightly.

'What's come?'

'The money. From DataTrak. It's in the account. I walked down to the bank to check the balance, and it's in there. We're rich.'

'Oh. And that's all you went out for?'

'What else would I be doing at six-thirty in the morning? I haven't gone completely bonkers.'

'I'm glad to hear it. I was thinking of calling the doctor. You've never been for a walk before – not voluntarily, anyway.'

'There are a lot of things I've never done before that I may start doing now. You just watch me.'

'I will,' she said lightly, but she meant it more seriously than he realised.

Without Teri, Skip had no one. There was no special confidant, no friend to whom he could turn and ask for advice and guidance – except, of course, God. Skip had been raised not as a God-fearing worshipper, but as someone who could talk to God whenever it was necessary, confident that his prayers would be listened to, if not answered. He kept his faith well hidden from public gaze and rarely spoke about it; he had learnt from early on in his business career that any such openness either encouraged the crazies or turned off the heathens. He also believed that his relationship with God was a particularly private affair and wouldn't easily withstand external attention.

London presented Skip with a whole new set of problems. He wanted to devote all his time and energy into making a huge success of his career, but he was already encountering the dry cynicism of the Brits at their worst. Few of them had any special desire to see things change, and they certainly weren't about to let an American come in and tell them what they were doing wrong. He desperately wanted to motivate them, to get them fired up with his brand of enthusiasm, but they remained sceptical and slow to move. He'd already got a name for some of the middle and junior managers in the company: the permafrost. However hot the blast of reality, they were not going to melt.

But problems, as Skip well knew from all his management training and diligent studies of the world's leading texts on the subject, were really only opportunities in disguise. His challenge was finding a way of converting one into the other. Present these guys with a new spin on life and things will get better – or so he'd imagined when he first arrived. Now he was finding out that the Brits didn't operate that way: they had to be dragged into the twentieth century, let alone the new millennium. He wished he had Teri beside him every night; she knew how to look at things differently, and always came up with a great solution when it all seemed so hopeless.

Teri was mad at him, he knew that much. Even though she did her best to hide it, she was distinctly unimpressed with Nick's plan. He felt bad about that, too, but what can a guy do? She'd consistently told him that, in a crunch, his career would come before hers; she was the one who'd been so positive about the move to London, when he was going through agonies trying to make up his mind. She didn't really have much justification for her current state of mind, when you thought about it. There again, he was asking her to take on a lot of responsibility. Life could be tough, and that was for sure.

In spite of this, Skip didn't falter. He knew what he had to do, and he still had Nick's blessing to do it. Other guys in the firm couldn't stand Nick, he knew that, but his patronage had got Skip the job and he was determined not to disappoint him. Skip had quickly appreciated the value of a mentor, especially one as powerful as Nick; at IBM he'd hitched his star to the wrong guy, a man who turned out to be a lush and was moved to special projects, never to be seen again. Skip didn't make the same mistake twice, a lesson of which Teri reminded him every so often. She was always keen to know where Nick stood in the DataTrak pecking order, and studied any reorganisation memos with special care to see if he was losing or gaining power. 'Don't be afraid to distance yourself from him if he looks like becoming a liability,' she'd once told Skip. 'Don't alienate him, and by all means stay friends outside work, but run a mile from anything he's associated with if it's going to fail.'

Solid advice, just like everything Teri said: she was so pragmatic, so wise, and he counted his blessings every day. Who else had such a tower of strength to rely on? In his eyes, the greatest thing about her was her humanity. Teri was neither vindictive nor insensitive. She could apply dispassionate logic to every situation, and yet she would never discount the human factor, constantly suggesting options that would do the least harm to the least number of people. She hated to see people hurt unnecessarily, particularly if they had a family to support; she was the one who'd told him to look after Michael Lensman's wife and child, and she'd follow it up with him to make sure he'd done the right thing.

Skip's mind couldn't always focus on these critical issues so, in recognition of this shortcoming, he rarely made a major decision without consulting Teri first. She could see things to which he was blind, step back from the fray to look at the bigger picture. He'd come to rely enormously on her judgement and tried to learn from her, but it wasn't easy: he'd go back to the office and be faced with a different set of challenges, all requiring her input before they could be effectively managed. Far from resenting this, Skip saw it as a wonderful partnership where she offered herself as a willing resource. And in return . . .?

He was less certain about his own contribution. He perceived himself as a good partner, attentive and, more importantly, consistent, but he could never quite put his finger on what it was that Teri loved about him. He was not one of those sparkling, exuberant types who could sweep a woman off her feet and keep her up there for ever; he was steadier than that, though, and there were fewer troughs in their relationship as a result. Maybe she loved this; maybe she needed the anchorage which he provided, although he doubted that she was this soft. He worried about himself as a resource for her: what did she take from him to balance the equation?

But his domestic concerns were small compared to what confronted him professionally. This was his big test, and he would pass it; that at least was certain. Teri would expect nothing less from him, and she'd eventually be there to see he achieved the success, and acclaim, he craved. When the going gets tough, the tough get going, and I'm one of them, he told himself. I can do this. I will do this.

The call came as Teri was stepping out of the shower, and she stood naked and dripping in the bedroom as she answered the phone.

'Is this Teri McMaster?' She didn't recognise the voice, which sounded female.

'It is. Who's this?'

'Have you opened your mail this morning?'

'No. Why?'

'Shame. Have a nice day.' The line went dead.

Teri dried and dressed herself quickly, puzzled by the call. She went out to the mailbox and unlocked it; inside was the normal pile of bills, flyers and unmissable opportunities, but there was only one letter she was interested in. It had an airmail sticker and the typewritten envelope was addressed to her. She hurried back inside and ripped it open. It was one page, laser-printed.

YOUR HUSBAND IS A SHIT.
THAT MAKES YOU A SHIT.
IF YOU'RE LUCKY, YOU MAY LIVE TO REGRET MARRYING HIM.
ENJOY LIFE WHILE YOU CAN.

That was all there was. Teri read it several times, then studied the envelope. It was from London, according to the postmark. She put it on the hall table and called Skip, but he was out. What kind of sick person does this? she thought as she ripped it up and put the torn pieces in the bin.

FOURTEEN

'Who the bloody hell can that be?' Michael said as the doorbell rang. It was eight-thirty in the evening, and he and Annie were in the middle of dinner.

'Jehovah's Witnesses?' Annie replied.

'I'll tell them I'm a Mormon,' he said over his shoulder as he went to the door. He opened it still expecting to confront beaming faces, and was therefore surprised when he saw that it was Pam. 'Oh!' he exclaimed.

'That's a nice welcome.'

'Sorry, Pam, it's . . . well, I didn't expect to see you.'

'That's all right. I should apologise really, turning up like this unannounced and everything.' Michael studied her face and thought she'd been crying. 'Can I come in for a moment?'

'Of course.'

Pam stepped into the hallway and looked along it to see Annie at the other end. 'Hallo,' Pam said. 'Sorry to barge in. I'm not disturbing you, am I?'

'Not really,' Annie said without any indication of enthusiasm for her visitor. She turned away and went back into the kitchen, and Michael ushered Pam into the sitting room at the front of the house.

'Sit down, Pam. Can I get you a drink?'

'No thanks. I'm driving.'

'So – what brings you to sunny Wimbledon?'

'Look, I'm really sorry about this. I had to see you. There are so many things going on, and I'm really confused and upset, and I thought you might be able to help me sort it all out.'

'I'll do my best. What's the problem?'

She snorted. 'Where do I start? Nick Zamboni's gone back, you know. Skip's now in complete charge, and he's already making a pig's ear of everything, trying to change it all around and making everyone feel totally sick. Pardon my French, but he's a real arsehole.'

'Give him a chance, Pam. He's very new, and he's still learning. I'm sure things will improve in time.'

'Well, that's very charitable, especially after what he did to you.'

Michael smiled. 'History,' he said. 'It's all water under the bridge.'

Pam rolled her eyes. 'So they gave you a good deal, then? They must have done, the way you're talking.'

'Let's just say I'm happy with the outcome.'

'Well anyway, he's a real pain and everyone's missing you a lot – including me.'

'That's nice to hear, but now you have to get on with Skip. He's not going to go away. He's Zamboni's man and he'll be there for the duration.'

Pam now spoke very softly. 'That isn't actually the main reason I came to see you.'

'No?'

'No. There's something much worse.'

She obviously wanted Michael to drag it out of her, so he played along. 'What's that?'

'Phone calls. Abusive ones.'

'To you?'

'No, not to me, but I've picked them up. Someone's been calling Skip, two or three times every day I reckon.'

'Saying what?'

'Basically, saying he's a real bastard and deserves to die and that he won't get away with it.'

Michael found this hard to believe. 'And this someone has said this to you?'

'Oh yeah, made no bones about it. "You tell your boss that I rang, and tell him what I told you," that kind of thing. It's really frightening.'

'Man or a woman?'

'It's pretty obvious that the voice is disguised, but I'd say it's a man.'

'Did you try 1471?'

'Yes, but he withheld his number.'

'Have you told Skip?'

'That's why I'm here. I didn't know what to do, and I thought I'd ask your advice.'

Michael took all this in and thought about it, nodding slowly as he did so. 'I don't really know what to say. I think he has a right to know. I'm sure I'd want to in the same situation. It all seems very bizarre. I couldn't imagine why anyone would want to terrorise him like that. He's pretty harmless.'

'Right,' Pam said, sounding as if she didn't totally agree with his assessment. 'That's what I'd thought. Who'd hold such a grudge that they'd do this to him?'

The lights finally flashed in Michael's head and he understood what Pam was saying. 'You don't think . . .? Are you suggesting that I might be doing this?'

'It had crossed my mind. After all, he shafted you.'

'Pam, I hope you know me better than that. I'm not the vindictive type. Yes, I'll admit I was very upset, and I would happily have murdered Skip or Nick at the time, but that's all in the past. I'm fine now – couldn't be more relaxed about it all. As I said, it's history and I've dealt with it. End of story.'

'You're sure?'

'Positive.'

'I'm really pleased to hear that, because I couldn't bear to think of you and Annie and Holly suffering from what he did to you. That would be too much, I reckon.'

'It's very kind of you to worry about us, and I'm touched. But you can stop right now.'

'It still doesn't change the fact that someone's making these phone calls.'

'No, and that must be very distressing for you. I think the best solution is for you to tell Skip – or if you can't bring yourself to do that, go and see Mary Strutter in Human

Resources and ask for her advice. She's very pragmatic. She'll know what to do.'

'I suppose you're right. Yeah, that's what I'll do. Thanks for that, Michael. You're a real friend.' Pam got up and smiled weakly. 'I'll leave you in peace now. Send my love to Annie and Holly, and my apologies for interrupting you.'

'No problem.' They walked together to the front door and Michael watched her walk to her car. When he turned round, Annie was standing right behind him.

'So what did she want?' she asked coldly.

'Reassurance, and that doesn't cost anything.'

'Except your supper's ruined.'

'It was only salad. How can it be ruined?'

'Because I ate it.'

'You pig!' he said, and they both laughed.

'You want to watch out for her,' Annie said later. 'She's trouble.'

'Oh, not really. She means well.'

'I wouldn't be so sure. I've always thought she was slightly unhinged.'

'Pam? Salt of the earth. Don't worry about her – I know how to handle her.'

'I hope you do.'

In Michael's time at DataTrak, staff meetings had never featured very heavily on the agenda. Don Retzer wasn't keen on them, preferring to send memos and e-mails if there was something to say; Michael too thought they were a waste of time and effort. The staff themselves didn't seem too concerned about the lack of any such forum: if someone wanted to know what was going on, they had only to call in on Brian and he would soon bring them up to speed. Brian was as effective as the World Service in collecting and disseminating information, and was often used for precisely this purpose. A secret divulged to him could be reliably expected to have been passed to ten other people within an hour of its disclosure.

Skip, inevitably, saw things differently. For him, staff

meetings were an integral part of working life, 'an opportunity for senior management to control and refine the internal communications process and cascade issues of enterprise-wide importance', as he'd said in one of his e-mails to Nick Zamboni. He therefore introduced weekly meetings – Monday morning at 0830 – at which attendance was nominally optional but practically mandatory. Instinctively Skip wanted to introduce more routine to the organisation – 'structured creativity', as he'd referred to it in the same e-mail – and regular meetings were one of the ways he sought to achieve this.

An ad hoc meeting, called at the last minute, therefore came as something of a surprise to the staff. Inevitably they turned to Brian as they trooped towards the largest meeting room, but he was unable to offer any clues. 'I honestly have no idea,' he said. 'Perhaps dear Skip has broken a fingernail or something equally vital to the well-being of our institution.' There wasn't much time for further speculation; Skip was waiting for them, standing at one end of the room by a huge video screen which was normally used for system demonstrations or conference calls. He looked sombre and, unusually, he didn't exude his normal coruscating bonhomie, avoiding eye contact and merely nodding at anyone who managed to catch his attention.

Skip eventually looked up when he felt everyone was assembled. 'Well, looks like we have a full house,' he said. 'Let's get started.' He stared down at the floor and shifted his weight on his feet. 'There's no easy way to tell you this. Many of you will have known Don Retzer. He ran this area with distinction and some notable success. It's therefore very painful to have to tell you that Don tragically took his own life last night. His wife, Jean, rang me this morning. She's obviously very distressed and we're going to be offering her all the support she needs. That's really all I have to say for now. Are there any questions?'

Skip surveyed the faces looking towards him, but no one volunteered to speak. 'This is a great shock for all of us, I know,' he continued. 'If any of you want to speak to me

108

privately, my door is always open. In due course we'll let you know about the funeral arrangements, as I'm sure many of you would like to pay your last respects to Don. Thank you for your time.'

They all filed out in silence. There would be no discussion of this news until they were well away from the office, certain that they were among friends and could speak openly. Whatever thoughts they had, they wanted to hold to themselves for now. The inquest would come later.

Michael shrugged and opened his hands in acknowledgement of his confusion. 'I simply had no idea,' he said. 'There was no hint, nothing, that it was all going so wrong for him. I still can't believe it.'

'Do you know what happened?' Annie asked.

'Pam didn't say. Apparently Skip was pretty vague, didn't go into detail. Jesus, committing suicide is a pretty desperate way of resolving your problems. I mean, he told me that Jean was a little bit shaky, but I didn't think it had got so bad for him. I wish I could have done more to help.'

'That's crazy, blaming yourself. Don was obviously very disturbed. You couldn't have changed that. It's those bastards from DataTrak. They're the ones you should be blaming.'

Michael thought about this. 'I'm not sure it's quite as simple as that. Yes, I know they're bastards, but you don't top yourself just because you lose your job.'

'I should hope not.'

'Precisely my point. I'm not walking around in a state of mortal depression – quite the opposite, in fact. It isn't worth it. Don must have had some serious things going on that we knew nothing about. Being fired wouldn't have knocked the stuffing out of him, not unless it was the final straw.'

'So what do you think about Pam's little story?' Michael had told Annie about the phone calls to Skip.

'Well, it certainly isn't me, I can promise you that. But, if you're suggesting it might have been Don, I'd find that very hard to swallow. That wasn't his style at all.'

'I didn't mean it was Don. But what if it was Jean?'

'Jean?'

'Why not? Let's suppose that Pam is telling the truth, and these calls really exist, other than in her head. Jean has all the motivation she needs to do that kind of thing. Perhaps it didn't mess up Don too much when he was fired, but he himself told you how upset she was. I don't think it's too far-fetched to think that she might make the calls to Skip.'

'But Pam said she thought it was a man calling.'

'I don't think it would be too difficult to sound like a man on the phone.'

'Maybe not. But I still find that hard to believe. And anyway, Skip had nothing to do with Don being fired. That was all Nick's doing.'

'Well, it's all getting out of hand, whatever the true story is. I think you should cut all your ties with DataTrak and get on with finding something else to keep you occupied. And I think Pam is a real problem. I'm sorry to have to say this, but I can't stand her.'

Michael smiled at Annie. 'I get the message,' he said.

'Good. And by the way, isn't it about time you started thinking about what you're going to do next? You've been loafing around the house and showing very little interest in doing anything constructive. It's time for action, I reckon.'

'I'm working on it. I will sort something out, Annie, I promise. Just give me a little leeway, OK?'

'Little being the operative word, I hope.'

'Trust me. I'll know when I'm ready to make a move. I'm keeping in touch with the headhunters, and they won't forget me.'

'They'd better not,' Annie replied. 'We need you working. I can't have you slopping around here all day.'

'Why? Because I'll find out about your secret lover?'

She slapped him hard on the side of the head. 'Go and get us a drink,' she said, 'before I murder you.'

FIFTEEN

A grey and tepid September rain fell across Heathrow on the morning Teri arrived. The rain came down almost unenthusiastically, as if it had no reason to be there other than to welcome holidaymakers and other unsuspecting travellers. For Teri this was no surprise, her memories of London being almost exclusively damp, but she would still have preferred some sunshine to herald her arrival.

As promised, Skip was waiting for her when she finally made it through customs. His grin was as big as ever and it warmed her as soon as she'd spotted him. They hugged and kissed without speaking, hardly knowing what to say to each other: they'd never been separated for this long before and they weren't quite sure how to start again. Teri was bursting to tell him her news – their news – but she felt she should let him go first; the baby wasn't going to go away, and it would probably be better if she was sitting down quietly in their hotel room before she broke it to him. She didn't really want him to start fussing and worrying whilst they were in the taxi.

Instead she let him talk about work and how he'd been getting on. She loved his vigour and his naked optimism, childish values that he'd never really discarded, and as he talked, she realised just how much she'd missed him. For Skip, coming to England was another big adventure which he treated with the same excitement as he must have experienced when his parents first took him to Disneyland; it was impossible for her not to be caught in this wave of euphoria, and her exhaustion was swept away by it. The trials of the last week melted in his glow, her anxiety for his

111

well-being allayed by his obvious verve and health. She thought, as the taxi edged them slowly along the M4 towards London, how stupid she'd been to worry that he might not be able to handle this new assignment: he was thriving under the pressure. He looked and sounded wonderful.

'So,' Skip said, 'do you want to know the plan?'

'The plan?'

'Yup. I know I'm not famous for my planning, but I've got a schedule worked out. You have a rest when we get to the hotel, and I'll make some calls and catch up on some paperwork. If you're up to it this afternoon we'll look at some apartments, have an early dinner and then hit the sack.'

'Apartments,' Teri said thoughtfully.

Skip teased her. 'Yeah. It's kind of a convention here that you live somewhere, you know?'

She smiled but she was worried. She had imagined that they would need a house with a little garden for their family, and wasn't thrilled about the idea of living three floors up with no elevator. She decided to approach the problem at a tangent. 'What's our housing allowance? Would it stretch to a house?'

'The way I see it, we could only afford a house if we lived further out. I don't know how you'd feel about it. I kind of assumed you'd want to be central, and I'm not so keen on a long commute.'

'OK. Well, I think we ought to look at all the options. If we can get a house, that'd be neat.'

Skip didn't pick up on her undertone and grinned at her. 'Whatever you want. I'll get the real-estate people to run up a new list. Top priority is making sure you're comfortable and happy. I'll go with whatever you decide, you know that.'

The crisis averted, Teri felt happier. She stared out of the window as the taxi carved its way through traffic and Skip continued to talk about work, her mind unable to fix on anything other than the baby and how it would change everything for them. She felt a little guilty at not sharing this with him, but she needed some time to think and readjust.

112

Skip would understand; he always did.

Once they'd reached the West End hotel, and Skip had unpacked her bags, she called room service and ordered a pot of tea and toast. After it had arrived, she made him sit down with her at the table. 'Skip, I have some important news,' she said. 'I'm pregnant.'

He shook his head in disbelief, his face eventually dissolving into a huge smile. 'You're kidding,' he said.

'Would I?'

'I can't . . . it's . . . gee, that's fantastic.'

'Skip McMaster – speechless at last. I never thought I'd see the day.'

He got out of his chair and came round to her, kneeling down to give her a gentle hug. 'You never said. How long have you known?'

'Oh, a couple of weeks. It's pretty early days. I didn't want to tell you on the phone. It was too special for that.'

'But . . . all that work I made you do. If I'd known . . .'

'That's one of the reasons I didn't tell you. You'd only have fussed and fretted and that wouldn't have done any of us any good. Anyway, that doesn't matter now. It's all behind us. I'm perfectly fit, and I've had a check-up and all's well. I'm eating like a horse, of course, but apparently that's normal.'

'And you're sure you're OK? You must be so tired.'

'Skip, I'm fine. Honestly. There's nothing to worry about. This kind of thing happens all the time you know, and we'll be no different to all the other couples. It's all going to be a breeze, believe me.'

'What has the doctor said?'

'Exactly that. I'll get regular check-ups while I'm here, and I was thinking I'd go back home when it gets close. I won't be able to fly much after seven months, but that'll be OK, won't it?'

'I guess. But I'm going to have to take really good care of you, and you're going to have to take it easy.'

'There you go. Two minutes and you're already fussing, just like I knew you would.'

'We should have some champagne.'

'Later. I'm going to put my poor swollen feet up for an hour or so. You get on with your work and I'll snooze. We have plenty of time to celebrate.'

'Your call. You are so clever. It's just unbelievable.'

'Well, you'd better start believing it, because you're going to be a father next year.'

'A father,' Skip said dreamily. Then he came back to reality. 'Do you know?'

'No. I just know it's healthy. Boy or girl, it doesn't matter, does it?'

'Absolutely not. Either way, junior's got to like baseball. That's rule one.'

'Get on with some work and stop fantasising.'

'A baby,' Skip said, and he stroked her hair. 'Who would have thought it after all this time?'

Charles Turkwood always looked forward to opening his mail. He rented a small serviced office in the Broadgate complex on the eastern fringe of the City – the monthly fee was horrendous, but he judged it important to have a prestigious address so that clients would take him seriously – and he was always in there by eight o'clock. With a cappuccino and a buttered bun from the local coffee shop, he would open all his letters and read his e-mails before he started on anything else.

This morning was especially good. A cheque had come in for a minor consulting project. He felt a little thrill at the prospect of going to the showroom at the weekend, armed with this money, to choose his new sports car. He put the cheque to one side and carefully sliced open all the other envelopes, binning most of the letters and flyers but saving a few for later perusal. He got to the final letter, plain white envelope with his name and address laser-printed correctly on it. There was a first-class stamp on it where normally, had it been a business letter, it would have been franked. He pulled out the paper inside and read it.

**YOU ARE A WHORE.
YOU RUIN PEOPLE'S LIVES.
YOU DON'T DESERVE TO LIVE.
PERHAPS YOU WON'T.**

Charles turned the paper over to see if there was anything on the back, but there wasn't. He placed the letter in the middle of his desk and stared at it, mesmerised by the message. After several minutes of thought, during which he tried to remember everyone who hated him or had a reason to persecute him, he decided not to call the police. He found a clear plastic folder, slipped the envelope and letter inside, then put the folder in a desk drawer. During the day he opened the drawer six or seven times and reread the letter, but he couldn't do anything to purge it from his thoughts. He left the office early and went for a drink. It shouldn't have worried him so much, but it did.

Jean Retzer was a thin, sharp-faced woman who rarely wore make-up to hide the thread veins in her cheeks. Although she had carried two children, she had never lost her bony, size eight figure. She looked incongruous next to Don, a very odd match to outsiders, and she was not a typical corporate wife, avoiding whenever possible the endless round of client entertainment and hospitality events. She kept a low profile at all times, preferring the solitude of home life and looking after her boys and husband to the opportunities of going out and meeting new people.

Jean could not cope with the aftermath of Don's death. Letters of condolence flooded through the front door, flowers were delivered and calls were made, but Jean tried to ignore all this alien activity. She was having far too much difficulty dealing with the loss of Don to know how to handle well-wishers, and she wanted them all to go away so that she could be left in peace to grieve.

She could not, however, stop the police from interfering. They made their call, coming with their notebooks and their radios as unwelcome intruders into the haven of her house, upsetting the boys merely by their presence. They asked blunt questions even as they protested their sensitivity to the situation, seemingly alert to any possibility that Don's suicide was not as clear-cut as it appeared. She herself was at a loss to explain why he might have done such a terrible thing: he could get depressed, just like anyone else, but he had never lost hope. She wondered if she'd ever really known him.

Underlying all her feelings was anger. She was furious that Don had taken himself away from her and the boys. As much as she hurt for herself, she ached for Oliver and Daniel: they were far too young to be asked to cope with such a loss. They were confused, withdrawn and largely silent, much as Jean herself behaved. But in them she did not see the rage that consumed her.

She needed to blame someone. It could not be his fault: he'd been driven to despair by what had happened to him, losing his sense of proportion and balance by the injustice of what had been laid at his door. Had she, in some unknown way, been responsible for pushing him to the brink? Was he so frustrated by his life with her that he couldn't bear it a moment longer? If this were the case, though, why hadn't he just walked out? There were easier ways to escape than suicide.

The black hole into which Don had fallen was, she concluded, a direct consequence of losing his job. He'd never said much about it, never revealed any true feelings on the subject, but she guessed it must have cut him to the bone. She had been devastated, enraged to an extent she'd not previously experienced, but he didn't appear to share her bitterness. He steered clear of condemnation when she tried to incite him – yes, she had attempted to goad him into some kind of action, she admitted to herself, if only to stir him from his torpor – and avoided discussion of DataTrak and its evils. They could still be in Vancouver, secure and content in their unchanging, uneventful ways, but DataTrak had ensured that didn't happen. She knew the real culprits, but was less certain of how to get her own back.

And she needed to. She needed to secure some

116

compensation for her loss, some satisfaction for the dreadful crimes committed against Don, and all paths led to DataTrak. Even in the midst of her grief, when she was trying to explain it all to her boys as they wept from incredulous agony, or wiping away her own smarting tears, Jean was thinking of the time when she could win some retribution. When the flowers from DataTrak had arrived – *We're all thinking of you and praying for you at this most tragic time* – she had told Daniel to toss them in the dustbin, still wrapped in the cellophane and tied with a big ribbon bow. How careless their gesture was, how revealing that they were able to jettison him so casually and then pretend to care when, in an irrevocable act of hopelessness, he'd killed himself. Their corporate commiseration had no value for her; it simply confirmed her darker suspicions about their motives.

There was no way she could stop them from attending the funeral, convention overriding all other emotions. They would come and shed their crocodile tears, promise their continuing support and then leave her to pick up the pieces, never to show their faces again. It would be a toxic charade, and she wanted no part of it. How could anyone help her to get through this? She staggered through the house, completing chores without attention, her mind fixed on the gaping emptiness of what lay ahead. There was no solace, no place to hide from the frightening void of her future, and she could only seek some small degree of ease by thinking of how she might get her revenge. Somebody had to pay. It was as simple as that.

Only one call had inspired her. Michael Lensman, who she knew had been close to Don, rang and sounded genuinely distressed. She believed him, sensed that he meant what he said, and his words touched her. Did he understand? Was he, too, suffering the same fate as Don? Could he help her to achieve her goal? She was too timid yet to ask outright, but she felt she might in time. Michael could be her ally, assisting her in her prosecution of the guilty parties. He would know how to apply pressure and get results. Jean clung to this notion and it became stronger. Emboldened, she resolved to talk to him at the funeral. He would know what to do, and he would want to do it. The thought of this collaboration was all she had left, and it would have to suffice.

SIXTEEN

Through the bathroom door Annie could hear Michael retching. 'Are you all right?' she asked.

'Fine,' he replied curtly. Annie hovered for a few moments, anxious about his health, and listened as he was sick again. Then there was silence and she crept away.

When he came downstairs his eyes were swollen and bloodshot. 'You look awful. Are you sure you feel OK?'

'Must've been something I ate,' he said weakly. 'I'll have a cup of tea and some tablets.'

Annie got him his tea and two paracetemol whilst Michael sat shaking at the kitchen table. 'What time do we have to leave?' she asked as she sat down with him. It was the day of Don's funeral.

'In about an hour.'

'You're sure Jean won't mind if we bring Holly?'

'Positive. Holly will liven up the proceedings, if nothing else.'

Annie had her suspicions about Michael's sudden illness, but wasn't prepared to divulge them. She thought she knew the provenance of his nausea: he was about to confront his former life, to see all his old colleagues, friends and, more importantly, enemies. It was a big test for him, and he was obviously reacting badly to the prospect. Under the table she crossed her fingers; please let this day go by as quickly as possible, she prayed to some unseen force.

After the funeral, when the mourners and well-wishers were all assembled at the Retzers' house in Parliament Hill, Jean marshalled her two boys – Oliver, aged sixteen, and Daniel, fourteen – to serve drinks and hand round the canapés she'd bought from Tesco's. Oliver was turning into a handsome young man. Before Don's death Jean had barely thought of him as more than the child she'd raised, but now she realised that he was maturing, growing towards independence and away from her. All of a sudden he seemed larger, more substantial, even slightly intimidating. With Daniel it was precisely the opposite: his sullenness exposed the immaturity of his emotions, and Jean wished she could sweep him up and cuddle him tightly until all the pain had subsided.

She had no idea of how to behave, of whether she should approach people or merely stand in a corner and wait for them to come to her. No one had taught her the protocol for her husband's wake. More than anything, she wanted to hide in a bedroom and let them get on with it; she would have preferred to be anywhere but here, with so many people she hardly knew and whom, in all likelihood, she would never see again.

She watched them as they split into their discrete groups like different tribes. The DataTrak enclave was in one corner of the sitting room; family friends in another; relatives mainly hovered in the kitchen, and a few hardy souls had stepped through the open French windows and were standing on the patio, mainly so that they could smoke. For the most part they avoided eye contact with her, but one or two came up to her directly and offered their sympathies before falling into silence, unsure of how to progress the conversation. What could they say to her? Have the roses been good this year? Does the life assurance pay out for suicides? Nice day for a funeral? Every interaction was stilted and uncomfortable. Few of the guests knew her well enough to find something relevant to say, even if they felt they should.

One of the early conversations was with Skip. He walked up to her confidently with Teri close behind and held out his hand to shake hers. 'Jean, I'm Skip McMaster,' he said, 'and this is my wife Teri. There's nothing one can say at a time like this, but I wanted to tell you how much I'm going to

120

miss Don. He was a fine man, and I'm very proud to have known him.'

'Thank you,' Jean replied. 'That's very kind.'

'You know, this is a bad time to be offering help, because everybody's going to be doing that. But I really want you to know that Teri and I will do whatever you need us to do. Anything at all, you just call and we'll get it done. You have my word on that.'

'I appreciate the offer, Skip, and I won't forget it, I promise.'

'Good.' He paused for a moment to signal that this most difficult part of the conversation was over. 'You must be so proud of your boys,' he continued.

'Yes, I suppose I am.'

'They'll be a great source of comfort to you, I guess, at a time like this.' Jean nodded dreamily, as if she weren't quite sure. 'Families need to pull together, don't they?'

Jean, who was hardly listening, looked over Skip's shoulder and saw Michael coming into the room. 'Quite,' she said. 'Look, would you excuse me? There's somebody I have to talk to. It's very kind of you to have come. I know Don would have been touched.'

Skip smiled and moved aside to let her pass. Jean walked across the room to Michael, who was still pale. 'Michael,' she said, putting her hand on his forearm. 'Thanks for coming.'

He turned and gave her a hug and kiss. 'Hallo, Jean. Annie's here, too. She's just in the loo with Holly.'

Jean smiled and raised her eyebrows. 'Oh God, I remember all that. Wherever they went, both boys had to have a look at the loo. I always thought it was like a dog cocking his leg in a new place.'

'So – how's it going?'

'Pretty much as grim as you'd think. What makes it so bad is that I can't believe he would have done this. I knew him pretty well. That sounds stupid, doesn't it? But some wives never really know their husbands, do they? I thought I knew Don, though. And that's what hurts – I obviously didn't.'

'I think you're being a bit hard on yourself. Who knows what was going on in his mind?'

'Not me, that's for sure. Look, I really want to talk to you, but now isn't a good time. Are you going to be staying for a bit?'

'To be frank, I hadn't planned to. There are quite a few people here I don't particularly want to see.' He nodded towards the corner where the DataTrak tribe was still in residence.

'Yes, I can understand that. But I do want to have a chat.' He saw the depth of sadness in her eyes, the despair in all her body language as if she'd suffered from some terrible beating, and he smiled at her.

'I'll wait,' he said. 'You catch up with me when you can. I'll probably be hiding in the garden shed, though.'

'Thanks, Michael. Don was right – you've always been a friend.'

Holly was at the far end of the garden, crouching as she earnestly studied a worm that was wriggling in the flower-bed. Michael and Annie stood on the patio in silence and watched her. They were caught unawares.

'Well hi there,' Skip said as he came up behind them, Teri with him.

'Hallo,' Michael replied, his flesh tingling as he turned to look at them. Annie turned too and waited to be introduced.

'This is Teri, my wife. And you must be Annie.' They all nodded hesitantly at each other. 'Sad day, huh?'

'Yes,' Michael said. 'Did you know Don well?'

'Unfortunately not. I met him once or twice, but that was about it. He was a great guy by all accounts.'

'He was.' There was a long pause as they all anxiously attempted to avoid any more sensitive ground.

'So Teri,' Annie said, 'how are you enjoying London?'

'Just fine, thank you. I only got in a couple of days ago, but I'm starting to get my bearings.'

'Have you found somewhere to live?'

'We've looked at some houses, and we're pretty keen on

one we've seen in Cobham. Do you know it at all?'

'Not really. We've driven through it, and it always looks very pretty. I think there are quite a lot of Americans there, aren't there?'

'That's what the agent said. I'm not sure whether that's good or not.' They all laughed nervously and looked down. Just as the silence became oppressive, Daniel, the younger of Jean's boys, came round with a tray of vol-au-vents and held them in the middle of their circle. Teri was the only one who declined.

'Teri's pregnant,' Skip blurted out as Daniel walked away.

'Oh, that's wonderful news,' Annie said. 'Congratulations. You must be very excited.'

'We are,' Skip replied, but Teri didn't look it. 'Anyway, Michael, how are things going?'

Michael swallowed hard and clenched his fist behind his back. 'Pretty good, thanks.'

'You fixed a new job yet? I shouldn't think it would take very long before someone smart snaps you up.'

Annie looked at Skip incredulously, then glanced across at Michael to see how he would react. Little jaw muscles flexed, but that was the only sign he gave. 'Early days,' he said. 'I'm not going to rush into anything.'

'Sounds like a sensible strategy. But if I can be of any assistance . . .'

Annie could control herself no longer. 'I think you've already done quite enough for Michael,' she said sharply. If she'd extravagantly broken wind she couldn't have hoped for a more embarrassed reaction. Skip's cheeks coloured and he shuffled his feet.

'Gee,' he said. 'I guess we should be going. Nice talking to you.' They all mumbled their goodbyes and Skip and Teri beat a hasty retreat.

'What do you think you're playing at?' Michael asked Annie when they were alone again.

Annie was unrepentant. 'Well, honestly, that was beyond the pale. The guy fires you and then says he wants to help. How fucking insincere can you get?'

123

Michael was surprised by her language. 'Annie, cool it. It doesn't matter, really. It's over. OK, he was a bit insensitive, but he's young and he's American and that's how it goes. I'm not upset, so you shouldn't be.'

'Maybe not, but I am. He's an arsehole, and it doesn't do any harm to let him know.'

When Annie was agitated there was little Michael could do to calm her down, so he chose to change the subject. 'Look, Jean wants to have a chat with me, and I've got to hang around. Why don't you take Holly home in the car, and I'll get the train back?'

'Now you want to get rid of me.'

'Not at all. Neither of us wants to be here, but I have to stay. I'm trying to be nice and helpful.'

'I know,' she said, a little mollified. 'You're right. I might start throwing the nibbles at someone from DataTrak. Give me the keys and I'll see you later.'

They collected Holly and went to the car. 'I'll be as quick as I can,' Michael said. 'Be good.'

'No – you be good. You're the one who's staying, remember?'

'I'll try my hardest. I'll follow your example, shall I?'

She smiled at him. 'You can be very cruel sometimes. I was only standing up for you.'

'I know, and I love you for it. Now go before you get us into any more trouble.'

It was past three in the afternoon before most of the guests had left. Michael had spoken to Brian, carefully avoiding too much debate about the circumstances of his resignation, and to Pam, who managed to tell him that the nuisance calls had stopped and she was going to let it drop.

Michael was sitting on his own with a glass of white wine when Jean finally came over to him. She looked tired and distracted, but she forced a weak smile as she sat next to him on the sofa. 'I hope I never have to do this again,' she said. He couldn't tell if it was meant to be a joke, so he said nothing. 'All these people, and I feel so alone.'

'Are you taking care of yourself?'

'I'm pretty much on automatic pilot at the moment. I don't want to eat but I make myself. The boys are being good, watching out for me and helping around the house. I don't know exactly how they feel. Outwardly, Olly is fairly chipper and keeps me sane. Daniel I worry about more. He spends a lot of time in his room, playing with his computer. He's obsessed with it, but I suppose that's just a defence mechanism. He was very close to Don, confided in him in a way he's never done with me. Fourteen's a difficult age at the best of times.'

'We all deal with it in different ways.'

'Night times are the worst. I don't like being in that big bed on my own. I walk round the house and turn on the radio, anything to take my mind off it.'

'What can I do to help?'

'I am going to ask you for help, and you're the only person I'll ask. I need to understand.'

'Well, I won't be much use on that. Don kept his thoughts to himself. Even when we last met and had lunch he was pretty guarded.'

'I don't mean about that. I mean about DataTrak, and what they did to him.'

'I see,' Michael said, although he didn't. 'I'm not terribly well up on that, either. I was away when it all happened.'

'But you know. You know how they treated him, because they did the same to you.'

'To a certain extent. They manoeuvred me into a corner so that I didn't have any option but to resign. With Don I think it was different. They eroded his confidence, chiselled away at him remorselessly over a longer period. Zamboni was always undermining his authority. He never let him do his job properly. That's really all there is to it.'

Jean closed her eyes and exhaled slowly through her nose. To Michael it looked as if she were entering some kind of trance, but she suddenly snapped out of it. 'How do you feel about that?' she asked.

Michael picked up on her rising emotion and tried to

assuage it. 'I suppose I've become inured to that kind of behaviour. It goes on all the time, much more than you'd imagine. I know it sounds cynical and jaded, but that's business. If you started taking it too personally you'd end up in a rubber room.'

'It's different for you, of course, I realise that. But I've lost my husband. Nothing can bring him back. The boys have lost a good father, and for no reason other than the fact that some bastards decided he was expendable at work.'

Michael didn't like where this was leading. 'What are you saying, Jean?'

'Isn't it obvious? Our lives have been ruined by DataTrak. I don't for one minute think that Don would have been brought to this if it hadn't been for Zamboni and his henchmen. You know, I keep on thinking about how it could have been if we'd never left Vancouver. We were happy there. Now everything's disintegrated. That hurts, Michael. It's like a hot knife in my stomach. How am I meant to deal with that?'

'The only thing I can say is that it takes time. Eventually you'll get some perspective on it. Right now I can quite understand how you must be feeling, but you need time to sort it all out. It will happen, I promise.' Michael recalled Don's concern about Jean's state of mind, and he wasn't about to encourage her by agreeing with her about the evils of Zamboni.

'You surprise me,' Jean said. 'I really thought you'd be more upset.'

'About what?' Michael asked defensively. 'Don? I'm incredibly upset, but that's because I've lost a true friend and because of what it means to you and the boys. But I can't make the connection you're suggesting. DataTrak may have been a contributory factor, I'll grant you that, but it can't have been the only cause.'

'Perhaps you're stronger. Who knows how things will affect different people? All I know is that I want Don and I can't have him and I can see clearly who's to blame for that. I'm not going to let it drop, Michael. I owe Don that much.'

Michael made a conciliatory gesture with his hands. 'And that's entirely your prerogative,' he said. 'In your situation I'd probably do the same thing.'

They were silent. From the kitchen they could hear family members rattling plates and glasses, hiding their awkwardness with activity.

'Will you help?' Jean asked quietly.

'You know I will. Whatever you want, you have my support. But, for what it's worth, I'll also give you my advice.'

'It's a deal, then. That's worth a lot to me. I won't rest until I've got justice, you know.'

There was nothing more that Michael could say. Jean was set upon a course of action that he could do little to alter. It was painful to see her like this, but he wasn't going to deter her. Only time, he hoped, could achieve that.

SEVENTEEN

Just watching Skip could make Teri exhausted. From the moment she had told him the news he had been in overdrive, buying baby manuals and vitamin supplements and calling her at all times of the day to make sure she was getting enough rest – 'Yes,' as she'd said tartly on one occasion, 'if only you'd stop ringing me when I'm asleep.'

They moved into the house in Cobham on a Friday, two days after Don's funeral. It was modern and sat in a large estate of similar properties, all with deep front lawns and shiny new cars in the drive. It had been redecorated – magnolia from top to bottom – and was fully furnished. Teri had arranged for most of their possessions to be put into storage in the States, but a small shipment of things she couldn't bear to be without was due to arrive within a month.

DataTrak arranged a lease car for them, and they spent the first weekend driving around the area, stopping at a pub for lunch and walking – but not too far, at Skip's insistence – until they felt they had some idea of the lie of the land. By Sunday evening Teri was shattered; she lay on a big leather sofa as Skip scuttled between her and the kitchen, making an enormous noise as he prepared cheese omelettes and salad, a highlight of his culinary repertoire. They ate in front of the television and tried to make sense of English humour.

'What do you think about Don?' Teri asked, lacking the perseverance to continue watching.

'It's tragic. He was one of the good guys.'

'Any idea why he did it?'

'None whatsoever. I guess things just got on top of him and he couldn't see a way out.'

'He was pretty badly beaten up by Zamboni, wasn't he?'

Skip put his fork down and finished chewing a lettuce leaf before answering. 'Everyone's been beaten up by Nick at one time or another,' he said. 'It happens. But that's just his way. He has a prickly personality and he's very impatient. After a while you get used to it, or you leave. I've had my share of beatings, but I know his heart's in the right place and usually he's in the right. What I couldn't stand is if he was coming over tough about something and he was patently wrong. But that doesn't happen with Nick. He knows this business inside out and he has very solid judgement.'

'So he was justified in what he did to Don?'

'I'd say. Don was a bit laid-back from what I hear. He tended to let things happen, rather than make them happen. Nick detests that. He's always in a hurry. You look at his direct reports and you'll see they're all the same – they're performers, producers. Nick insists on that.'

'And that includes you?' Teri asked, smiling a little.

'I guess it does. But the jury's still out here, which is why I have to work so hard at it. Nick's watching me, and he's not going to give me very much time to turn things around. As long as I deliver, we'll be in good shape.'

'So you're not planning to make the same mistakes as Don?'

He grinned at her. 'Absolutely not. Any mistakes I make will be mine alone.'

'That's what I like to hear. If you're going to screw up, be unique about it.' Skip moved over to sit beside her and massaged her feet. 'I could get used to this, you know. Peel me a grape, and all that stuff? I like being pregnant if this is what's involved.'

'And I like you being pregnant. It's a good feeling.'

Teri was totally relaxed and enjoying the attention when the phone rang. 'I've got it,' Skip said, jumping up and racing over to the phone. 'This is Skip McMaster.'

The voice that replied was muffled and strange, as if being heavily disguised. 'Everything OK in your little nest?'

'Who is this?' Skip asked.

129

'You won't escape, you know. You can run, but you can't hide. Is Teri there?'

'What is this? What are you talking about?'

'Those who know say Skip's been a naughty boy. Naughty boys get punished. Think about it.'

'You've lost me. I'm hanging up.' But he didn't.

'You'll work it out. Ask Teri. She knows.' There was a pause. 'Oh, I have to go now. Have a nice life.'

Skip was left holding the receiver as the line was cut. He shook his head as he replaced the handset and, when he turned round, Teri was staring at him.

'Secret lover?' she said innocently.

'I wish. No, just some crank caller.'

Teri pulled herself upright on the sofa, suddenly animated. 'Tell me what they said.'

'Nothing much. Some junk about me being naughty and being punished for it.' He shrugged to show how unimportant it was but Teri was not to be put off.

'Tell me exactly what they said, Skip. I need to know.'

'Hey, OK. It was weird. Like I said, they said I'd been a naughty boy and had to be punished. They said, "You can run but you can't hide". Asked if you were here – said you'd understand. Then they rang off.'

'They mentioned me by name?'

'Yeah. It's no big deal, is it?'

Teri sighed. 'Well, it wouldn't be, except . . . I was meaning to tell you but I never got round to it. There was a call when I was back home. Asked me if I'd got a letter. I said I hadn't and they said that was a shame. When I collected the mail it was there.'

Now Skip was anxious. 'And?'

'It was an airmail letter. Just one page, printed, basically saying that you were a bastard and therefore so was I and that, if I was lucky, I might live to regret marrying you. That was it. No name, no hints otherwise as to who might have sent it.'

'Why didn't you tell me about this?'

'To be honest, I didn't want to worry you, and then I

forgot all about it. It didn't seem so important at the time.'

'Did you keep the letter?'

'Trashed it.'

'Damn. It's totally bizarre. I mean, who on earth would want to do something like this?'

'That's what I thought – some sick person with a warped sense of humour, maybe. Anyway, I hadn't thought any more about it – until now.'

Skip sat down next to Teri and rubbed his hand across the back of his neck. 'Well, sounds like someone doesn't like us, but I'm damned if I can figure who. Any ideas?'

'Could be that man at the dry-cleaner's you never paid for your suit – remember?'

'Teri, be serious. Anyway, I did pay him, just a little late.'

'So who is it?'

'I don't know, but we have to do something about it. We'll have to get our number changed for a start. Maybe I should call the police. What do you think?'

'I think they'll be pretty underwhelmed. We have nothing to tell them. We could call the phone company and tell them we have a nuisance caller. They should be able to do something. But first up you've got to stop making enemies, you hear?' Teri stroked his arm. 'Don't worry, Skip. Don't let it get to you. Whoever it is wants us to be upset about this, wants a reaction. If we stay calm and ignore it, it'll go away.'

'You're right, of course. It's just a bit spooky, that's all. We've only been here five minutes and already some weirdo knows our number.'

'Welcome to England. Now, as I recall, you were in the middle of massaging my feet and you hadn't finished with the left one. Get back to work.'

'At your service, princess.' Teri slipped back down on the sofa and Skip did as he was told.

Having bought a new computer, Michael had set it up in a spare bedroom and seemed to be determined to use it as much as he could. He produced a new CV which he asked

Annie to proof and approve: in return, she made him promise that he would send it out to as many headhunters as he could think of.

Annie was still at the stage where she was prepared to give him the benefit of the doubt. Her tolerance threshold had increased since she'd come face to face with Skip. She knew she was being unreasonable, but she'd immediately taken against him and had found him superficial and glib. The smile, the look, the casual, easygoing manner all added up, in her mind at least, to a package she thought repellent. Skip typified everything she despised about corporate life, and her brief confrontation with him had crystallised all the unformed prejudices she held.

And, now that she had seen for herself what Skip was like, the whole affair was beginning to affect Annie more than Michael. She was no longer able to dismiss events with the sang-froid she'd previously applied; it wasn't simply a matter of saying: 'Well, that's business and we must move on', regardless of Michael's benign acceptance. Now the thing was personal: the enemy had a face and she could focus her resentment on it. OK, she said to herself, so Michael had come out of it unscathed so far, but what about her and Holly? Were they totally insignificant? Did anyone care how they felt?

Annie was confused by her own reaction. She wasn't normally like this and had, as far as she could judge, handled the deal with a fair amount of good grace and resignation. It wasn't in her constitution to simmer with anger over the past – that was more often Michael's problem, and yet he was now the one who had the sanguine view, the pragmatism to consign it all to history's rubbish bin. She was left in the unlikely position of battling to come to terms with what it meant and how they would live with it; she was the one who felt abandoned, let down, her life callously dismantled. Michael was fine, and that was one thing, but it was quite another to assume that she, too, could ride it out and let it go. For that matter, Michael himself was guilty of making that assumption; he had behaved as if, as long as he was able to endure the pain, there would be no related effect on her and Holly.

She couldn't blame him for this: after all, hadn't she played the role of good and supportive wife to such perfection that he would have expected nothing less from her now? She had painted herself into this corner and, once there, couldn't see a way out. Much as she would have liked to discuss it with Michael, and tell him how she now felt, she knew it couldn't happen. He wouldn't understand; more importantly, she didn't want him destabilised by hearing of her own wild and irrational thoughts. But this consideration for him didn't stop her entertaining such thoughts, making her restless and frustrated. I am stronger than this, she told herself. I cannot allow this to bring me down.

But it did. She could not escape from this hiatus, where she was caught between the memory of a happy and secure past and the prospect of an uncertain future. If Michael had walked straight into a new job – or if he'd even made the effort to find one, which she knew he hadn't – she could have jettisoned everything which now disturbed her. She would have had something to look forward to rather than the wreckage of what was past. Conversely, Michael seemed almost too comfortable in this no-man's land, quite happy to be directionless as he sat upstairs and played with his computer. He had made no serious effort to find employment and was apparently unmoved by what had occurred, only demonstrating any emotion over Don Retzer's suicide. Annie desperately wanted to confront him and spur him into action for her sake as much as his, but she knew what the reaction would be: give me more time, he would say. And she would; that was the only way she knew.

His new ability to surprise her manifested itself one morning. She and Holly were having breakfast when he came downstairs wearing his best suit. 'Interview,' he said brightly in explanation.

'Interview? You didn't tell me about this. Who with?'

'Bloomberg. I didn't want to say anything until I was sure I'd made it on to the shortlist. I'm going to see one of the heads of global sales and marketing. Dealing-room products, just like DataTrak only better. I've got to be there at ten-thirty.'

'Well, you look like a top banana in that suit so you're bound to get it. That's wonderful news.'

'Let's not get too excited yet. There's a long way to go. But I do know some people there, so I think I've got a fighting chance.'

'Have they mentioned money?'

'Not yet, but it's got to be competitive. Some of their sales people make a fortune.' He smiled at her and Holly. 'Wish me luck.'

'You don't need luck,' she chided. 'You're a brilliant salesman and if they've got any sense they'll hire you on the spot. Don't undersell yourself – you know what you're like.'

'There's no chance of that. I'm feeling pretty confident about this one. They need me, and they'll have to pay to get me – as simple as that.'

'That's what I like to hear. You are going to have breakfast before you go, aren't you?'

'I'm too excited to eat. Don't worry, I'll be fine. I'll call you.'

'We'll be standing by the phone.'

Michael checked himself in the hall mirror on the way out and needlessly adjusted his tie. Annie felt a tingle of excitement run up and down her body: was this, she wondered, the beginning of the end? She watched Holly eating her cereal and wished for good things to happen. They deserved a little bit of good fortune.

Later, when Annie was upstairs, she wandered into the spare bedroom where Michael had his computer. He had kept the desk very tidy and uncluttered, with the PC in the middle of it. Annoyingly, the screen had been switched off, because Annie was curious to see what he'd been working on. Feeling like an intruder, she was reluctant to poke around too much, but she couldn't resist flicking through the neat pile of papers sitting in a plastic tray on the edge of the desk.

There were bills, and clean copies of his CV, nothing particularly interesting. Disappointed, she pulled at the top drawer of his desk and was surprised that it was locked. What did he have to hide, she wondered? She looked around the room for the keys, and eventually found them behind a photo of Holly that he'd put on the mantelpiece over the unused fireplace. Now her hands sweated a little. Was this terribly wrong, to invade his private space? How would she feel if he did the same? Curiosity overcame her doubts, and she unlocked the drawer.

A box of white A4 lay inside the top drawer. She looked at the top sheet and read the single typed paragraph on it.

Police today were making house-to-house enquiries in an effort to piece together the last known movements of Skip and Teri McMaster, who were found dead in their car in the garage of their Cobham home at the weekend. They had apparently died from exhaust fumes. A police spokesman said that, although it appeared to be a case of suicide, they were keeping an open mind and continuing with their investigation. He added that there was no obvious motive for the murder of the two Americans, who had recently arrived in Britain. A neighbour said that they seemed to be a very friendly couple who were settling in well.

At first Annie couldn't take it in, and she had to read it several times before it registered with her. Feeling cold and sick, she quickly closed and locked the drawer and put the keys back behind the photo. Then she stood in the centre of the room with her fists tightly clenched, tears brimming in her eyes and her head throbbing. It was too hard for her to think straight, and she let her emotions take over, sobbing as the full horror of what she'd read engulfed her.

EIGHTEEN

Pam lay fully clothed on her bed and listened to the sounds of the house as it lived its own life, performing automatic, programmed acts to keep itself running. She had known that she would call in sick on this day, had already planned it as she was tidying up her desk and squaring things away to prepare for her absence. Even when she was genuinely ill she felt guilty about taking time off; without a good reason, however, she felt even worse, as if she were committing the most terrible act of treason which would inevitably result in discovery and punishment. In spite of this, she was committed to her path: she needed the time and space to think about what she had done and what she might do to follow up on it.

Cliff had already gone. He had a lot of work on now that the summer was drawing to a close, and he would be out for long days, pruning, clipping, clearing and tidying up other people's gardens. He could be the laziest person she knew but, when he was busy and the money was rolling in – sometimes in cash, more often in traceable cheques – he applied himself well and knuckled down to work. She was proud of him for this; so many of the boys she had met before she settled on him had become complete wasters, unable to hold down a job and drifting helplessly into petty crime or a life on the social. Cliff, she reckoned, could easily have gone the same way, but he had matured and seemed to recognise that there was more to life than a single path between the job centre, the pub and the bookies'.

He had no idea about her, though, and what she was going through. He existed in a world where everything was simple, where there were no doubts about his role and his relationship

136

with her. It never crossed his mind that there were deeper, darker parts of the soul – hers in particular – black pools which harboured strange motivations and dangerous desires. His was a monochromatic, unimaginative universe where men and women might not understand each other but still managed to get along as long as they both knew their place. It was as straightforward as that, and there was no need to question the natural order of things.

How Pam wished for the same clarity of thought, the same blind acceptance of events and consequences. It had been like that once, of course, she could still see that: there had been a time when everything happened pretty much as she'd expected, and the road ahead was free from uncertainty and nasty surprises. Get married, set up home, save a little bit each month, one day even have some kiddies: that was the way it happened, and she'd had no reason to believe it would be otherwise for her and Cliff – no reason, that was, until Michael had walked into her life.

Michael shone with a different light. He existed in what seemed to her to be a parallel universe, capable of higher thought and nobler deeds than other men: even as she told herself that he was unreachable, a prize that was beyond her grasp, she still ached at the prospect of a long life without him, never touching his face or feeling his hot, sweet breath on her neck. She knew that he had no interest in her, but that only increased her discomfort because, had he been more accessible, more responsive, it would somehow have lessened the aura which surrounded him. As long as he was remote, he was unbearably attractive to her; the dream for her would always be better than the reality. At least she could manage the fantasy so that nothing went wrong. In real life, that didn't happen.

Her quandary, as she slipped off the bed and went downstairs, was hurting her head. There were so many things she could do, actions she could take which might alter events and, just possibly, change his perception of her, that she didn't know where to start. Michael was strong, seemingly unharmed by all the vicious attacks on him, and that was her main problem. She wanted to do something so stunning, so completely winning, that he would have no option but to reward her with what she craved most: his attention. Going to his house had been a misjudgement. He had not reacted as she'd expected, remaining calm and bringing her down to earth without any fuss. He was good like that: in all the time she'd known him, he'd never really lost his temper, always maintaining a level head even in the worst situations. He could be scratchy, or short, but never truly angry or rude. She so badly wanted to melt that ice, to see him fired up and aggressive, for no greater reason than it might also open his eyes to what she could offer him.

And what was on offer was utter devotion. Pam was convinced that Michael was not as happy as she could make him, hopeful that she could deliver a different, higher level of delight to his life. Yes, she accepted that, purely physically, she had little with which to tempt him – overweight and plain, as she harshly appraised herself – but she believed she could overcome these inadequacies by the intensity of her dedication to him and his happiness. Annie – well, Annie was a typical product of her upbringing, too certain and pushy for Pam's liking, too concerned with her own well-being to spend enough time attending to Michael's. Pam found her to be a bit of a snob, always looking down her nose when they met, behaving as if she was superior just because she had some money and was thin – and owned Michael. That was the right word – ownership – that was how it seemed to Pam. Annie owned something valuable but didn't know it, was almost casual about what she possessed, as if having it was all that mattered and there was no need to maintain and enhance it, like some expensive oil painting on the wall that only needed an occasional dusting and would just appreciate with age. Michael needed more than that; he needed to be cherished and nurtured, and that was precisely what Pam could do for him.

She could no longer control the passion which had spread like an unchecked cancer, and her reason began to desert her. Every part of her felt sore, her clothes rubbing against

138

her skin like wire wool, her whole body throbbing with the abrasion of her desire. She was being driven by emotions she'd hardly known were possible, their strength forcing her to consider the worst possible solutions to her disease; the heat of her anxiety was unbearable, and she longed for the cool touch of normality to bring down the fever. But in her confusion, in the maelstrom of infatuation and jealousy and revenge and doubt, she could not reach back to that orderly time when everything was straight and level. Even though it was only in her imagination, Pam had gone too far, had travelled along a path which closed behind her with every step she took. There was no turning back, no way out. Whatever the consequences, she was too committed now to stop.

As a rule, Michael didn't lie to Annie. There was no need to: their marriage was based on trust, a partnership of two equals, and he had no secrets from her. In any case, he was a bad liar. His eyes grew large and glassy and his tongue thickened whenever he attempted deception and he'd long since given it up as a talent he didn't possess.

So he was surprised at how easy it had been when he'd had to. He knew that Annie wanted to believe him – had no reason not to – and that she would never imagine that he'd actively deceive her over such an important matter. A job interview at Bloomberg – how simple it was to convince her that it was reality, that he was trying to do what she wanted and was making a proper effort. He needed to get her off his back, and this was the best way he knew how. He could string her along with this for as long as it took, feeding her little morsels of news to show that it was all progressing but, hey! these things take time and the right guy isn't going to be in town for another two weeks and it looks like the job description's going to change and they're having a reorganisation and . . . well, there were a thousand reasons for the delay, and he knew them all.

What he didn't know was how it was all going to end. Eventually – in three, six, nine months? – he was going to have to face the music, not just about the illusory job but the fact that all his ambition had seeped away, to be replaced by a void where there should have been hope and hunger. It was as if someone had stuck a big drain hose into his guts and sucked out everything which kept him going, leaving only the vital organs so that at least his metabolism could function. Every limb felt heavy, every blink of his eyelids an effort: his mind was fixed in a permanent state of inactivity, to such an extent that nothing could hold his attention – nothing, that was, except the fact that he was adrift and feckless, floating in tideless water. He was passively aware of his critical condition, like a patient on the operating table who, when the anaesthetic wears off before the procedure is complete, is powerless to tell anyone. He knew what was going on, but he had no way of heading it off.

This impotence didn't worry him – except that it worried him that he wasn't worried. He was perfectly content to let things run their course, to watch almost as a disinterested third party as his world spun by. He knew he should have been concerned, and he should be doing something active about it, but he was disabled by the enervating effect of everything that had happened, to him and to those around him. He had, fleetingly, been animated by Don's suicide, interested in helping Jean to sort out her life, but these feelings were soon overwhelmed by a heavy, deadening malaise which weakened muscle and sinew as well as thought.

He sat in a café and chewed a buttered bun at the very moment when Annie would be thinking he was at Bloomberg. He watched the office workers popping in and out but felt no empathy with them, even though he was dressed in their uniform and they would not have given him a second glance, so conventional did he look. He was no longer part of their tribe, no more the thrusting executive with important deadlines and major deals to close. Stripped of this, he was pointless: there was no affiliation, no objective, no anything. Beneath his suit and tie he was hollow, incapable even of feeling the pain of exclusion from this club. He wasn't tired, but he wanted to sleep: at least in his dreams he still functioned as he had before, his unconscious mind active in a way he couldn't consciously replicate. Perversely, sleep had become the refuge from this desert: most other people wanted to escape from reality through it, but he enjoyed it mostly because it took him back to where he had been.

When he walked out on to the pavement he looked at buildings he knew so well with different eyes, as if he was a tourist and had never seen them before. He couldn't imagine what was going on inside them, what commerce and activity was being transacted; he was a stranger to it, excluded by his loss of office, the surrender of his security pass and calling cards and mobile phone. These accoutrements of business, previously taken for granted and valued so little, now assumed major significance as he tried to survive without them, weapons in his arsenal that had been confiscated so that he felt threatened and vulnerable.

Michael took a long, circular route around the City, strolling past the offices of many of his former clients and ending up at Broadgate, a huge soulless sprawl of ugly buildings around Liverpool Street station. He walked around the circle of shops and restaurants which bounded the ice rink in the centre of the development; his name was known in many of the restaurants, having been a frequent client in the days when he would entertain his customers with expensive lunches washed down with overpriced wine. He wondered if they would still greet him so effusively, now that he was without office and any money he spent would be his own, his credit cards no longer carrying the DataTrak title. He guessed that he could walk into any of these places and see half a dozen people he knew, men and women still on the corporate merry-go-round and oblivious to the real world. What would he say to them: 'Yes, it's true – I've given it all up and I'm happier now than I've ever been'? He doubted it: they'd hardly believe it, just as he did not believe it. He craved fresh admission to their exclusive society, but utterly lacked the will and determination to reapply for membership.

He grew tired just thinking about it. He needed to sit

down and rest, but he was uneasy in this hostile environment. He had already forgotten some of the rituals of City life, his confidence sapped by his absence from the daily routines. He only felt truly safe in his room at home, sat in front of his computer with the door shut and Annie downstairs. He would look out of the window and watch the top of a tree swaying in the gentle wind, or stand up and see passers-by and neighbours as they carried on their business in the street. It was so comforting, this slow, repetitive and formless existence, as if he were living his life by proxy through the people and events he watched from his window. It helped to take his mind off all the more important issues, the crisis he was facing but would not address.

Michael was about to turn on his heel and head for the tube when he heard his name being called from behind. 'Michael?' a man's voice said, more a question than a salutation, as if the person wasn't quite sure it was him. Michael turned to look over his shoulder; at first he saw no one familiar, but then his name was called again and he located the source of the voice. Standing at a small coffee kiosk was Charles Turkwood. He was clutching a polystyrene cup and was grinning broadly. He waved his hand to call Michael over. There was a moment of hesitation as Michael's brain seemed to stall, unable to register what he was witnessing, before he moved one foot in front of the other and walked slowly towards Turkwood.

'Well,' Turkwood said. 'Fancy meeting you here. How the devil are you?'

Michael was still incapable of pulling his thoughts together. 'Fine,' he answered mechanically. 'You?'

'Never better. I'm just taking a quick injection of caffeine before going on to a meeting. Will you join me?'

'Er, well, I'm in a bit of a hurry,' he lied to cover his astonishment.

'Go on, I'm buying, and you don't hear that very often from a consultant.'

'OK. I'll have one of those.' Turkwood ordered two more double espressos and paid for them. He handed one to

Michael and they moved across to a bench to sit down.

'So what's the story with Mr Lensman?' Turkwood asked brightly.

Still trying to deal with the shock of this warm welcome, Michael was guarded and suspicious. 'No story that I know of. Why – what have you heard?'

'Nothing much. I had lunch with your Skip McMaster – a strange fish, I must say – but I haven't heard a peep from you. Have you been in hiding?'

Michael couldn't tell if he was being wound up, or whether Turkwood really didn't know. 'No, I'm not in hiding,' he replied. 'I'm history, that's all. I resigned from DataTrak. I thought they would have told you.'

Turkwood thought about this news and sipped his coffee. 'Resigned, have you? Where are you going?'

'Nowhere. I'm taking some time out to think about what I want to do next. But . . . I'm amazed you don't already know about all this.'

'Are you? It doesn't surprise me. Everyone at DataTrak's been behaving very oddly since the Morgan Stanley business. They were mightily aggrieved they didn't win it, as I'm sure you know. I told Skip you'd done an excellent job, put in a good word for you, but they're not happy.' Turkwood stopped talking and his expression changed dramatically. 'Oh, good Lord,' he exclaimed, 'your departure doesn't have anything to do with that, does it?'

Now Michael didn't know how to react. Was Turkwood a very good actor? He appeared to be genuinely horrified at the idea, and yet Michael had him down as the instigator of all his troubles. 'As a matter of fact, it does. I resigned by mutual agreement. You didn't hear that from me, by the way. And, no offence intended, I was given the strong impression that you had something to do with it.'

'Me?' Turkwood said in a shocked voice. 'How come?'

'It sounds stupid now, but it was suggested that you'd lodged a complaint. They said you'd accused me of trying to bribe you to get the Morgan Stanley business.'

Turkwood's face was impassive, and then he laughed, a

big laugh that rocked his shoulders. 'Come off it, old boy, that's just too fantastic for words. You're pulling my plonker, aren't you?'

'I wish I was. But it's true. In fact, they were so convincing that I almost believed it, too.'

Turkwood stopped laughing. 'Good God, that's obscene. It's more than that, it's slanderous. I should call my solicitor – and I hope you've called yours.'

'Well, I can't advise you on that,' Michael said quietly, 'but in my case there wasn't much point. Sooner or later they would have got me out. Better that I took the money and ran as soon as possible.'

'Very noble. What a bunch of bastards. Of course, we should have known after what they did to poor old Don. Fortunately I was able to help him out a bit, give him some work.'

'You've heard about Don – I mean, recently?'

'Haven't spoken to him for some time, now you mention it. Why do you ask?'

'He committed suicide.'

'Oh my Lord,' Turkwood said, obviously shaken. 'I had no idea. He had a family, didn't he?'

'A wife and two boys. They're devastated, as you'd expect.'

'It gets more bizarre every minute. Look, I've got to run off to this meeting, but it shouldn't take long. If you hang around I'll buy you a spot of lunch. We can talk things through. It sounds to me as if you've been seriously maltreated, and I can't abide that. You're a damned good salesman, always were. If I can help in any way . . .'

'That's very kind of you, Charles, but I have to be getting back. Tell you what, give me your card and I'll call you next time I'm up, I promise. I'm very glad I ran into you – otherwise we might never have sorted this out.'

'Too right, old boy. The lunch offer stands, in any event. But tell me one thing – how do you want me to deal with DataTrak? I must say I'm very ticked off about them using me like that. It stinks. But I don't want to tread on your toes.'

'Can you leave it with me for a bit? I'm still trying to get everything straight. I'll come back to you – but, for the time being at least, I'd appreciate it if you'd say nothing.'

'Consider it done. What a shocking way to run a business, though. I can tell you right now, DataTrak is off my shortlist. They won't win any more business if I have anything to do with it.' Turkwood got up and tossed his empty cup into a bin by the kiosk. 'Call me, please. I'd like that.'

He walked off, leaving Michael sitting alone. Now he knew for sure what he'd suspected all along: the whole thing had been a sham, and Turkwood was an innocent party to it. He remembered his mother's advice, 'Always go with your first instincts', and these returned to him, shaking him into a new state of awareness. There were some things he could tolerate, some indiscretions he could ignore, but these people had gone beyond the boundaries of acceptability. Finally, after everything he'd been prepared to overlook, Michael was starting to understand the true nature of his predicament.

NINETEEN

The house in Cobham had enough rooms, as Teri said, to accommodate the Red Army if it ever dropped by for the night. Upstairs there were five bedrooms and three bathrooms – one en suite – and downstairs there was a large kitchen, a sitting room, dining room, cloakroom and a study. Skip had set up his home office in the study – the den, as they called it – with a computer and modem, fax machine, separate phone line and a two-drawer filing cabinet. There was no window in this room, but the lighting was good and Skip bought an extra Anglepoise lamp for the desk. On most evenings he would get home from work, have dinner with Teri and then retire for an hour or so to the den to catch up with his paperwork. For Skip the job had no thresholds; there was no delineation between home and office, and he worked wherever and whenever he needed to. Teri understood this: it was part of the bargain.

She had quickly found her bearings in Cobham and was beginning to appreciate the English way of life. Shops weren't always open, and neither were pubs. Everyone drove on the wrong side of the road and she was particularly careful whenever she crossed the street, instinctively looking the wrong way first. But she was intrigued by the English and their reserve: they didn't speak unless spoken to, and they kept their opinions to themselves. They were polite in a remote sort of way, and seemed pretty uninterested in her. No doubt, she thought, they were well used to Americans here and did not view them as especially interesting. She liked that; she didn't want to be looked at like an alien.

She'd returned from a shopping trip and was in the kitchen

unpacking the bags. Everything was so small – the packets, the cuts of meat, even the oven and the dishwasher – and she wondered whether it was something to do with the legacy of rationing. Had the Brits never recovered from the privations of the war? She liked to buy in bulk, but the supermarkets here were very mean with their portions. She smiled as she stored the groceries and filled the fridge; it was certainly different, and none the less exciting for that.

Teri was just putting away the last of the shopping when there was a knock at the door. Around here they were constantly badgered by all manner of salesmen and hawkers, all wanting to cash in on the evident wealth of the neighbourhood. She'd already bought too many dusters, too much handmade soap and a supply of fresh fish that would keep them – and the Red Army – going for about a year if they ate nothing else. The kitchen knives had been through the grinder's machine, and she'd fended off assorted gardeners, handymen, driveway specialists and roofing contractors. Another caller would be given a polite but firm refusal.

She padded to the door and opened it. There was no one on the step and she looked left and right but couldn't see anyone standing at the side. Then she looked down and saw a brown A4 Jiffy bag leaning against the wall of the porch. She looked up hurriedly to try to spot the person who'd delivered it – nothing. The estate was quiet at this time of day; over on the other side there was a window cleaner up a ladder but otherwise the place was deserted. The corporate wives were all out at aerobics classes, or spending money, or lunching on lettuce leaves and mineral water or, more enticingly as far as Teri was concerned, conducting torrid affairs with their gardeners behind the drawn curtains.

She stooped down stiffly, her back aching already from the baby, and picked up the package. She put her hand on the small of her back to rub it as she looked at the envelope.

BY HAND – PRIVATE & CONFIDENTIAL
TERI MCMASTER

The letters had been carefully handwritten with thick black marker pen. She turned the package over but there was no more writing on it.

Closing the door, she walked back to the sitting room and slumped into an oversized armchair. She carefully opened the bag – they were so useful and she didn't like to waste it – and peered inside. She was expecting to find something fragile in it, but there was only a thin sheaf of papers as far as she could see. She pulled them out and, dropping the bag to the floor, she put them on her lap.

The first piece of paper was blank, so she turned it over and saw what was underneath. It was a folded sheet of paper, not A4 but much longer and thinner. Unfolding it, she saw what appeared to be official markings printed across the longer side of the paper. Then she saw the words CERTIFICATE OF DEATH, boldly printed and centred below the markings. There were several boxes beneath this, each filled with more printed words. Her eyes fell on one line:

FULL NAME OF DECEASED: Teri Carlton McMaster (née Andersen)

There was another line beneath this with her current address, then a single entry:

DATE OF DEATH:????

She stared incredulously at the form. To her untrained eye it looked exactly how a death certificate should look. All her other details were there – date and place of birth, spouse, next of kin – and her eyes skittered across the page as she held it fully open. She noticed that, where there should have been signatures, the spaces had been left blank. She put it carefully on the arm of her chair and looked at the next piece of paper. On this, which was plain A4, someone had typed:

ONLY YOU CAN STOP THIS BEING ISSUED.

FOR SKIP, IT MAY ALREADY BE TOO LATE.
GET OUT WHILE YOU CAN.
YOU'RE NOT WELCOME HERE.

Teri hurriedly scrabbled through all the other sheets of paper but they were blank. She returned to the certificate and read it again: every element of it was filled in correctly. Whoever had done this knew a lot about her. Suddenly it was very personal, very close. Her skin started to itch and she felt the presence of evil in the room with her. Unsteadily getting to her feet, she went back to the front door and opened it. The window cleaner was putting his ladders back on the roof of his van. A green Mercedes estate car pulled out of a drive two houses down from her. A dog barked aimlessly.

She slammed the door shut and put the security chain in place. She went round every window and door checking the locks, then rushed to the phone to call Skip. As she was about to pick up the receiver the phone rang, making her jump. She picked it up, hoping it was Skip.

'Hallo,' she said nervously.

'You got it, then. That's good.' The voice was almost familiar, almost placeable, but she couldn't even determine whether it was a man or a woman.

'Who is this?' she screamed. 'Why are you doing this to us?'

'Teri, Teri,' the caller said calmly. 'Surely you know. Surely he's told you.'

'I don't understand.' Teri was starting to sob. 'Please leave us alone.'

'I'm sorry. I can't do that. It's gone too far. You must realise that. There's no turning back.'

Teri was now greatly distressed. 'What do you want? Is it money? We'll pay. Whatever you want. Just leave us in peace. We've done nothing wrong.'

'Too late. I'll be in touch.'

She was left holding the receiver, fat tears flooding down her cheeks. Her head began to swim and she slid down the wall and slumped on to the floor. Very slowly, she listed to the right and collapsed, unconscious, the phone crashing down beside her.

Annie had been sick. She'd lost count of how many times she'd knelt in front of the lavatory bowl, or bent over the kitchen sink, but she had nothing more to evacuate from her stomach. She wanted a glass of wine – a bottle, or two – to try to deaden the pain, but she knew that wasn't the best idea. Michael hadn't called, and it was half past four in the afternoon. Holly was being as irritating as she could be, wanting attention and asking lots of stupid questions and generally adding to Annie's misery, but she held firm and refused to snap. She needed a clear head; she needed a coherent plan to deal with this. As everything caved in around her, she had to be strong. She alone could restore some reason to the situation.

She had set Michael's office back exactly the way it had been before her discovery, but she still didn't know whether to disclose to him what she'd found. Obviously he was imbalanced, ill, unable to cope, however much he'd tried to hide it from her. If she confronted him the whole thing could explode and he might lose it completely. She didn't want that – but what was the alternative? Pretend everything was all right? Ignore the facts? That wasn't her style: unlike Michael, she needed to confront these problems head-on. Bewildered, frightened, she tried to come up with excuses, mitigating factors that would set it all in perspective.

And, though she battled against it, she kept on returning to the idea that it was somehow all her fault. She could have stopped this, the madness and the deception and the despair which had crept into his life. Had she reacted differently – perhaps, even, had she encouraged him to demonstrate more anger and rage – this would never have happened. She'd been too timid, too keen to let him alone and give him the oasis she thought he needed; how much better it would have been if she'd prompted him to vent it, baited him until it all spilled out and was quickly spent. She was to blame; poor Michael had received the worst possible treatment from her. How naive she had been.

'You stupid bitch!' she shouted as she stood at the sink and drank a glass of water. But she wasn't sure if she was chastising herself because of what she'd done – or not done – or because she felt such revulsion at her facility to take the blame for Michael's condition. In terms of self-esteem, Annie was heavily in debit. She'd never felt so inadequate, so incapable of handling her own life, let alone managing with Holly and Michael. Since the wake, and her outburst at Skip, she'd made a drastic re-evaluation of her own worth. The growth of her private anger, her suppressed feelings of resentment, had been accompanied by a plunge in her estimation of herself. She wasn't as tough as she'd thought; she wasn't a good wife and mother; all this compassionate, understanding, supportive act was just a pile of bullshit, designed to conceal the fact that she was weak and useless. She'd failed herself and by association had failed her family. The proof of that, if it were needed, came with the words Michael had typed and hidden upstairs. His mind was warped and she'd let it happen.

How could she ever have imagined that he was coping? What possessed her? It was so dumb that it defied belief. Now she had to face the consequences of her deficiency. He would come home, bright-eyed and bushy-tailed, speaking of the fantastic opportunity and holding out the promise of the good life again, and what would she do? Wouldn't she do what she had always done, playing the game and hiding her feelings so that life would be calm and even until . . . until the next time? Would there be other events, other crises which sent him over the edge? Once you let it go, you can never recover. She thought of infidelity: if he ever touched another woman, she'd kick him out. She'd seen too many women let them back, seen how they'd swallowed their principles to keep the peace. She'd sworn that wouldn't happen with her. But this was a similar conundrum: how far do you go to avoid disruption? Was it worth it, in the end? Now, faced with a living reality rather than a vague notion, she didn't know how to react.

And, when his key rattled in the lock and she heard him drop his briefcase on the hall floor, she was still wrestling with those questions. Michael walked into the kitchen and kissed her. 'Good day?' he asked, but she knew he didn't want to talk about her day.

She got her excuses in straight away. 'Average. The curse is coming and I'm a bit hormonal.'

'Oh.'

'So come on, tell me what happened.'

He went to the fridge and pulled out a beer. 'Promising, but inconclusive,' he said before taking a swig. 'Do you want a drink?'

She looked at the clock on the wall. 'It's a bit early. Oh, what the hell. I'll have some white wine.'

He poured her a glass and handed it to her. 'Where's Holly?' he asked.

'In her room.'

'I'll go up.'

'No, leave her. She's happy. I want to hear about the interview.'

'Well, as I said, it's all a bit up in the air. I know they want me, but it isn't quite as simple as that. It looks like they're planning a major reorganisation, and they have to schedule me into that. It could take a bit of time.'

'But you think it'll happen eventually?'

'I'd be very surprised if it doesn't.'

She was very careful about phrasing her next question. 'You've been gone a long time. Were you there the whole day?'

'Pretty much. They gave me lunch, which was nice. I'm sorry, I should have phoned.'

'That's OK. I knew it would be something like that.'

'Anyway, they said they'll be in touch again. I called the headhunter and he said he'd let me know their feedback.'

Something was wrong about him, Annie could tell: there was a hint of falseness in his tone, as if he wasn't telling her everything. 'You don't seem too excited,' she suggested.

'I think I'm just tired. It was a pretty full day, and I'm not used to it, that's all. No, I'm very pleased with how it all went.' Holly raced into the kitchen and hugged Michael's legs, and he swept her up into his arms. 'How's my favourite daughter?' he said, kissing her forehead.

'Daddy, you've only got one daughter – me!'

'So you must be my favourite.'

Annie watched them and smiled weakly. He was good at this. He knew how to avoid the uncomfortable discussions that she so often wanted. There was no opening, no crack for her to prise apart so that she could determine what was really going on in his tortured mind. She felt a wave of nausea and sipped her wine to quell it. Tonight, just tonight, she would avoid it too – it could wait until the morning. A deep sleep, assisted by wine, would help to focus her mind on what was important. Right now, she was frightened, but she didn't want to answer the nagging question of what, or who, frightened her.

When Skip found that he couldn't open the front door he went to the side gate that led into the garden and round the back of the house. That, too, was bolted from the inside. Puzzled, but not unduly worried, he walked to the front again and peered through the sitting-room window, not entirely certain of what he was looking for. There was no sign of any life, and he thought Teri must be upstairs. He went to the front door and rapped lightly.

He waited patiently until he heard some movement in the hallway. 'Who is it?' Teri asked loudly.

'It's me. Who'd you think it would be?'

'Oh.' He heard the security chain rattling and then the door opened. 'Hiya.' Teri looked drained; her eyes were puffy and there were dark crescents beneath them. Her shoulders drooped with exhaustion.

Skip kissed her on the lips and stepped inside. 'What's with all the security?' he asked as they walked back to the kitchen. She stopped walking and turned to look at him, her face blank.

'I think I'm losing my mind,' she said. 'It must be the

153

baby messing with my hormones.'

'You're taking those homeopathic tablets, aren't you?' he asked, concern in his voice.

'Yes, I'm taking the tablets. All ninety-six of them.'

'Bad day, huh?'

'You could say that.' She moved on and went to the kitchen, getting Skip a glass of pink lemonade from the fridge. He was addicted to the stuff and she'd had to instigate quite a search to find a regular supply. He took it, thanked her, and sat down at the table.

'Want to tell me about it?'

'Just one of those days I'd prefer to forget. How about you – how's my hard-charging senior executive?' She was trying to be light but Skip could tell she was depressed.

'Regular day – meetings, calls, more meetings and a mountain of paperwork. I tell you, we're the principal perpetrators of global deforestation, the amount of paper we generate. I thought this was meant to be the electronic age.' Teri raised her eyebrows and attempted a pale impression of a smile. 'So, shall I cook tonight?' he continued. 'You look all in.'

'That'd be nice,' she said without any real conviction. Then she sat opposite him and laid her hands on the table. 'I was thinking – and I'll quite understand if you say you can't – but wouldn't it be neat if we went away for a few days? We haven't seen much of England yet, and I'd really like to go to the Lake District or the West Country or somewhere. You know, get away from it all and just be together on our own.' There was a pleading undertone which Skip picked up, suggesting she was almost desperate.

'I guess we could. If we did it over a weekend, I could take the Friday and Monday. I could certainly use the break, and the office will just have to get along without me.' He grinned, pleased that he could do this for her and wanting to show how easy it was for him to fall in with her wishes. He needed to see her smile, to watch her face light up; he hated finding her like this. 'Got any plans?'

'No, but I'll get going on it tomorrow. Thank you. It means a lot to me.'

This formality worried him more. She never spoke like this: theirs was an easy, casual relationship, where things like that didn't need to be said. He put his hand over hers and rubbed gently. 'What is it, babe? What's eating you?'

She pulled away suddenly and stood up, turning so that she had her back to him. 'Pay no attention,' she said quietly. 'It's nothing, OK?'

'Sure,' he replied. 'How do you do, my name's Skip McMaster, remember? What's going on here?'

She snapped back. 'Drop it, OK? I'll be fine.'

Skip got up and went behind her, putting his hands on her shoulders and massaging them. 'Princess, you're worrying me. The baby's all right, isn't it?'

'Perfect. It's the mother that's got all the problems, and all the pills in the world can't sort her out.'

He continued to move his hands over her neck and shoulders but she didn't react, her head stiff and unmoving. 'I guess you're tired. Why don't you go up to bed and I'll bring you something to eat? Room service, no extra charge.'

She wriggled away from his touch and turned to face him. There were tears in her eyes. 'Skip, don't ever leave me.'

He reeled back in mock surprise. 'Not something I was planning, not right away anyhow.'

'I'm serious.'

'So am I. What's brought this on?'

'Just . . . well, I don't know what I'd do without you, that's all.'

She pushed herself against him, hugging him so tightly that it felt as if she wanted to climb inside him. After several silent minutes she released him. 'Go on,' she said, brighter now, 'go into your den and I'll start dinner. Forget what I said. I'm feeling much better.'

He nodded, grinned at her, then did as he was told. A fax he was expecting sat in the delivery tray of the machine and he pulled it out, sorting the pages back into their original order. But the bottom page was not part of the same transmission. It was immediately striking because it had large

155

bold-print letters centred on it. His attention was immediately drawn to it.

> YOU KNOW WHAT YOU DID.
> THERE'S NO ESCAPE FROM IT.
> THINGS CAN ONLY GET WORSE.
> ASK TERI IF YOU DON'T BELIEVE ME.

He looked at the heading of the page to see if there was an identifier, but there was only the date, time and his fax number. He carefully stroked his hair as he held the paper. Should he tell her? The state she was in, this would blow her mind. He decided against it, but also made a mental note to sort this out, once and for all, in the morning.

TWENTY

Brian Shale could not recall a more embarrassing moment in his life. He had been sitting in trap one, as the men referred to the end lavatory cubicle, taking his time as he scanned the *Sporting Life*. It had been a noisy session, punctuated by sighs and gasps of relief; he regarded this early morning ritual as sacrosanct, and his colleagues could set their watches by it. But, when he'd finally finished and opened the door, he was horrified to see Skip standing outside, leaning against the washbasin unit.

'Hi,' Skip said.

'Hallo.' Brian didn't know where to look.

'Sorry to interrupt you like this, but I've got a problem and I need your help.'

'I see.' Brian answered warily as he tossed the paper on the unit and turned on a tap.

'I'll get right to it. Teri and I have had some bad things happening to us – hate mail, crank calls, that kind of stuff.'

Brian continued washing his hands and looked at Skip's reflection in the mirror. 'Sounds nasty. Any idea who it might be?'

'I was kind of hoping you could fill me in on that. You know, whenever a new guy comes in there's bound to be some resentment, and that's totally understandable. You make changes, unsettle things a bit, people get nervous. So I was wondering – you're plugged into the grapevine. Hell, you are the grapevine. Anything's going on, Brian's the first to know about it. I figured you might have heard something, might know where all this is coming from.'

157

Brian frowned and shook his head. 'Can't help you, I'm afraid. If it's bad, you should call the police. If not, I'd just ignore it. But I haven't heard a dicky bird about it. It's not the sort of thing people would advertise.' He shook his hands over the basin and turned to the paper-towel dispenser.

'Who hates me here? I want to know – I can take it. I'm not here to win a popularity contest.'

'Hate is a very strong word. You're right, there are certain people who are uncomfortable with what you're doing, but nobody likes change when it affects them. That's only natural. But I wouldn't say that what you're doing would be enough to engender real hatred. That's too extreme. And I can't think of anybody in this office who would stoop to the kind of level you're describing. We're a pretty civilised bunch here, as I hope you've realised by now.'

'I have, and that's what makes the whole thing so disturbing. There's real venom behind all this, as if someone's really got it in for me and Teri. Professional, constructive criticism I can take, but this goes way beyond that. It's personal, and very distressing, especially for Teri.'

Brian finished drying his hands and tossed the towels into the bin. 'Do you want to tell me what's been said?'

'Let's just say it's vicious. Someone's bent out of shape about something I've done, and I can't figure out what the hell it is. If I knew, I could fix it.'

'Well, I'm very sorry for you and Teri, but my mind's a blank. Your best bet is to call in the police. Get your phone numbers changed, go ex-directory, get them to put a trace on the line. That's all I can suggest.'

Skip seemed to ignore this advice. 'And you're sure you've heard nothing?'

'Not a sausage. If I do, I'll let you know.'

Skip nodded thoughtfully. 'Well, it was worth a try. I really appreciate your help with this, and I'd be grateful if you didn't mention it to anyone else.'

'My lips are sealed. All conversations in this room are strictly privileged.'

'Oh, yeah,' Skip said, seeing the humour of it. 'Sorry about that.'

'Well, not such a bad idea. Most of the critical decisions in this organisation get made at the coffee machine or in here.'

'I guess. Thanks, Brian.'

Brian left, but Skip stayed where he was. He told himself never to play poker with Brian: he was excellent at giving nothing away.

Jean Retzer wore a flowery patterned skirt with an elasticated waist, a plain white muslin blouse and square-toed leather shoes. Her clothes could have come from an Oxfam shop, relics from the seventies; her hair, too, was cut unfashionably. She sat in Mary Strutter's office with her hands folded in her lap, waiting patiently but with a determined look on her face. She'd been offered coffee but had declined; Mary's secretary didn't know what to do with her.

'Mary may be some time,' she'd said.

'I'll wait. I have plenty of time,' Jean had replied.

Forty minutes later, Mary walked into her office and glared at Jean behind her back. This was something she didn't need.

'Mrs Retzer,' she said crisply. 'Good to see you. How is it all going?'

'Much as you'd expect.'

'I'm afraid I'm really tied up today, and I apologise for that. If you could make an appointment . . .'

'This won't take long. I'm sure you have a little time for the widow of one of your former employees.'

The word 'widow' had the desired effect and Mary smiled sympathetically. 'Always. What can I do for you?'

'Compensation. That's what I'm here for.'

'Compensation? I'm not sure I follow you. We are paying you Don's full pension, aren't we?'

'Yes. Do you think that's adequate? Does that clear your conscience?'

'I don't think my conscience needs clearing, does it?'

'Doesn't it? Doesn't it bother you that one of your senior managers, whom you fired, then commits suicide? Doesn't that strike you as something more than a little coincidental?'

Mary was surprised by the harshness of Jean's tone. 'Frankly, no. I wasn't privy to your husband's inner thoughts, so I have no way of knowing what drove him to take his own life. I'm sorry to sound so blunt, but that's how I see it. Obviously you see it differently.'

'Obviously. But it's not just me. Michael Lensman agrees with me.'

'Michael Lensman?' Mary exclaimed. 'What's he got to do with this?'

'He and I have compared notes, as you'd say. It's abundantly clear that DataTrak victimised Don and Michael in much the same way. Your actions were unjustifiable and, in Don's case, directly contributed to his death. You should watch out for Michael, make sure he doesn't suffer the same fate.'

Mary looked at her watch. 'Look, Jean, I know you're distressed and under a lot of pressure. You're confused and angry, I can see, and you want to vent some of that on DataTrak. But please, let me assure you, this is a hopeless line you're taking. We aren't liable, any lawyer will tell you that. I think we've been more than fair with you. We're paying the pension, meeting our obligations in full without any question, and there's nothing more we can do.'

Jean was unimpressed. 'Corporate manslaughter. That's the phrase that springs to mind.'

'Jean. Be reasonable. Making wild accusations like that can only get you into trouble, and that's just what you don't need right now. OK, you can say it to me and it won't go any further. Others might not be quite so understanding.'

'So you're saying there'll be no more help? You're washing your hands. I'm left to pick up the pieces, and DataTrak sails on, wrecking other people's lives without a backward glance.'

'No, that's not how I'd put it. But I would caution you – if you persist, we'll defend ourselves vigorously. We can't allow you to say these things, you know.'

'Why – because they're true? You try and stop me. I've been wronged, and so have my children. It's time for you to recognise that, make some redress. You owe me that. I will make DataTrak honour the debt.'

'We're getting nowhere with this,' Mary said tetchily. 'If you have a claim, submit it to us in writing and we'll review it. That's all I have to say.' She stood up from the desk. 'Thank you for coming in. Now, I have another meeting and I'm already late. My secretary will see you out.'

Jean stayed where she was for a moment, then got up slowly. 'I won't be brushed off,' she said menacingly. 'Tell your bosses that.' She swept out of the office and Mary was left shaking her head. This kind of thing wasn't in her job description, of that she was sure.

'Why?'

'Come on, Annie, you know as well as I do. I'm stuck in a rut. I looked at myself last night and realised just how grey I've become. I'm lifeless. I need to get out of here. I'm suffocating.' Annie looked at his face and knew he was right: his skin was flat and dull, and his eyes didn't sparkle. But she felt a keen slight from his proposal. Michael wanted to go away 'for a few days' on his own, somewhere by the sea where it was peaceful and he had time to think. He had not come to bed the previous night, sitting alone in his office with the radio on whilst she lay awake and tortured herself with her imagination. He had sprung this on her at breakfast.

'But why now? You've had weeks of doing nothing, plenty of time to think things through, as you put it. Surely you don't need any more time, do you?'

'You really don't get it, do you? My life's been shattered, and it's only just hit me. Oh, it's fine for you and Holly, I know. You can just get on with things the same as always. But I'm drifting here, Annie. I'm going nowhere, vegetating. It's driving me mad.'

Annie chose to ignore his barbed accusation. 'But you

161

were doing so well. You've handled it marvellously. God, when I think of what it might have been like, but you've been brilliant. I don't see the point.'

'The point is, I have to do this and I'm going to. I'm sorry if that upsets you, but that's how it is. Discussion over, OK?'

'No! Not OK!' Annie shouted, making Holly jump as she drank her orange juice. 'Sorry, love. Michael, can we continue this conversation in the other room?'

They left Holly to her breakfast and went into the sitting room, remaining standing. 'Look,' Annie continued, calmer now, 'I cannot handle this. You come back from a job interview and all's right with the world, then in the blink of an eye you're saying you need to get away from us. I'd say that's pretty strange behaviour, wouldn't you? What do you want? We're giving you all the support and encouragement we can, but you seem determined to be awkward. Nothing we do is right. We have to resolve this. I'm not prepared to carry on like this any longer.'

'But don't you see? It's not you, it's me. I'm the problem, and I'm trying to deal with it. This isn't meant to be a comment on you and Holly. I just have to straighten it all out in my own mind. Then I'll be fine, I promise. Trust me.'

When he said that, Annie immediately thought of his writing. Could she trust him? Did she really have a single clue as to what he was doing or thinking? She couldn't trust herself and her feelings, let alone his. Everything was crumbling before her eyes, and she was powerless to stop it. Everything Michael said was irrational, however much he tried to imbue it with calm reason. Everything was taking on a new and disturbing shape, running out of control without a brake.

She sighed. 'Do what you want,' she said, resigned to it. 'But you'd better make damned sure that when you come back you've put all this crap behind you. This is the last chance, Michael. I don't want you coming back in the same frame of mind you are in now. I won't stand for that. We've suffered quite enough from your mood swings for one lifetime, thank you.'

'I will. It'll be the new, improved me.' He tried to kiss her but she turned her head away. She'd had enough and, for the first time ever, she wanted him to be gone.

Skip breezed up to Pam's workstation. 'Pam,' he said, flashing the sickliest smile she'd ever seen, 'I need you to organise some things for me. Got a moment?' He jerked his head to show her she should follow him into his office. Once inside he closed the door and went to stand behind his desk, putting his hands on his hips. 'I want you to get on to the phone company, have all our personal numbers changed and made ex-directory. I've written a list down here.' He handed her a slip of paper with his brown ink all over it. 'Can you get that done today?'

'Of course,' she said, a small frown appearing on her face.

'Nothing to worry about. We're just getting a lot of wrong numbers, and a lot of calls for the last tenants,' he lied. 'This should sort it out.'

'Right.'

'Oh, and by the way, you don't need to tell anyone the new numbers. I'll deal with that.'

'I'm happy to do it, if you want. It'd be no trouble.'

'No thanks. I'll deal with that.'

'Was there anything else?' Pam asked.

'That does it. Thanks. Oh, no, there was one other thing. How are you feeling?'

'Sorry?'

'Well, you were off sick yesterday. I just wondered . . .'

She stuttered her reply. 'Oh, yes, thanks for asking. No, much better. Twenty-four-hour flu, it must have been. Came and went.'

'Great. Good to have you back.'

Pam nodded weakly and left his office. She went straight to her phone to call BT. Recovering rapidly from her embarrassment over Skip's concern for her health, she felt very happy to be entrusted with this task. This was one project she'd take special care over; he'd expect nothing less, and she'd do it well.

TWENTY-ONE

Skip had a naive belief in the principles of law and order. Someone did something wrong, they should be punished for it – but, in keeping with his faith, he also reserved a good deal of sympathy for the offender and a wish to see forgiveness and rehabilitation. He carried no spite, no misdirected sense of retribution: we are all sinners, and we all need help. In this, he and Teri differed somewhat, as she was keener on straight punishment without the garnish of compassion and understanding. Skip suspected that, when it came to a situation where she was the victim, she'd expect the full weight of the law to be on her side and hang the rest of it.

With this in mind, he called into the local police station on his way home from work. Skip would dearly have liked to have dealt with the problem himself – it was a small challenge, an irritation that could be easily managed if he worked on it a little – but he felt some duty to Teri to engage the services of the professionals. If they chose to give it scant attention that would be completely understandable, but at least he'd have made the effort. He expected a tepid response, and he was not disappointed.

The desk sergeant, a balding, overweight man with a florid face and huge forearms covered in thick white hairs, ambled in a few moments after Skip had rung the bell. 'Hello, sir,' he said without any real interest.

'Good evening. I'm wondering if you can help me with a small problem I've got.'

'That's what we're here for,' the sergeant replied, still detached and giving the full impression that Skip's small problem was nothing to do with him and was unlikely to become so.

'My name's Skip McMaster and I live in Richmond Court. My wife and I moved in a few weeks back. We've been getting some weird calls and faxes.'

'Weird?'

'Yeah, like nuisance. It's very upsetting for my wife, so I thought I'd report it.' Skip shrugged to show that, as far as he was concerned, it was no big deal.

'I see.' The sergeant put his big hands on the counter between them. 'Calls and faxes, you say. So there's some hard-copy evidence, is there?'

'Yup. I brought a fax with me, thought it might help.' He pulled out the folded paper from his inside top pocket and pushed it across the counter.

The sergeant unfolded it, read it briefly, then put it down in front of him. 'Does this mean anything to you, sir?'

'Not really. It just doesn't make any sense.'

'And who is Teri – your wife?'

'That's correct.'

'What about the calls? Can you give me any information on those?'

'Roughly speaking, they take the same line as the fax. We've done something wrong, as far as this guy's concerned, and they're pretty beaten up about it.'

'This guy? You know it's a man, then?'

'No, sorry, that's just an assumption. In fact, the voice is kind of androgynous, if you know what I mean. Could be a man or a woman.'

'You're American, sir? Have you recently moved here?'

'Right on both counts. We're from Ohio.'

'Is that the potato state?'

'No, that's Idaho.' Skip was starting to get a little frustrated, wishing he hadn't bothered.

'My mistake. Anyway, the point I was getting at is whether this has started since you arrived here, or whether it's a continuation of something that was going on in Ohio.'

'Actually, my wife did receive one letter – air mail, she

says – and a call when she was still there.'

'I don't suppose you have that letter, do you?'

'Unfortunately not. She tossed it.'

'Tossed it,' the sergeant repeated, as if trying the expression to see how it sounded with an English accent. 'Pity. Can't be helped though. She wasn't to know.'

'So, is there anything to be done?'

The sergeant sucked his teeth, considering where to set this in the list of priorities. 'Have you changed your phone number?'

'It's in hand.'

'And you've contacted BT to tell them? You know they have a nuisance-call service?'

'I didn't, but I'll get on to it.'

'Well then, what we can do is send someone round to take all the details and follow up on anything promising. But I'll be frank with you, sir – don't hold your breath. We're at full stretch here, and it's not going to get anyone terribly excited. Better that you know in advance, so you don't get your hopes too high. Our experience is that these cranks tend to get bored, especially when you change your number and get BT involved. They move on to someone else.'

'I can see that. It's just . . . well, as you can see from the fax, it's a little personal. I don't know what you think, but it doesn't strike me as random. Seems like we've been targeted for whatever reason.'

The sergeant dropped his shoulders. 'Oh, I wouldn't put too much store by that,' he said. 'They want you to think that. It's more sinister that way. Unless, of course . . .' He left the statement hanging, raising one eyebrow languidly.

'Unless?'

'Unless you know who it is.'

Skip grinned a little. 'If I did, officer, do you think I'd be here now? I'd far prefer to leave you guys out of this.'

'I couldn't possibly recommend that course of action, sir, but if you do know, well, it's up to you how you deal with it. As often as not, a polite warning is all that's needed, if you get my meaning.'

167

'Completely. Look, I don't want to take up any more of your time. I'll tell you what. We'll see what happens once the numbers are changed and we've contacted the nuisance service. If this person persists, I'll come back to you. Otherwise, forget it.'

'Very sensible. Now, if I can just take a note of your details for my register . . .'

Once the information had been filed, and Skip was on his way home, he began to feel rather stupid. After all, he reasoned, this was hardly the Boston Strangler they were dealing with. The policeman had been sensible and soothing, his diffidence an indication of how insignificant the whole thing was. Skip dismissed it from his mind and started to focus again on work and other more pressing issues, setting his life into its proper perspective. He hoped Teri was back on form and ready to present him with her ideas for a break; they needed one.

The phone rang at two in the morning, and Skip's hand fumbled for the bedside light before his mind clicked into gear and he kept the room in darkness. Teri was sleeping badly, and he wanted to take the call – which he imagined would be from Nick Zamboni – in his den.

He picked it up on the third ring and, without waiting, said: 'Could you hold just a short moment? I'm going to take this downstairs.' He found the hold button and pushed it, then replaced the receiver. 'Go back to sleep, hon,' he said quietly before slipping out of bed and rushing downstairs to the den. He was thirsty but didn't have time to get a drink. He picked up the extension phone in his study. 'Sorry about that.'

'How sweet,' the caller said. 'You don't want to disturb her. The mother needs her rest.' The same voice, flat and neutral. It chilled him, but he held steady.

'This isn't going to work, you know.'

'What?'

'This intimidation, whatever game it is you think you're playing. Why don't you give it a rest?'

'But Skip, we've only just begun. And we're having so much fun, aren't we? I mean, we're building a good relationship here.'

'I'm going to hang up now.' As before, he didn't.

'I only called to find out how it went with the police. Were they interested? Should I be worried?'

Skip was stunned. Was this an educated guess, or did he – she? it? – really know? 'I tell you, buddy, you have every reason to be terrified. I'm getting mad, and that's not a good thing to happen. You're sick, you hear?'

'Thanks for that. I'll bear it in mind. But look, what does it say in the Bible? Turn the other cheek, that's it. So start turning. I'm just warming up.'

Skip found himself shaking – from anger or fear, he couldn't tell. But he deliberately tried to calm things down. 'It would help if I knew why you were doing this. Maybe we can sort something out, face to face, you know, deal with it.'

'Nice idea, but I don't think so. You know, anyway. Time to pay, Skippy. I'll be in touch. Sweet dreams. Oh, before I go, there was one more thing.'

'I'm not listening.'

'Yeah? Well, you'd better. You can change your phone numbers a hundred times and I'll always know. You can move house, and I'll find you. I'm psychic that way. Gotta run. But it's been good talking to you.'

The caller cut the line and Skip slumped into his captain's chair in front of his desk. He felt sweat pouring down his sides from his armpits. Closing his eyes, he moved his head up so that it faced the ceiling. He was sitting like that when a cold hand touched his shoulder, making him start.

'Skip?' Teri said from behind him.

'Wow!' he said. 'You scared the life out of me.' He swung round in the chair. 'Nick,' he lied. 'He has no concept of time zones.'

'It wasn't Nick. I listened upstairs.'

'Oh.' A beat passed as he tried to think of something to say. 'Hey, babe, this is all going to go away.' He got up and hugged her tightly, rubbing one hand down her back.

'It isn't,' she mumbled into his neck. 'It's gone too far for that. And you can stop humouring me. You wouldn't have gone to the police if you believed that for a moment.'

'Just a precaution. Just laying down a marker.'

'It hasn't worked, has it? Whoever it is is playing for keeps. We need to get out of here. I am scared to death, I don't mind telling you.'

Skip thought for an instant. 'Is there something else? Has something else happened?'

'I got another letter. This one wasn't so obscure.'

'Where is it?'

'In the kitchen drawer, with all the other papers. I'm sorry, I should have said.'

'Yeah, you should have. I'll look at it and take it down to the station tomorrow.'

They stood in the den, still with their arms around each other, and then she pulled her head back so that she could look him in the eye. 'Skip?' she asked nervously. 'Is there anything you want to tell me? I mean, do you know what this is all about? Because this is truth or dare time. I have to know.'

'Teri, I promise you with all my heart that I have no idea what this is all about, none whatsoever. This is coming out of left field for me as much as you.'

'But you would tell me, right? You would, wouldn't you?'

'You know I would.'

'Because I couldn't take it if something came out later and you'd known all along and you hadn't told me, even if you thought it was for my own protection. I'd much rather hear it from your own lips, right here and now.'

'Teri,' he said, somewhat hurt. 'What do you think of me? I wouldn't do that.'

'Good. Then we're in this together.'

'For ever,' he replied. He kissed her and closed his eyes. 'We'll get through this, I know we will. It isn't going to harm us.' But secretly he suspected that it already had.

Michael left at six o'clock in the morning. He had tried to pretend that the atmosphere between them didn't exist, that he didn't notice how tense and terse Annie was, but it was a poor show. She had lain awake for most of the night, racked by alternating emotions – anger and guilt, remorse and bile, doubt and certainty – as he slept untroubled next to her. He was up at five, randomly stuffing clothes into a tote bag and clattering around in the bathroom. Annie was desperate to know where he was going but, in view of her earlier outburst, she couldn't bring herself to ask him. To his mother? Unlikely, given that Peter would be there. But where else did he know, and where else would he find what he was looking for? By the minute he was becoming more enigmatic, more unpredictable, just as he'd promised – 'There are a lot of things I've never done before that I may start doing now. You just watch me' – but not in a pleasant way. This was too hard on her, too much to ask of her.

When he'd finished packing, and was showered and dressed, he leant over her in the bed. 'I know you're awake,' he said quietly. 'Don't let's leave it like this. I love you so much.'

She kept her eyes closed. 'It's a funny way you have of showing it,' she murmured.

'I can't explain it to myself, let alone to you,' he replied, sitting on the edge of the bed and turning so that his hands rested on either side of her head. 'But I'm not running away, I promise. I simply have this need, and it's got to be fulfilled. I'll be back before you know it.'

'Somehow I doubt that.'

'Well, I will. Be good. I'll call you.' He waited a moment, hoping for a reaction, but got nothing from her. 'I'll kiss Holly on my way out. Send her my love, won't you?'

Annie nodded, unwilling still to open her eyes and look at him. She heard him sigh as his weight lifted from the bed. When he had gone, and she heard the front door closing,

171

Annie turned on her pillow and let out a long, low moan. The pain was almost unbearable.

TWENTY-TWO

September was always a strange month for business. Workers returned reluctantly from their holidays, still tingling from too much sun and unaccustomed diets, their metabolisms taking time to adjust again to office coffee and M&S sandwiches at lunchtime. Few deals were signed in September, hard as the sales force at DataTrak pushed: their proposals and contracts sat on buyers' desks like the first leaves of autumn in the garden, not yet important enough to clear away.

For Skip it was frustration beyond endurance. His thirty-day plan had come and gone, atrophied by creeping sloth; his grand designs lay in ruins, and he began to appreciate the full nature of his challenge. A special sales team meeting was called, in which he offered extra cash incentives for anyone who could close a deal by 30 September. Their eyes twinkled, but he could see from the body language that, in their hearts, they knew the bonuses would be hard earnt. His division was twenty per cent under budget on the revenue side, and twelve per cent over budget on expenditure: a large proportion of the latter was due to his own package, which had inflated the cost of running the business. Skip spent every minute of the day worrying about Zamboni and when he would finally intervene: a weekly update was e-mailed to him – sales pipeline, closed and lost deals, headline financials – but, to date, there had been no reaction.

Now he sat with his financial controller, a Pakistani called Walid who could transform figures into almost any shape required but who could not, as he had made plain, redress the imbalance between income and costs without some external assistance. They had gone through every line of the budget, every single expenditure, making adjustments and agreeing on cutbacks.

'Of course,' Walid said, his head wobbling as it always did when he was offering his own opinion, 'the biggest single expenditure remains your staff. You've got some fat in there, no doubt.'

'Fat?' Skip asked. 'We're running on empty as it is. I was planning to ask Zamboni for more resources.'

'Bad idea,' Walid said, head now swaying around more than ever. 'Nick has a headcount freeze. He's looking to cut staff, not add.'

Skip was a little intimidated by Walid, even though nominally he reported to him. He knew that Walid and Nick had long phone conversations, and worried about what was said in them. He needed to tread carefully. 'Are you saying that we should let some people go?'

'Your call, Skip. I'm just saying that it's an obvious area for savings, if that's what you want to do.'

'But it's expensive, isn't it, firing people?'

'Depends how you do it. You could get Mary to draw up a list of staff and how much it would cost to let them go. Pick the ones with not much service, or the ones on a low base salary. If they complain, you can drag it out so that, if you need to pay more, it wouldn't hit this year's numbers. Defer the cost and take a bet that next year will be better.'

'That sounds a tad unethical,' Skip said honestly.

'I'm the financial controller, not the company chaplain,' Walid responded immediately, giving Skip the impression that he'd said this many times before.

'So I'll call Mary, set the ball rolling. I guess there's no harm in taking a look, even if I decide to do nothing.'

The head wobbled again. 'Do nothing isn't your best option, Skip. In fact, I'd say it isn't an option at all. Nick will be all over you like a rash if you leave things as they are. He wants action.'

Skip knew that this was a genuine message, one sent to Walid by Nick with the express intention of it being delivered onwards. 'Straight up, what are our chances of hitting budget?' he asked without really wanting to know the answer.

'The way things are now, I think it's about as likely as England regaining the Ashes.' Skip didn't understand this, but gathered it was a highly improbable scenario. 'Your best bet is to accept that now but show you're doing something about it. You can always blame it on your predecessors, in any event. That's what I'd do.'

'Problem is, I've made commitments – in writing. Nick doesn't throw those away.'

'Well, that is a problem, but it's not insurmountable. For a start, your forecasts included the Morgan Stanley deal. That went pear-shaped and it wasn't anything to do with you. You acted in good faith on other people's information, which turned out to be way off the mark. Take that out of the equation and it looks a little better.'

The Morgan Stanley deal: for a reason he couldn't quite put his finger on, mention of that deal made Skip shiver with unease. Ever since his lunch with Charles Turkwood he'd had the feeling that Nick almost wanted the deal to disintegrate and was relieved when it did. It was all tied up with Michael Lensman and the way he was axed. There was a rotten smell surrounding that whole affair, a whiff of an intrigue to which he was not a party and yet in which he had been a significant player. He asked himself if Walid knew more than he did.

'Do you think I should call Nick?' He didn't want to ask for advice, but knew he needed it badly.

'What for? We're sending him all the data he can handle, and he's not stupid. He can read between the lines. He'll call you when he's ready.' Walid seemed to be protecting something – his special relationship with Nick, perhaps? He was clearly enjoying the power it bestowed on him, way beyond the terms of his job description.

'OK. Let's roll with the staffing angle, get it progressed so that when Nick calls we can demonstrate our commitment to setting things back on track. I'll talk to Mary when we're finished up here.'

Walid sat completely still, his head now properly fixed to his neck. 'Was there anything else?' he asked.

'I guess not. But let me know if he speaks to you, OK? I want to be kept in the loop.'

'You've got it,' Walid said, but Skip doubted his word.

Walid gathered up his bundles of papers and left the office. Skip stood up and turned to look out of his window. He had striven so hard to get here, to place himself at the centre of activity, but now it was all going wrong and he couldn't work out a recovery plan. On top of this, Teri was having panic attacks at home, calling frequently and urging him to come back early. It was all melting away as he stood and watched helplessly, and the person on whom he'd most depended was incapable of restoring order, riven as she was by her own anxieties. He closed his eyes and prayed, not for divine intervention but merely for some guidance. Show me a light, Lord, to get me through this darkness. He'd never needed it as much as he did now.

With a curious and unknown symmetry, Michael was thinking of sales targets as he drove down the M4. He'd rented a car in Wimbledon – a Golf GTI, like they'd had before Holly was born – and was in the fast lane, doing ninety with the sunroof open. With them he never drove above seventy; Annie called him 'Mr Vanden Plas' because of his sedate speed and careful road manners. But, on his own and with nothing to stop him, he was enjoying the thrill of sweeping past everything else on the motorway. He was feeling released, unfettered by all the distractions and obstructions that were tying him up at home. Thirty-two years old and the weight of the world on his shoulders: it wasn't fair and he didn't deserve it. That's what had started him thinking about the sales targets. No one of his age should be given such enormous responsibility; it was unreasonable to expect him to cope with that, and raise a family at the same time, let alone deal with all the problems of managing a sales team.

He smiled as he thought about Skip and the heat he'd

probably be feeling by now. Zamboni would be climbing all over him, wanting to know why the region was still under budget and why he hadn't fired more people – or perhaps, more improbably, Skip had turned it around and Nick was actually pleased with his performance. That would be a turn-up for the books: Zamboni never praised anyone, was never satisfied and could always find reason to complain. Skip would be discovering that. And Michael couldn't care less. It wasn't his problem.

Except . . . part of his problem was inextricably linked to Skip. Much as he tried to deny it, the hurt was still there, the injury still nagging. Whichever way he looked at it, the path of blame always led back to DataTrak. So maybe I would have left of my own accord, he thought; maybe I wasn't as happy as I'd made out, but that would have been my decision, taken in my time and at my pace. Those arseholes had no right to accelerate the process, however much justification they believed they had – and Turkwood's revelations only served to harden that contention.

As he hit a snarl-up on the interchange with the M5, Michael reviewed the situation. No job, and no desire for one; home life increasingly claustrophobic, with Annie's subtle but unmistakable chiselling of his fragile confidence; and a blossoming desire to identify and punish the real culprits. What a prospect: Michael told himself that only a fool could fail to see how he needed a break before he imploded. Good God, hadn't he suffered enough without Annie getting in on the act? She claimed to be supportive, but he couldn't see it; she just wanted to push him back to work, sweep the past under the carpet and pretend it never happened. OK, so she'd lashed out at Skip in a surprising and uncharacteristic display of vitriol, but that wasn't enough. She didn't – couldn't – share his sense of injustice, didn't see it all as clearly as he did. When he really needed her sympathy, all he got were bland words and emptiness.

Once through the traffic, and motoring nicely again on the M5, he tried to establish a strategy. Frustratingly, what he truly wanted was for things to be the same, but different.

He wasn't ready to reject it all, the infrastructure he'd built around his life, but he longed for some new impetus, something to get his adrenalin pumping again without having to slog through the same morass. Should they up sticks and move – emigrate, even? He'd enjoyed his time in New York, found it stimulating and vibrant, and he wondered if they shouldn't go there and leave everything behind. It was an option, anyway, and should be given due consideration.

But what did he want to do with the rest of his life? Wherever they went, he would still be there; he couldn't change the way he was, the way he felt, the reactions he had to different stimuli. He had the presence of mind to realise that, however much he changed the wallpaper and the habitat, Michael Lensman was who he was. He was fully formed, already set in his ways, locked in his skin: he had to accommodate that and exist within the boundaries it created. Yes, even at his age, he was set on a course, values moulded and unchangeable. It was frightening but unavoidable. And it begged the question: what did he hope to achieve by running away now? He was in the car with himself and he carried the same mind that had been festering in Wimbledon. How could he escape that?

He hit the end of the motorway, and began the long descent towards the south Devon coast. He remembered a holiday there with his parents – the only one, as far as he could recall, they'd ever taken in this country – in a large, dusty house overlooking the sea near Salcombe. How old was he – nine, ten? His strongest memory was of his desperate desire to be alone on a beach and explore the caves and rock pools, all the while being implored by his mother to take Peter with him. He had wanted to sit on an isolated rock above the waves and read his book, but Peter was always there, always bothering him. He secretly wished that Peter might slip and crack his head open and he could watch as his puny brain oozed out. But, despite these frustrations, that holiday had been a good one, good enough that he wanted to go back and revitalise some of the memories.

178

He reached Salcombe by eleven o'clock in the morning, and began to look for B&B signs. The school holidays were over, and he imagined it would be easy to find a room. He drove past several likely houses but didn't stop, wanting to take his time before making a decision. Finally he saw a sign at the side of the road – 'Foresters Arms, Rooms Available, Good Beer and Food' – and, on impulse, he followed the sign into a turning which led a hundred yards up a steep track to an old building covered with ivy and flanked by trees. Two cars were parked to one side; otherwise there was no indication of any life.

He parked by the other cars, got out and stretched extravagantly. Two hundred and fifty miles non-stop: he was stiff and uncertain on his feet. Looking around, he saw that the pub stood on the edge of a forest which ran all the way up the hill, possibly half a mile away. Beneath him he could see the bay of Salcombe and the broad, flat sweep of the sea. He inhaled deeply, the thick air working its way into his system to get the blood flowing again. Lazily, he made his way to the open front door of the pub and walked in. It was a simple room, unadorned by nautical artifacts and horse brasses or other such abominations. It was also empty. He went to the bar and coughed loudly, then waited. Eventually he heard some unseen movement and a woman walked through to stand behind the bar.

She was tall – almost too tall for the low ceiling – with straight blonde hair tied back in a pony tail. Her face was tanned, as were her forearms, which had a light down on them. She wore faded blue jeans with a white studded belt, and a white T-shirt with small fake pearls stitched to it across the chest. She was, he guessed, in her mid-thirties.

'Hallo,' she said.

'Hallo. I was wondering, do you have a room?'

'We do. Just for tonight, is it?'

He liked her accent – not too broad, but definitely West Country. It was like clotted cream. 'Probably longer. A week, maybe?'

'I'll just check.' She disappeared and he found himself

watching her backside as she moved; it was nice, in proportion with the rest of her.

She returned, nodding and grinning. 'We can give you the front room with en suite, looks over the bay. Thirty-two quid a night, full breakfast included, pay in advance if you would.'

'Excellent.' He pulled a large wedge of notes from his back pocket and counted out the money on the counter. She picked it up and turned round to get some change from a small pot on a shelf behind her. No till, he thought: how quaint.

'You have some luggage, then?' she asked as she put the change in his hand. He stared briefly at her long tanned fingers, the nails unpainted and filed short but nicely rounded.

'It's in the car. I'll get it.' He wheeled away lightly and went to retrieve his tote bag from the boot. Unnoticed, many of the knots inside him were beginning to loosen, the sea air, the luck at finding this spot, the woman's warmth all combining to ease the tension.

Once back inside, she led him up some very narrow stairs to a small landing. 'Through here,' she said, pushing a door open. She stood there, back to the door, and he had to push past her, his upper arm just making contact with her breasts. She didn't flinch at this, but he did.

'All right, is it?' she asked as he looked around. There was a double bed with white linen, a chest of drawers and a small desk and chair under the window. There were two prints on the walls, both of ships in heavy seas.

He smiled and looked back at her. 'Perfect.'

'Bathroom's through there,' she said, pointing to a door at the other side of the room.

'Great.'

'You'll be on holiday, then?'

'R and R,' he replied, but she looked blank. 'Rest and recuperation.'

'Oh. Right.' She nodded slowly, but seemed unwilling to leave. 'Bed's brand new,' she added.

'Wonderful. Thank you. I'm sure it'll all be marvellous.'

'I'll leave you to it, then. When you're ready, come down and I'll give you all the information.'

He wondered what information that could be, but didn't ask. She made him slightly uncomfortable, the lazy way she spoke and moved, as if on a different time line. He smiled at her again and she pulled herself away from the door, closing it behind her as she left. He immediately moved to check if there was a lock on the door, which there was. It was almost ethereal, as if he'd stepped into an alternative reality where nothing was quite as it seemed. The woman had spooked him, that was the only way to describe it, and he couldn't shake off the sensation. He sat on the edge of the bed, unable to pull himself together.

After a while he got up and went to the window to open it. He stared out at the bay, still dazed, his mind dislocated from his body. The air was fresh and moist, and he concentrated on his breathing, large gulps in and out, but it didn't help to recover his bearings. He was consumed by lethargy, as if the air were too thick for normal movement and thought. He tried to bring himself back to the normal world, to think as Michael Lensman, but the fight was too much. The stillness seeped into his bone marrow, immobilising him in its grip. He wanted to lie down – but, more than that, he wanted to win back some vigour. Dragging himself away from the window, he picked up his bag and pulled out all his clothes, spreading them carelessly on the bed.

He decided a shower might sort him out, so he stripped off and went into the bathroom. It was a tight little space, and a powerful extractor fan leapt into action when he pulled the light cord. There was a shower cubicle, a tiny washbasin and a lavatory. He opened the cubicle and switched on the tap, then returned to the bedroom to find his washbag. And there she was, standing in the doorway with a big white towel in her hand.

'I forgot this,' she said, seemingly completely unabashed by his nakedness. She held it out for him, her eyes focused on his. He didn't know what to do: she was teasing him, and he was utterly defenceless. There was no point trying to cover himself so he took two steps towards her and grabbed the towel, letting it fall immediately so that it covered his front.

With no apology, she left again. He could just hear the shower running above the roaring of blood through his veins. What the hell's going on here? he asked himself as he stood clutching the towel.

TWENTY-THREE

'Pam, would you come in and close the door?' It was the closest Pam had ever heard Skip come to having impatience in his tone; normally he was so calm, always smiling, always charming. It drove her half mad, so she was quietly satisfied at this edge of temper.

He had told her that, whenever she went into his office, she should bring her daybook with her. The daybooks were another 'Skip special', as all his initiatives were known: every person in the office was issued with an A4 lined book and was instructed to record the details of every conversation and meeting in it, transferring the relevant information to the electronic database at the end of the day. So far the results had been sporadic at best; had Skip looked at Pam's, he would have found various shopping lists and personal reminders of things to do. Brian Shale, she knew, recorded sick jokes and drew vulgar cartoons in his.

She carried her daybook and a pen in with her. Another annoying task had been to find a supply of the brown-ink pens he liked so much, and now she found herself holding one. She sat down in front of his desk and waited for instructions.

'Pam, I'm expecting an important visitor here at three-thirty. Whatever I'm doing, wherever I am, you're to interrupt me. I have to be here. Reception will call you, and you are to meet him and take him straight to the conference room. I don't want him coming in here, OK?'

'Fine. What's his name?'

'Dunbar. Mr Dunbar.' He placed special emphasis on the 'Mister'. 'Could you get some coffee organised, too?'

'No problem.' She wrote it down, more for show than anything else.

'Great. Now, give me an update on the phone numbers. Where do we stand?'

This was her chance to prove to him how dedicated she was. 'BT will be sending all the documentation to your house in the next couple of days. You'll need to sign some forms and then they'll switch the numbers over. They'll be ex-directory.'

'Do you have the numbers?'

Pam blushed a little. 'No. I thought you wanted them kept secret. That's why all the papers are going to your house rather than here.'

'Right. Good thinking. But I think I could trust you with them, couldn't I?' He grinned at her, but she noticed it didn't have its usual dazzle factor. For the first time she saw tiredness in his face and movement, and she wanted to write that down in her daybook – 'Skip knackered' – but thought better of it.

'I suppose so,' she replied.

'I know so. And as we're on the subject, I wanted to let you know that I think you're doing a super job here. It can't have been easy, and I'm really grateful for all the effort you've put in.'

Now her face reddened more – from guilt, or just unease, she couldn't say. Unused to praise, even from Michael, she didn't know how to react. It was worse because it came from Skip, the man who had thrown this part of her life into such turmoil and for whom she held nothing but contempt. 'Oh, well,' she stammered, 'I mean, it's not a problem.'

'Well, you let me know if I'm ever out of line. I'm the new kid on the block – but you know all the rules. Keep me on the straight and narrow, won't you?' She nodded but could find nothing to say, her chin sinking towards her chest to hide her embarrassment. He sensed it and moved on. 'So, three-thirty, OK? Mr Dunbar.'

'No problem.' She closed her daybook with a slap, got up and left. Back at her workstation she saw a new delivery of internal mail in the in-tray. There was a reusable orange envelope on top, marked 'Strictly Private & Confidential', addressed to Skip and sent from Mary Strutter. Her fingers hovered over it; all correspondence from Human Resources was interesting, and she desperately wanted to see what was inside. It could wait, though. He was going to a meeting in thirty minutes, and he'd never know.

Detective Sergeant Chris Dunbar was certainly no older than Skip, and was almost as well turned out. He wore a sharp blue double-breasted suit with a white shirt and a patterned red tie. His brogues shone from frequent polishing. He had short brown hair which was controlled with some kind of lotion. To Skip he was a revelation: he'd been expecting someone altogether more crumpled and weary. This guy looked as if he worked out. They sat opposite each other at one end of the large conference table. Dunbar had flipped open a little black notebook and laid it on the table with a smart pen. Skip put a manila folder down as well.

After Skip had poured the coffee he looked steadily at Dunbar. 'Look, I really appreciate you coming in here. I hope you'll understand why I didn't want to do this at home – my wife is jumpy enough as it is.'

'Not a problem,' Dunbar said briskly, opening his hands. 'So what do we have here?'

'Ordinarily I'd ignore this kind of thing but, as I told your officer, this is pretty personal stuff. After I'd come down to the station we got another call, late at night, and whoever it was knew everything that was going on, seemed to know that we'd got the police involved. I have to admit, it's got me kind of scared, not to mention what it's done to my wife.'

'You have some documentation there?' Dunbar asked, nodding at the folder.

'It's pretty sick. There's even a fake death certificate in there.'

'We can test it for prints, but we'll need to take yours and your wife's – Teri, isn't it? Will that be a problem?'

'I'll handle it. She'll understand.'

'Good. Before we get started, I need to get a few facts

185

straight. I'm going to have to ask you a couple of questions that may be a little close to the bone.'

'Shoot. I've got nothing to hide.'

Dunbar smiled briefly, then got serious. 'Do you know who's doing this?' He let the question hang in the air, seemingly willing to wait all day for an answer.

'No,' Skip replied firmly.

'You see, more often than not, these people know their targets. They have a reason, however obscure, for what they're doing. It all gets out of proportion in their heads and this is the only way they can see to get their own back for whatever it is that's bugging them. Could be a jilted lover, could be someone from work. You see what I'm getting at?'

'I do, but it doesn't help in my case. There are no skeletons in the cupboard, if that's what you're looking for.'

'So no reason at all that you can think of why someone would want to do this to you and Teri?'

'Zip.'

Dunbar rocked in his chair slowly. 'Can I ask you about work? You've not been here long, have you? Did you replace someone? Have you fired anybody since you've been here? Anything like that, anything that might get up someone's nose, even if you didn't realise it at the time?'

In a slow dawn of realisation, a gradual lifting of the mist, Skip began to put it all together. He felt the rush of stupidity, the blindness of his stare, something so obvious that he'd never thought to look at it properly. It hurt badly, but he didn't want that to show. 'You know, now that you come to mention it, there are a couple of things I ought to tell you on that score. I've not given any thought to them till now. I did replace a guy – Don Retzer. What's more, he committed suicide recently.'

Dunbar picked up his notebook and poised his pen over it. 'Don Retzer?' he asked, and Skip spelt the name out for him. 'And he has a family?'

'A wife and two kids – nice boys.'

'OK, we can look at that for a start. You said there were a couple of things?'

'Yes. We had to let someone go – Michael Lensman.' Skip felt treacherous as he spelt out the surname, a Judas. This was not how it should be. 'I guess – and it's only a guess, as I never heard this from him – he might have thought he was going to take Don's job. But I don't for one moment think . . .'

'No, well, you never do, do you? But this sounds promising. There's something to go on here.' Dunbar was now writing as he spoke. 'Have you stayed in touch with this Lensman fellow? Do you know what he's up to?'

'I've seen him once, at Don's funeral. He seemed fine. He's a regular kind of guy. I can't see that being a very productive line of enquiry.' Skip was furiously trying to deny what was being implied, even as it became apparent to him that this was, indeed, fertile ground.

'You never know. It's worth following up, anyway. Do you have addresses for these people?'

'I can get them and phone them through to you.'

'Why don't you get them now? I'll wait.' Skip nodded reluctantly and reached for the phone on the middle of the table. He punched Mary's number and asked her to bring the details along to the conference room. As they waited Dunbar helped himself to the manila folder and studied the documents, his face impassive. When he'd finished he closed the file and put it in his briefcase. 'I imagine you won't be wanting this back,' he said.

'It's all yours. I never want to see it again.'

Mary knocked and then came in. She was interested in Dunbar but didn't want to intrude, so she handed Skip a piece of paper and left immediately. Skip looked at it before giving it to Dunbar.

'Please talk to your wife,' Dunbar said. 'Get her to come down to the station. It'll make our job much easier.'

'I will. But what do we do in the meantime?'

'Let's see what happens once your numbers have been changed. If the calls persist, we'll have to think about putting in some hardware to trace them. But I'm hopeful that, once we've had a chat with these people, it will all grind to a halt.'

'If it is anything to do with them – and I know that's a big if – will you charge them with anything?'

'That's down to you. We can warn them off, scare them out of their wits, and that should suffice. Anything more than that is at your discretion.'

'If it comes to that, I guess we'll pass. I don't want to prolong the agony.'

Dunbar closed his notebook and stood up. 'That's probably a very wise decision. Well, I have everything I need. We'll take it from here. You'll let me know if there are any developments at your end.' He produced a card and handed it to Skip. 'Call me on the mobile.'

'When do you think you'll . . . get round to them?'

'Today, tomorrow – sometime very soon, anyway.'

Skip saw him off the premises and then went back to his office. The whole thing was corrosive, he thought; here he was, pointing the finger at people he hardly knew, making their lives a misery with nothing more than some flimsy, irrational conclusions to justify the action. He'd have to stop in at church on the way home and ask for forgiveness.

Michael looked at the digital clock on his bedside table: Jesus, it was six o'clock. He'd slept away the entire afternoon, collapsing on to his bed after taking a shower. He pulled himself up and found some clean clothes, dressing slowly in a effort to regain some liveliness. He had no idea of what he was going to do next: go down to the bar, go for a walk, drive into Salcombe? He was starving and thirsty; perhaps a quick pint downstairs, while he picked up the information she'd promised, would restore him. And then he started thinking of her again. What had occurred was so unlikely that he felt it might have been a dream; she couldn't really have walked into his room like that, could she? These things didn't happen in real life.

After checking himself in the bathroom mirror, he went downstairs leaving the room unlocked. She hadn't given him a key, and he needed one, needed the security. He didn't want her or anyone else poking around when he wasn't there.

He reached the bar and walked over to the counter. A couple of late holidaymakers were sitting at a table by the window, maps opened in front of them. He nodded at them in a pale attempt at civility, then turned his back to them. She was standing there, right in front of him, smiling knowingly. God, it was disconcerting.

'You've surfaced, then?' she asked. She was dressed differently now: a sleeveless pink T-shirt, white denim miniskirt and cream espadrilles. He knew, just from the most casual glance, that she wasn't wearing a bra.

'This sea air is pretty potent,' he said, trying to keep his eyes away from her breasts. 'Knocked the stuffing out of me.'

'You're fit now, though. So, what can I get you?' The voice again, like polished walnut, provocative, enticing, mellow.

'A pint of cider, I think.' She reached up to get a glass from a shelf above the bar, and her T-shirt rose to reveal a thin strip of golden midriff. Michael was suddenly very interested in a sodden beer mat on the counter. She poured the cider and placed it in front of him.

'One pound ninety, please.' He handed her a fiver, waited for change from the pot, took it from her hand. 'So you'll be wanting all the information,' she said. 'Breakfast's at eight-thirty. We lock the front door at midnight, unless you make arrangements beforehand. We can get you a newspaper in the morning if you tell us what you want. Evening meals from seven to ten, lunch from twelve to two. That's about it.'

'Sounds good. By the way, do you have a key for my room?'

'Silly me. Must've forgotten it. It's right here.' She got the key from under the counter and placed it in front of him. 'Another thing I forgot – your name. Need it for our register, see?'

'Of course. Michael . . .' He hesitated. What the hell. 'Michael McMaster.' It sounded quite good, and he briefly enjoyed the deception. But why had he done it? He couldn't say, just a reflex reaction.

'Well, Michael, I'm Debby. Pleased to meet you.'

He wanted to ask Debby many other things – no ring on

189

the wedding finger, no man around or anyone else for that matter, just her filling up the space in front of him, everywhere he looked. But he didn't. This was a dangerous game and he wasn't up for it. She could fool around all she liked, but he wasn't going to respond.

He sat nursing his pint and watched as more customers arrived, but his attention always came back to her. She moved with a fluency that was distracting, every action imbued with some exotic promise. When she pulled the beer pump her breasts protruded and her nipples showed through the T-shirt, and he couldn't resist staring, even if she did notice. In a quiet moment she handed him a brochure on the South Hams, as the area was known. 'Useful, that'll be,' she said. 'You can keep it.'

He read it only because it was something to do, something to keep his mind off her. He looked at the old clock behind the bar, and remembered he should call Annie. He hadn't even thought about her and Holly, but couldn't decide if this was good or bad. 'Do you have a phone?' he asked.

'Not a public one, but you can use ours. Come on, I'll show you.' She lifted a hinged section of the bar to let him through, then led him to a door which led into private quarters. 'Just here,' she said. 'There's a pot for the money. Not calling Australia, are you?' she joked.

'No, no, just London. Thanks.' He dialled their number, waited until he thought the answering machine was going to cut in, but Annie picked up in time.

'Hi, it's me,' he said, loudly as if he thought he needed to speak up from so far away.

'Oh.'

'Everything all right there?'

'What do you think?'

'Annie,' he said, and then wasn't sure what he wanted to say. 'Annie, I'm OK, really. This isn't a premature mid-life crisis. I still love you, more than ever in fact.' He had to say this, uncharacteristic as it was. She had to hear it.

'So glad,' she replied flatly. 'Where are you?'

'Devon. Salcombe.' He didn't want to tell her more, about

190

how beautiful and restful it was, conscious that she would resent it still further.

'How nice for you. Look, Holly's in the bath. I can't stay. What will I do if there's a crisis? Is there some way of getting in touch, or are you determined to be awkward?'

'No, there's a phone here.' He read the number out for her. 'They'll get a message to me. I'm not going anywhere.'

'You already have, remember?' Nothing to say, no way to counter this. 'When will you be back, assuming you're coming back?'

'Soon. A week, maybe less, once I've got it all clear. I'm mending already.'

'We'll expect you when we see you, then.' Not approval, just acceptance. She put the phone down before he had a chance to say more, the first time she'd ever done that. He could recall the times they used to be on the phone when they were courting, when neither would hang up first. How things had changed.

He replaced the receiver and dropped a pound coin into the pot. As he turned, he saw Debby at the door; had she been listening to the whole exchange? She didn't move immediately, unconcerned at being caught like this. Then she smiled at him in the most peculiar way, as if she understood everything. He swallowed hard and tried to return the smile, but found his facial muscles wouldn't work properly. This is fire, he told himself, and you don't want to get burned.

TWENTY-FOUR

'She's barking, Chris. You know how they look when they're not really there? Well, that's how your Mrs Retzer looks. She's all sweetness and light on the surface, but underneath . . . well, stark raving bonkers.'

Chris Dunbar was sitting in his car, listening on his mobile to a colleague from north London who'd done him a favour and dropped in to see Jean. He was smiling at this description of her. 'But could she be doing it?' he asked.

'Who knows? She didn't seem very concerned, I'll say that. Anyway, I put the wind up her, like you asked, said it was a very serious matter. She shrugged, didn't react. I don't know. Sorry.'

'OK. Thanks for that, Steve, I owe you one.'

'Bloody right. Cheers.'

Dunbar looked at his watch, calculating that he'd give the Lensmans a few more minutes before knocking on their door. He'd parked a hundred yards away from their house – smart, in a good neighbourhood – and waited. Eight in the morning; would they be up and doing? He didn't want to intrude in case it was all for nothing. He waited five minutes, got bored, and climbed out of the car.

He knocked on the front door and listened for a dog – they hated coppers, seemed to sense them and normally went berserk – but, to his relief there was no barking. The door opened and a good-looking woman stood before him.

'Mrs Lensman?' he asked, discreetly showing his warrant card.

'Yes.' She was puzzled, frightened, a perfectly natural reaction.

'Detective Sergeant Dunbar. Is your husband at home?'

She was cautious. Holly was clinging to her legs, peeping round to see him. 'No, I'm afraid he's not. Why – is he in some kind of trouble?'

'No, not that I know of,' he said, smiling. 'Just making some routine enquiries, that's all.'

'Well, I'm afraid he's not here and I don't know when he'll be back.' Polite, but guarded.

'Could I come in for just a few moments?' he asked. 'Easier than . . .' He jerked his head backwards to let her know that he was conscious of what the neighbours might say.

'Yes, sorry, of course.' Annie pulled the door fully open and led him into the sitting room. 'Can I get you a cup of tea? The pot's fresh.'

'That'd be lovely. White, no sugar.' He looked around the room whilst she was gone, Holly staring at him from the doorway, unable to come in or go out. It was a beautiful room, he thought: pale apricot walls, lined curtains, lots of photographs and books on the shelves, valuable prints hanging everywhere. Class, that's what it was; these people had class. He didn't usually encounter that, not in his line of work, and he'd forgotten how it looked and smelt.

He was standing in the centre of the room when Annie returned, two floral mugs in her hands. 'Here we are,' she said, slightly more relaxed. 'Please, take a seat.' He sat in a big armchair, less comfortable than it looked, and she settled down on a sofa with Holly practically stitched to her side.

Dunbar pulled out his notebook and pen. 'You say your husband's away.'

'Yes. Just for a few days. He hasn't been well.'

'Really?'

'Stress, I think.'

'Tell me about it.' He added a snort to show he understood. 'He's lost his job recently, I hear. That must be tough.'

'Yes, but . . . how do you know that?' She bristled a little.

Dunbar weighed up the odds, tried to assess her: not as frail as she looked, he guessed, so he took the gamble. 'There's been a complaint. We have to follow it up. Couple called

193

Skip and Teri McMaster. They've been the object of some very unpleasant calls and faxes. Doesn't seem to be any rhyme or reason to it, so we're really working in the dark here. Your husband – Michael? – he worked with Skip briefly, didn't he?'

'Very briefly,' Annie corrected him.

'There was bad feeling between them?'

'There wasn't time for that. Skip arrived, Michael left. It's business. Happens all the time, so I'm told.' She was brisk, matter-of-fact, giving nothing away.

'I see.' He wrote something in his book. 'As far as you know, have you or your husband been in touch with the McMasters since then?'

'We met them at a funeral. That's the only time.'

'That would be Don Retzer's funeral, right?'

'Right. Gosh, you do know a lot already. Michael worked with Don, as I'm sure you're aware.'

'Yes, I'd heard that. Anyway, I was wondering if you could think of any reason why the McMasters would be picked on like this. I mean, can you recall any major incident that might have sparked this off?'

Annie thought about this, letting the question seep into her. 'Shouldn't you be asking them that?' she replied defensively.

'That's the thing, you see. They're stumped, but he suggested I had a word with your husband.'

'I can't imagine why. They hardly knew each other. Unless . . . unless Skip is saying . . .' Dunbar could see the thought arriving on her face, changing it to a look of utter disbelief. 'But you can't be serious. That's absurd.'

'Yes, well, as I said, we have to chase down every eventuality, however far-fetched. But I would like to speak to Michael at some stage. Perhaps he could call me?'

'I can't promise that, I'm afraid. He's practically incommunicado. He does need complete rest, you see.'

'I understand, but if you speak to him, could you ask?' Don't push it, he told himself; something's not quite right here.

194

'I'll try. Do you have a card?' He pulled one out and put it on the coffee table between them. 'So is that it? I'm free to go?' The attempt at lightness was strained; she clearly wasn't enjoying this.

He smiled at her and Holly. 'That's it. No more questions. I'm sorry to have troubled you. You've been very helpful.'

'Have I?'

'Yes, of course. I wish everyone was as cooperative as you. Make my life a lot easier.' He drained his mug and stood up. 'Thank you, Mrs Lensman. And thank you, young lady,' he added, looking at Holly, who immediately curled up more tightly. 'I'll see myself out.' He left them sitting there and walked out into the fresh morning air. Like a stone in his shoe, this brief meeting had given him an uneasy sensation. She was too brittle, too watchful of what she'd said. A nice woman, but who knows? He chided himself for his cynicism; after a while you begin to suspect everybody, and that's downright unhealthy. Still, worth pursuing . . .

Michael did not wake up naturally. A distant knocking on the door roused him, and he carefully opened his eyes, already aware that even this small action was likely to be accompanied by a heavy thumping in his head. Perhaps that's what the noise had been, the first stirrings of a major hangover. He couldn't remember how, or when, he'd got to bed. His last clear memory was of a pint of local cider, murky and pretty flat, being put in front of him by Debby. How many of those did he have? His stomach grumbled ominously, suggesting he hadn't eaten and its liquid contents were still deciding which way to go. He groaned as there was another light knock on the door.

'Coming,' he said throatily, swinging his legs over the side of the bed. Without thinking further he stood up, his legs hardly strong enough to support his weight. He opened the door – unlocked, to no great surprise – and Debby was standing there, a big tray in her hands. She brushed past him and put the tray on the bed.

'Thought you might prefer this up here,' she said. He was

relieved to realise that he was wearing his pants – and his socks.

'Thanks.'

'How are you feeling?'

'I don't know yet.' He didn't want to admit to anything, and certainly didn't want to ask her what had happened.

'Here, have a cup of tea. It'll do you good.'

He looked at the tray: toast, orange juice, bacon and eggs and a pot of tea. His stomach jumped somersaults at the prospect. 'Yes,' he replied. 'That'd be nice.' He sat on the bed and poured himself a cup, then drank down the orange juice in a single gulp.

'So, you still on for today?' she asked, smiling knowingly. He looked at her blankly. 'You don't remember, do you?'

'I'm sorry, it's all a bit hazy.' He'd have liked to have shaken his head but didn't want to risk it.

'I thought you were a bit pickled. You hold it pretty well, though. That cider's felled stronger men than you.'

'I don't . . . I mean, did I . . . ?'

'You didn't do anything to be ashamed of, if that's what you're asking. You were a lamb. Good as gold. Had a bit of a struggle getting up these stairs, I must say.'

'God, I haven't drunk that much for ages. I don't normally. Can't imagine what got into me.'

Debby went to open the curtains – had he drawn them last night? – and the light flooded in. Michael turned his head away. 'Anyway,' she said, 'you did say last night that you'd like to go to this little cove I know. Very secluded it is. See, it's my day off. We can take a picnic, if you're up to it.'

Horrified at this report, Michael prevaricated. 'I don't know,' he said weakly. The thought of spending the day on the beach alone with her sparked conflicting emotions, and he wasn't at all sure which he wanted to prevail.

'Best cure for a hangover, swimming in the sea. Be right as rain by lunchtime.' She turned from the window to look at him, her body bathed in light. She was wearing a short sundress and, as far as he could see, nothing else. The fact that she was barefoot he found exquisitely sexy; for some

196

reason he was always randy when he had a hangover, and today was no different. Below his waist he could feel the reaction to her, and he immediately knew which of his mixed emotions would win the battle.

'Sounds good to me,' he said.

She moved towards him, long golden limbs fluent and loose. 'Great. You eat your breakfast, come down when you're ready and we'll go. You won't be disappointed.'

As she was leaving he had a sudden thought. 'The thing is, I don't have any swimming trunks.' He knew it sounded stupid but little things like that worried him.

Debby looked over her shoulder and he could see a wicked smile on her face. 'Don't need 'em,' she replied, then left.

Just as she had promised, the cove was completely isolated. Debby directed as he drove through winding, single-track lanes with tall hedgerows until they reached a steep farm track leading down practically to the water's edge. They had to walk for about ten minutes across shingle before finally climbing over an outcrop of rocks, arriving at a deserted pebble beach. 'There, what did I tell you?' she announced triumphantly. 'No grockles ever come here.'

'Grockles?'

'Tourists. Like you, I suppose.' She laughed.

'Oh.' He looked around as she laid out two large beach towels and set the picnic basket down. 'Well, I'm not surprised. It's pretty well hidden.'

'Local secrets,' she said mysteriously. As he watched her, she pulled the sundress over her head. He swallowed hard, hoping against hope that he wouldn't see what he suspected was coming, but he did. She was naked. His head was still throbbing from the after-effects of the cider, but now other parts of him throbbed more. His mouth fell open in amazement.

Casually, without any sense of embarrassment, Debby crouched down and got a bottle of suntan lotion from the basket. She stood up again and rubbed the lotion all over her front whilst he concentrated very hard on staring at the sea. She lay down on her towel and brought her arms up to put her hands behind her head.

'Do you get many days like this in September?' he asked, his back to her.

'No. Rain and mist mostly, cold as hell. But sometimes we have really good weather, even this late. Got to take advantage, haven't we?'

Michael was trapped. He had to turn round eventually, pretend this meant nothing to him and he could handle it, but he couldn't see how. It was there, almost presented to him on a plate, and he didn't have a damned clue of how to deal with it. Was he meant to strip off? He was wearing a T-shirt and some old tennis shorts, and he pulled his shirt off to reveal his milky torso.

'You'll need some lotion,' she said, obviously watching him. 'Come here and I'll do your back.'

He closed his eyes, as if that would make it go away. Still clutching his T-shirt, he turned and tried not to stare. He stepped over to her as she sat up with the bottle of lotion in one hand, a large squirt of it on the fingertips of the other. He meekly sat down with his back to her and felt the cold lotion on her soft fingers as she rubbed across his shoulders and down his back. The stirrings he felt were growing in intensity, straining inside his shorts. She patted him when she'd finished and he swiftly flipped over so that he was lying on his stomach. Suddenly the cold sea seemed very appealing, the only solution to his problem, but he didn't want to get up.

'Going to take them off?' she asked in his ear. 'There's no one here to see, except me, and I already have.'

'Maybe later,' he replied hoarsely. He lay completely still, stiff and uncomfortable, paralysed by the situation and his inability to do anything about it.

'You men. You're all big kiddies really, aren't you?'

'Something like that.' He wished she would stop.

'I'm not going to eat you, you know.'

He summoned up all his fragile confidence. 'Look, Debby, I'm way out of my depth here. I'm a married man, I've always been faithful. This is quite difficult for me, and I think you know that. This doesn't happen to me. I came down here for a break. My head's all screwed up and I don't need this.'

'Don't need what? Nothing's going to happen, 'less you want it to.'

Courageously he turned on to his side to face her. Her skin shimmered in the sunlight and he couldn't help admiring the beauty of it. 'It doesn't work like that,' he said firmly.

Her eyes stayed closed against the sun as she spoke. 'Bit of fun, that's all it would be. Help with your R and R, as you call it. Seems like you need it, whatever you say.'

They were silent then, Michael still on his side, his head leaning on one hand. She was too gorgeous for words, such a temptation, but he also considered the consequences. Nothing was that simple, however beguiling it appeared. There would be regret and guilt and pain and deception – was it worth it?

'Tell me about you,' he said after a few minutes, wondering if she was awake.

'Nothing much to tell. Been here for ever.'

'The pub? You own it?'

'In a way.'

'What does that mean?'

'Legally, it's my husband's. But after his accident . . . well, he can't run it, so I do it all.'

'You're married? I had no idea.'

'Why should you? Does it make a difference? He's in a wheelchair, spends all day in his room with his binoculars, no good to me he is.'

'I'm sorry. I didn't realise.'

'No need to apologise.' Debby sat up and pulled her legs up, wrapping her arms round them. 'It's not as though . . .' She seemed to think better of what she was going to say. Now there was a different tone to her luscious voice, more vulnerable. 'Thanks for asking, though. You're a good man, aren't you?'

'Not really.' And then he added, despite himself: 'I wouldn't be here with you if I was.'

She put her hand on his forearm. 'It'll be OK, I promise.' She left her hand there for too long, looking into his eyes. As if to break the spell, he jumped up, suddenly emboldened.

'Fancy a swim?' he asked. Before she could answer, he had pulled off his shorts and was running towards the sea. He dived in and the chilled water was the most refreshing tonic he had ever experienced. When he surfaced he looked round and she was standing, waist high, in the water behind him. She waded slowly out to him as he found his footing on the shifting pebbles, coming right up to stand in front of him. She put her arms round his neck and kissed him on the mouth. At first he tried not to yield, but the feeling was too profound, the need too great. Waves slapped over their bodies as they held the embrace. She slipped one hand down his back, over his buttocks until her fingers were grasping him. He was too excited to move, the cold water no longer having any effect.

It was brief and powerful, the most intense encounter he'd ever had. When it was over, and they stood as still as they could in the tide, their legs shaking, Michael expected to feel sick. But he didn't. Instead, he felt released, as if this had been a cathartic exercise of such strength that it had extracted all the furies from him. He rested his head on her shoulder and planted gentle kisses on it.

'Come on,' she said softly. She led him out of the water and back to their towels, and they both lay down, too exhausted to speak or move.

Later, when his skin was dry, she sat up suddenly. 'Oh, I forgot to tell you,' she said. 'Your wife rang earlier, left a message, wants you to call her.'

TWENTY-FIVE

Teri knew at once. She was curled up on her bed, and the cramps in her stomach told her before the blood came. She reeled towards the bathroom, tears smearing her face, and stripped off all her clothes. Physically, she'd always been strong, with a mind to go with it, but she'd been struck low by the pressures of the last few weeks and the tiny life within her would be the first to suffer, as she well knew. The blood was everywhere, thickened by other fluids, and she stood helplessly as it seeped out of her. She sobbed as she put her hands gingerly between her thighs, unable to do anything to stop this relentless process. She pulled one hand away and looked at it in awe, turning it around slowly in front of her face as if mesmerised by what she saw. She was witnessing the end of a life that had been closer to her than anything else, a life that had been a part of her without ever having been seen, and her only reaction was to twitch spasmodically as it ebbed away from her, a trail of evidence down the insides of her legs.

Mechanically she stumbled back to the bedroom and dialled Skip's number, now shaking violently.

Pam answered. 'He's not here, I'm afraid. He's gone to a meeting.'

'Do you have the number where he is? I'm really unwell and I must speak to him.'

'Just hang on a moment, Teri.' Silence on the line: Skip had left instructions as to how to be contacted. Then Pam was back. 'Teri, someone's calling him right now. Is there anything we can do? Shall I call an ambulance?'

'Yes, yes, do,' Teri replied desperately. 'It's really bad,

201

Pam, tell him, for God's sake.'

'OK, Teri, just lie down and we'll get an ambulance to you. It's on its way shortly.'

Teri dropped the bloodstained phone and collapsed on to the bed, still shaking uncontrollably. She had nothing left to give, no means of resistance, and she let nature take its course without the fight to prevent it, even if she could.

'She's very weak. She lost a lot of blood, of course. But she's going to be all right.' The doctor, a young woman, stood with Skip in a quiet waiting room at the hospital.

Skip's eyes were watery but he kept his composure. 'That's what really matters, I guess,' he said, struggling to control himself.

'This is always hard, I know, but there's no reason at all why you shouldn't try again. Lots of first-time pregnancies end this way, and the mums go on to have healthy babies. Your wife is very strong otherwise, so there's nothing to worry about. Just give it a few months.' He nodded without really hearing what she was saying. 'We'll keep her in overnight, just to monitor her progress, then she can go home in the morning.'

'What should I do?'

'Give her plenty of bed rest, make her eat properly. Keep an eye on her. She's going to be depressed, naturally, so you need to watch out for that. I wouldn't leave her on her own at first. Stay with her if you can. She'll need your support.'

'Thanks, doctor.' Skip was dazed and hardly knew where he was. She turned to leave. 'Do you have a chapel here?'

'Yes. Just follow the signs to the end of the corridor. It's a bit rudimentary, I'm afraid.'

'Doesn't matter.' She left and closed the door very quietly, the signal for Skip to release all his tears. Mysterious ways, he thought as he cried.

It was after five in the afternoon when Debby and Michael returned to the pub. He was prickly from all the exposure to the sun, and uneasy about how to behave with her. Her manner didn't change – friendly, relaxed, as if nothing important had passed between them – and she left him to go on up to his room and shower. He scrubbed himself vigorously, hoping to remove all traces of her scent, but there was a part of him that couldn't dispel the elation he had felt, something that no amount of soap and water could erase.

He called Annie, heart thumping as he worried that something in his voice would betray him. But she wasn't listening for that. 'Where the hell have you been?' she snapped.

'Sorry. I went out for a drive, lost track of the time. What is it, anyway? Is Holly all right?'

'Yes, Holly's fine and so am I, thanks for asking. But you may not be.'

His heart pounded even faster – could she know? What had Debby said to her? 'Why? What's happened?'

'We had a visit from a policeman today. Very nice, very polite, but he wants to speak to you.'

'Me? Christ, what have I done?'

'You tell me, Michael. What have you done?'

'Nothing that I'm aware of. What's this all about?'

'Your great friends Skip and Teri have been receiving nasty phone calls and faxes. It sounds to me like they think you may be behind it all.' A heavy pause, so that he could take it in. 'Are you, Michael?'

'Jesus! No, of course I'm not. What makes you think that?'

'I'm not sure what to think about you any more,' Annie said wearily. 'Nothing would surprise me.'

Wheels turned as he considered this condemnation. What Pam had said about some phone calls to Skip; how Annie had suggested it might be Jean Retzer; how easy it would be to point the finger at him, just as Pam had been inclined to do; it all added up to serious trouble.

'Surely you know me better than that,' he said.

'Do I? I don't know what you're doing down there. I don't know what's going on in your head. All I know is you're not the Michael I thought I knew. Something's changed, and it isn't me. I still have to carry on while you bugger around messing up our lives. So tell me, what should I think?'

203

'I don't know, Annie, I really don't. I'm trying my hardest, believe me, but it isn't enough for you at the moment. But please, please don't think that I'd do anything like that. God knows I'm messed up right now, but that . . . no, please.'

'Don't try and make me feel guilty, Michael. That's always your trick, isn't it? Turn it back on me as if it's my fault. I'm not the one who's gone away. I'm not the one sitting in isolation in front of a computer writing sick stories.'

'What?' he exclaimed. 'Oh God, that, that thing I wrote? It was just a bit of fun, to get it out of my system, my way of dealing with it. How did you find that?'

She ignored his question. 'So what else are you hiding, Michael, that's what I want to know? How many surprises have you got in store?'

'Look,' he said, vainly trying to restore calm to the conversation, 'I'm coming back. This is getting out of hand. I can explain everything.'

'I suggest you explain everything first to the police,' she said curtly. 'I don't want you back until this is sorted out. We don't have a future unless you do. Do you understand that?'

Her ultimatum hit him like a keen slap on the face. 'OK, OK, that's no problem. Give me his name and number and I'll call him right now.' Annie read out all the details and he jotted them down. 'I'm going to call him, then I'm coming home.'

'Don't bother if you don't,' she said with finality, then put the phone down. Michael looked to the door, acutely aware that, if she wanted, Debby could have heard every word. But she wasn't there, a small relief in the face of so much disturbance.

He called Dunbar's number. When it answered, he straightened himself. 'Hallo. This is Michael Lensman. My wife tells me you want to speak to me.' Friendly, accommodating, cooperative; there was no need for anything less.

'Ah. Mr Lensman, thanks for calling. Are you at home?'

'No. I'm down in Devon. Is that a problem?'

'Probably not.' Dunbar waited. 'Has your wife filled you in?'

'Briefly. But, how can I help?'

'Well, basically nothing to be too concerned about. We're talking to everyone who might have a reason, however tenuous, to do this sort of thing to Mr and Mrs McMaster. But I was wondering, when are you coming back? I'd prefer to do this in person.'

'I was thinking of leaving tomorrow morning. I'll be back by teatime, I should think.'

'Excellent. I'll call round about seven, shall I? Give you a chance to get unpacked.' A small laugh – good, he's relaxed, no problem here, just routine.

'Perfect. I'll see you then.'

'Thank you, Mr Lensman. Enjoy the rest of your holiday.'

Michael replaced the receiver and wrung his hands together. He noticed they were shaking badly. For the first time ever, he needed a drink to steady his nerves. Then he thought about Debby again, and how she, too, could dissipate his worries. No, he told himself, that isn't the answer, but he wanted her badly, another first. He needed to lose himself in her soft folds, to have her wrapped around him for protection from all that threatened him.

In all the excitement, Pam had completely forgotten about the envelope from Human Resources. She must have swept it up with a lot of other papers for Skip and put it in his in-tray without remembering to untie the thin red string which held the flap down. Now things had calmed down – Skip wasn't coming back in a hurry, that was for sure, and the rest of the office was empty at seven o'clock in the evening – she slid into his office and retrieved it from his desk. She went back to her desk and sat down, a tingle of elation at having so much freedom.

Teri was pretty ill; she hadn't heard a word since that call, but she reckoned it must be something serious, something to do with that precious baby Skip was always banging on about. He called her twenty times a day and she was no better, smug bitch. They were so bloody conceited, so satisfied with what they'd got, never for a moment thinking about other people and what they had to put up with. Skip with his expensive suits and Teri with her condescending attitude, Lord and Lady Bountiful they were, too consumed with their own good fortune by far. A setback like this might wake them up to the real world, and not before time. Cliff wouldn't understand, wouldn't know what she was talking about, he just got on and mowed the lawns and never gave anything a second thought. But Pam wanted more, deserved it in a way; Michael was gone, the one thing she had that was really valuable, that friendship, that bond, which he might not have admitted to but he certainly knew was there, just in the way he spoke to her like an equal, like there was nothing to separate them. And now Skip had gone and ruined all that. It was too much.

She unravelled the string and peered into the envelope as if there might be a letter bomb inside. She slid her hand in to pull out the papers held together with a red paper clip. She placed the bundle on the desk and settled down to read.

STRICTLY PRIVATE AND CONFIDENTIAL

Skip—

Re: EARLY TERMINATION PACKAGES

The attached workings show the fully loaded cost of each member of your staff, including corporate overhead. The final column details the estimated expense of termination in this financial year. For your information I have highlighted the personnel who appear to represent the most cost-effective option if you decide to offer them redundancy terms. Depending on the timing, we can defer some of these costs until the next budget cycle.

Please let me know how you want to proceed.

Mary

Pam unclipped the rest of the pages and studied them. She searched for her name first, and had to look twice before it registered. 'SHINE, PAMELA' was highlighted in fluorescent pink. She read all the numbers against her entry – salary, length of service, total expense and estimated cost of termination – before it fully dawned on her. Mary Strutter was recommending that Pam be made redundant.

Her eyes swelled as the figures danced before them. What had Skip said? 'I wanted to let you know that I think you're doing a super job here.' Oh yeah, super job, Mr High and Bloody Mighty, so super that you want to fire me. The indignation rose and her chest heaved expansively. So that was it; not content with firing Michael, not satisfied with seeing Don Retzer top himself, now Skip was planning to axe a whole bunch more. It can't happen; it just can't. The madness has got to stop.

Still fuming, Pam went to the photocopier with all the papers and took five copies, then went back to her workstation and carefully rearranged the originals, clipping them together and replacing them in the envelope. She tied the red string back around the cardboard spools and put the envelope in Skip's in-tray, exactly where it had been. She filed four of the copies in her desk drawer and locked it, putting the key in her handbag with the remaining copy.

She had no coherent idea of what she should do next. Brian Shale, she could tell him, but he was a clown and couldn't be trusted with such sensitive information. But then it came to her in a blinding shaft of light: Michael would know. He always knew what to do. She could rely on him to give her the guidance she needed. After all she'd done for him, all the devotion she'd shown, he would come through for her. He was so wise, so strong, that he could put it all right. She'd have to tell him everything, of course, lay her cards on the table, but that didn't worry her. It was time for that. They'd come too far together now. He'd understand, see it was right. He was the only one who would.

'So, are you going to tell me about it?' Debby asked. They

lay next to each other in his bed, the heat of their passion only slowly receding.

'Tell you what?' Michael replied, torpor engulfing him.

'What your trouble is.'

'My trouble,' he repeated. 'I don't follow you.'

'Well, my sweet,' she said in that buttery voice, 'you make love to me like there's a fire. I've never known anything like it. Then you're all sullen and moody. Seems like you've got some big trouble in your life.'

'I don't mean to be sullen and moody. I'm just drained, that's all. You take it all out of me.'

'And the rest,' she said, disbelief in her voice. 'Too late to feel guilty, you know. And no point, neither. No one's going to get hurt over this. It's just shagging, that's all it is.'

He was relieved to hear her say that. 'I have to go back.'

'I know. Didn't expect anything else. Didn't want anything else. But I can listen, if that's what you want.'

He sighed deeply. 'My life's disintegrated. That's all. Everything I thought I had, everything that was . . . important to me, it's all gone away, and I can't seem to get it back.'

'Then don't try. Get something new instead.'

'But I don't know if I want anything new, that's the problem. I liked what I had before.'

'So why are you here with me now?' she asked, a little mischief in her tone.

'Don't ask me that. It's not fair.'

'I know. Only teasing. But you can have something different. You know that now, and it doesn't change a thing. You can do things different, like I have, but you've still got what you had, if you see what I mean. I'm not too good with words, not like you.'

'No, I think I understand exactly what you mean. Like you and your husband?'

'That's it. He's still here, and I'm still married to him, but I've had to change some things. I don't want you to think I go about sleeping with all the guests, because I don't, see, but I don't mind this and I reckon he doesn't either. We've had to learn how to cope with it, that's all.'

'And are you happy?'

'Sort of – at least, as much as anyone's entitled to, I expect. That's all you can ask for, isn't it?'

'I wish I had your clarity,' Michael said honestly.

'Takes time. That's the point. Can't expect it all to land in your lap straight off.'

'That's good advice, and I'll take it for now.'

They were quiet for a few minutes, and then she turned on her side and put her hand on his stomach. 'I bet your wife's a bit different to me, though,' she said, almost sadly.

'Yes, just a bit.' He thought for a moment. 'Not better or worse, just different.'

'There you are, then.' Her hand moved lower. 'So enjoy it while you can. Then go back, free and clear and no questions asked. That's the deal, isn't it?'

He rolled over to face her. 'You're a wonderful woman, Debby, and I don't deserve . . .' She put a finger to his lips to stop him speaking any more. She moved her fingertips softly against his face.

'Don't forget me, that's all. Never forget how this felt.' And he melted into her embrace.

TWENTY-SIX

Skip was fussing round Teri, straightening bedding that didn't need it, when the phone rang. Her face told him all he needed to know about how frightened she'd become: just the noise of the bell consumed her with terror.

'I'll let it ring,' he said.

'No,' she said firmly. 'It might be important.'

His shoulders sagged and he picked it up. 'Skip McMaster,' he said with as much authority as he could muster.

'Hi. Chris Dunbar here.'

'Oh, thank goodness it's you,' Skip replied with true feeling.

'Just thought I'd update you. We've visited Jean Retzer. As you'd expect, she's a little off kilter, but we don't think she's involved. We've given her a little encouragement to stop, though, if it is her. I also called on Mrs Lensman, and I'm going to be seeing her husband tonight.'

'That's good.'

'Well, it's not going as fast as any of us would like, but we'll get there in the end. Do you have any news to report? Any more calls?'

'No, all quiet on that front, I'm pleased to say.'

'And your wife? She's going to come down with you for the fingerprints?'

'Could you hold just one moment?' Skip looked at Teri, who was staring at him with an anxious face. 'Look, it's not so easy right now. My wife's rather unwell, and she'll need a couple of days to recover. I don't think I can do that yet.'

'Sorry to hear that. Nothing serious, I hope.'

'Er . . . no, no, she's going to be fine. Thanks for asking.'

'OK, but you'll let me know, right? We've lifted a lot of

prints from those papers you gave me. We need to eliminate yours.'

'I understand.'

'Anyway, after I've spoken to Mr Lensman I'll be in touch. Send your wife my best wishes.'

Skip bit his top lip and put the phone down. Teri's face seemed flattened, as if all the features had been punched in; where there had once been sparkle and vitality, there was now nothing, just emptiness behind the eyes. He hurt for her.

He sat down on the edge of the bed. 'The police are doing everything they can,' he said as he took her hand in his. 'They've spoken to Jean, and they're going to see Michael Lensman. They're being really helpful.'

'It's a little late for that,' Teri replied, her mouth twisted against the misery inside.

'I know, I know,' he said softly. 'We have to be strong now. This is God's way of testing us.'

'Please,' she said forcefully, 'can you leave him out of this? It's kind of hard for me to see that right at this moment. All I know is we had a baby and we've lost it. Now what did we do to deserve that? How does that square with God's will?' Tears began to brim in her eyes.

'I don't have the answer to that, but I know we can pull through this. We'll go away, get some rest, come back fitter and stronger.'

'We can't escape, Skip. We're trapped by this, wherever we go. Scar tissue, you know?'

There was nothing for him to say. It had all gone so terribly, irrevocably wrong, and she was facing up to it without hope. He couldn't agree with her, and yet how could he make her see? He stroked her hair lightly. 'Do you want to rest? Shall I leave you alone?'

'Leave, stay, it doesn't change a thing.' She was weak, he could see, too feeble to think rationally. He shook his head slowly.

'You need to sleep. I'll leave you now.' He got up and began walking softly to the door.

211

'Don't,' she said. 'Just be with me, Skip. I can't face this on my own.'

He turned back and went to lie next to her. 'I'm here for you always,' he said. 'You know that.'

He watched her as she drifted away into troubled sleep, her body and mind still smarting from the crisis she had faced alone. He was helpless to alleviate the suffering, and that was the worst part.

Michael felt both relief and alarm when he realised that Annie and Holly were not there. All the way back he had been readying himself for the confrontation, which would have been difficult enough without the further complication of his having something new to hide. Acutely aware of Debby's distinctive scent, he had continuously sniffed himself in the car to see if he could pick up any traces of it, even though he had scrubbed his skin until it was almost raw.

In preparation for the row – and he fully expected a major fight – he had rehearsed his lines over and over again. He was sorry, and he knew that wasn't enough, but even this brief time away had made him appreciate how valuable Annie and Holly were to him, how much he had missed them and how he would never again make the mistake of taking them for granted. He was ready to face up to the future, had spent too much time thinking about what he'd done rather than what he was doing (he especially liked that phrase), and would now fully apply himself to getting another job as quickly as possible.

There were big holes in all of this, he knew: how would he explain the deception about the Bloomberg job, for example? But he comforted himself with the fact that he needed to get through this day, and others would have to wait until they arrived. If he could successfully negotiate a truce with Annie, and get the police off his back, the rest would somehow fall into place. One day at a time, just like the alcoholics said.

He had recurring thoughts of Debby, but they didn't overly concern him: her own pragmatism had served to lessen the impact and significance of this encounter, relegating it to nothing much more than an ill-judged but harmless aberration. He had been weak when she found him; now he was stronger for the experience and, with a little effort, he could consign the memory to a dark and rarely visited recess of his soul. He felt a gentle twinge of conscience at the callous way in which he was willing to treat this, but Debby had been compliant, and what Annie didn't know couldn't hurt her. If this was the limitation of his bad behaviour, it wasn't the end of the world.

Having conquered his doubts, he could focus on the twin challenge of Annie and this policeman. He had, he reasoned, nothing to fear from either. Annie would bluster, sulk, make his life a general misery for a few days, then relent when she got bored of the effect. The policeman was on a fishing expedition and could probably be dismissed within twenty minutes. Michael could grit his teeth, ride the storm and come out the other side intact. He had to smile as he said to himself: 'Worse things happen at sea.' Yes, he'd had some things happen to him in the sea recently, but they weren't at all bad . . .

Seeing that the car wasn't there, Michael let himself in. He called out for Annie just in case, but the house was empty. It looked eerily tidy and clean – no toys scattered on the floor, no pile of washing in the kitchen, the dishwasher unloaded – as if there had been an orderly retreat. He didn't like the smell or feel of it. He went from room to room and found all the beds made, all the cushions plumped up, all the linen folded and put away. Happily, most of their clothes were still there, as far as he could make out. His bedroom office was just as he'd left it, although he now knew that Annie had been in there, rifling through his papers. That was crass; he should never have written such a pile of rubbish, let alone printed it out and kept it. She was right to have been alarmed, however misguided. What had he been thinking of?

He tried not to worry about their absence. He made himself a cup of tea and opened the few items of mail that were waiting for him on the kitchen table. He had hoped to find an explanatory note from Annie, but didn't. At a loose end, he unpacked his tote bag and spilled the contents on to the kitchen floor before shoving them all into the washing machine. Unused to such domestic chores, he fiddled with the switches for some time before he could make it work. He was watching it for recognisable action when he heard someone at the front door; the kitchen clock showed that it was only four-thirty. The policeman wasn't due until seven. Perhaps Annie was back and this was Holly, impatient as always to get in. He raced to the door to open it; Pam was standing there.

'My goodness,' he said. 'Hallo, stranger.' Looking at her, he could see she'd been crying.

'Can I come in?' she asked and, without waiting for an answer, she barged past him. He chased after her to the sitting room. This he didn't need. 'Michael, we have to talk. You have to help me.'

'What's happened?' he asked, curiosity getting the better of him.

Pam collapsed on to the sofa, her formless shape accentuated by the way in which she slumped backwards. 'It's all gone so terribly wrong. You're the only person who can help me.'

'OK, take your time. What's the story?'

'That bastard Skip,' she spat. 'He's gone too far this time.'

'Oh,' Michael said, somewhat disappointed that they were on the DataTrak path yet again.

'He's drawn up a list of people he wants to fire.' She paused, hoping vainly for some reaction. 'I'm on it.'

'Surely not. The office would collapse without you.'

She failed to recognise the irony in his voice. 'Obviously he doesn't think so. There are about eight of us lined up for the chop. The guy's been there five minutes and he thinks he can do this.'

'How do you know this? Has he announced it?' Michael already knew the answer; he'd always been aware that nothing was ever kept secret for too long, especially when Pam controlled the mail.

'Not yet, but it's coming, believe me. I've seen the memo from Mary Strutter.'

'I see. But . . . I'm not quite sure how I can help.'

'Oh Michael,' she began, and then the crying started, a distinctly unattractive sobbing and sniffing which, more than anything, annoyed him. She managed to talk between her snivels. 'Don't you realise, even after all we've been through? Isn't it obvious?'

Perhaps it was the recent overdose of sea air; perhaps it was because he hadn't felt this good for a long time; but, whatever the reason, Michael wanted to laugh. Pam looked and sounded ridiculous; the whole situation was farcical. This pudgy little woman was having a fit in front of him, and he had no idea why. 'What?' he said, suppressing the urge to giggle.

'It's so bloody stupid. I'm sorry, I'm making a fool of myself. But I can't go on any longer. I need you, Michael. You're . . . you're my best friend. You're the only one I can turn to. You've always looked after me, you have. And now, now all this is going on, I know I can rely on you.'

So this was it. Pam had been brought so low that he was her only hope of salvation. God, she must be desperate, he thought to himself. 'Well, OK, what do you want me to do?' he asked, fascinated by her declaration.

She collected herself, wiping her eyes with her fingers. 'You know, when you left, I thought I was going to die, I was that upset. I couldn't face the thought of not seeing you every day. That sounds silly, doesn't it? But we had something, didn't we? I mean, we were a good team. You took care of me and I took care of you. It was mutual, Michael, you have to admit.'

He nodded slowly. 'We worked very well together,' he confirmed, trying to keep it neutral.

'But it was more than that, wasn't it?'

'How do you mean?'

She moaned and rolled her bleary eyes. 'God, do I have to spell it out?' she whimpered. He waited, hoping she would. 'We . . . we, well, we meant something to each other, didn't we, I mean, beyond work?'

'I'm not sure I'm following you, Pam.' But he was; Michael was deliberately avoiding the issue.

'Don't you feel it?' she asked, pleading now. 'Isn't there anything there for you as well?'

He sighed, tiring of the game. 'Pam, I'm very fond of you. But that's as far as it goes, I'm afraid. We had a superb working relationship – full stop.' It was time to put her out of her misery, but this only started her off again.

'Oh Christ,' she wailed. He watched impassively as she sobbed; then, in a moment's weakness, he went to sit down beside her and put his arm round her chubby shoulder. He pulled out a handkerchief from his pocket and pushed it into her hand.

'Pam,' he said softly. 'This is no good. You have to trust me on this one. You're a big girl now, and I know you can handle it. I'll do whatever I can for you within reason, just as I always have. But you mustn't mistake that for anything else. I care about you, of course I do, and I hate to see you like this. Come on, stop those tears now – they're ruining your mascara.'

She looked up at him and forced a little smile. 'What happened, Michael?' she asked, truly puzzling him.

'Nothing.' It was all he could think of to say.

'You'll always be my friend, won't you – my special friend?'

'You have my word.'

'Whatever happens?'

'Whatever,' he said, without the faintest clue of what she was talking about.

'I've done some stupid things, I know. But I'm going to put it all right, you'll see.' She seemed to be more composed now, basking in his physical attention. 'I'll get things sorted, and we'll forget this has ever occurred.'

'That's my girl,' he said, and he squeezed her shoulder. 'And look, if you need some help on the redundancy thing, you'll let me know, right? I can't promise anything, but I'll see what I can do.'

'Oh that,' she said dismissively. 'No, thanks for the offer, but I know how to deal with that.'

'OK, but the offer stands.' He removed his arm from around her and stood up. 'Now, I hate to be rude, but I have an important visitor coming soon, and I need to get ready.'

'Yeah, no problem.' She pulled herself up and straightened her clothes. 'I must look a proper sight.'

'No one's looking,' he said generously.

As they reached the front door, she turned to face him. 'Thanks for everything, Michael. I really don't know what I'd do without you.' She kissed him, quite unexpectedly, on the cheek. 'You're special.'

She was halfway down the path when she stopped. 'Oh, have you heard?' she said brightly. 'Skip's wife lost the baby. Had a miscarriage.' And she was on her way before he had a chance to react.

It was, as Michael had calculated, a breeze. Detective Sergeant Chris Dunbar was as nice as any policeman could be. He had a cup of tea and they sat in the sitting room and went over the facts of the case. Dunbar gave every indication that he found the whole thing slightly tedious, and was almost apologetic about disturbing Michael.

'We have to do this,' he said. 'Procedure.'

'I completely understand,' Michael replied. 'Happy to help. I really sympathise with Skip and Teri. They don't deserve it.'

'That's very generous of you, and I'm sure they'd be touched,' Dunbar said. 'After all, there must have been a bit of ill feeling on your side, in view of what happened.'

'Not at all. It's purely business. Nowadays they say that you're no one unless you've been made redundant at least once in your career. It happens all the time. You just have to take it in your stride and move on.'

'Don Retzer didn't, did he?'

The observation surprised Michael, but he was happy to steer the conversation in a different direction. 'Well, I think there must have been more to it than that. I knew Don quite well, and I can't believe he'd have committed suicide simply because he lost his job.'

'His wife wouldn't agree with you on that. She's convinced that was precisely the reason.'

'I'm not an expert in these matters, obviously, but I'd say she's a little unstable at the moment. Wouldn't we all be in her position?' He smiled knowingly at Dunbar, but got nothing in return.

'And you? Your wife told me you were a little under the weather.'

'Delayed reaction, I suppose. I needed to get away. Nothing more sinister than that.'

Dunbar changed tack again. 'So you have absolutely no idea who could be doing this to the McMasters?'

'Beats me. It sounds really bizarre. I mean, they lead a pretty blameless life, I'd imagine.'

'Not according to someone.' Dunbar flipped his notebook shut and put it in his breast pocket. 'That's it, then. I'm done. I do appreciate your help, Mr Lensman.' He got up and they shook hands. 'Oh,' he continued, shaking his head, 'my memory's like a sieve today. This is going to sound terrible, but there's nothing to worry about. Would you mind going down to your local station and giving a set of fingerprints? Yourself and your wife? Just for elimination purposes.' He smiled reassuringly.

'Consider it done. As soon as my wife gets back, we'll get it sorted.'

'Now your wife's away?'

'Back tonight,' Michael said, without knowing if it were true. 'We'll do it first thing tomorrow.'

'Much obliged,' Dunbar said. 'Show them my card and they'll know what to do.'

By nine o'clock Michael was starting to fret. No call from Annie, no word to say where they were and when – whether? – they were coming back. He would have called her mother but lacked the courage to do it. Instead he sat and watched television distractedly, jumping at any sound outside the house. All other fears having been dismissed, this one ate

218

away at him. What game was she playing? What did she know, and what did she think she knew? He drifted into uneasy sleep on the sofa, the questions still plaguing him.

TWENTY-SEVEN

Skip sat in the captain's chair in his den, a pile of papers in front of him. The office had sent them over by courier, and he was meant to be working on them, but his thoughts wouldn't settle on such mundane matters. Every thirty minutes he crept up the stairs and looked in on Teri; reluctantly he'd agreed to let her take some sedatives, and her sleep was becoming deeper and more peaceful. She still looked dreadful, bloodless, and he ached at the very sight of her. When he was in the den this image of her shimmered before him, blurring his sight to everything else. The phone would ring, the fax would beep into life, but he remained fixated by the vision of her, drawn and sallow, her head hardly seeming to touch the pillow beneath it.

He had just returned to the den and was shuffling the papers unenthusiastically when the phone rang again. Nobody, it seemed, could make any decisions at the office without his prior approval: his big hopes for staff empowerment clearly weren't making much headway. He wearily picked up the call.

'Yup,' he said.

'You got close.' It was the caller, the first time for several days. The number had been changed but, because it was now his link with the office, Skip had disclosed it.

'I beg your pardon?' Recovering from the initial shock, he slipped his finger towards the recall button and pressed it, just as the phone company had instructed him. From that, and the time of the call, they could trace it. He looked at his watch and wrote down the time: nine-twenty-seven a.m.

'I thought you were smart. I was wrong.'

'Meaning?'

'The police. The cops. Call them in and it raises the stakes.'

'They're on to you, you know that,' Skip said flatly. Stay calm, keep talking.

'Yeah? We'll see about that.' That voice, neither man nor woman, but familiar too – where had he heard it?

'It's only a matter of time, buddy. And by the way, I'm beginning to lose interest.'

'Sad. Very sad. My heart bleeds. Come on Skip, you can do better than that.'

'It's all over. Quit while you're ahead, that's my advice.'

'Always so free with your advice, that's what I like about you. Pity you don't follow it yourself. Pity you haven't always been so understanding. You wreck lives, Skip. That's the truth of it. You're the one who should quit, while you still can.'

Skip was unwillingly drawn in. 'I don't get this. What am I supposed to have done?'

'Think it through and you'll get there. Good and evil, right and wrong. You know all that stuff. You hurt us, and you must be punished – you know, an eye for an eye. You're big on all that Bible crap, right?'

'Us?' It was the first time this had been used, and it might be a clue, a window, a breakthrough. 'Who's us?'

'Time to go. And remember, you were close.'

When he had put the phone down, Skip forced himself to go through the whole conversation again. There were hints, intentional or not, lying just beyond his grasp. Us – what did that mean? You were close – a sure sign that, somehow, he had worried the caller. He remembered to call the nuisance line and give them all the details before returning to the problem. They promised an answer later in the day. In the meantime, he turned it all over one more time. He knew that voice, however vaguely. With luck – and, dare he hope,

221

God's help – they were getting there. It was a small palliative to set against their greater pain, but it would have to suffice for now.

Motionless on the landing, hardly daring to breathe lest she was caught, Jean Retzer clenched her fists as the wave of nausea crested in her stomach. She'd suspected, of course, right from the moment when that policeman had been to see her. It was all so obvious, so . . . logical, yet she'd been wrapped up in her own obsessions – yes, she admitted to herself now, they were exactly that – that she'd lost her natural senses, those instincts which would normally have picked this up a mile off. She'd been absorbed with bitterness and vengeance, when all around her there were signals flashing like beacons, flares sent up into the darkness which she'd failed to spot.

But how to react? How do you deal with this? Don would have known; he'd have developed a plan in an instant, known immediately what to do next. He had the means, the serenity, to take the right approach and keep the lid on it all. She was merely an admiring, at times envious, onlooker as he dealt with these special, intimate problems with the skill of one who has been there himself. How she needed him now.

She slid noiselessly into her bedroom and lay down. The weariness from this battle was finally overwhelming her, the spoils no longer worth the fight. She'd put them through this, an unnecessary and spiteful crusade with no clear aim. No wonder, then . . . as a wife she knew she'd been a failure, confirmed irrevocably by Don, but now, as a mother, she was facing further humiliation. Could she go through more? How much strength was left in this puny body? Whichever way she looked at it, her life's work was spilt horribly at her feet. The whispered conversation she had overheard resounded in her ears to lend authority to her despair.

Having failed to gain any proper rest, Michael had given up trying to sleep. Increasingly concerned, he had prowled about the house aimlessly, his imagination running unchecked as he agonised over their continuing absence. It was so out of character for Annie to do this, despite ample provocation; she didn't run away from problems – unlike him, he accepted – preferring to confront them, air her grievances and settle everything there and then. For her to have left, whether temporarily or not, suggested a deeper wound, something which couldn't be healed with a straightforward, old-fashioned row.

Worse still was the fact that she hadn't called, hadn't left any indication of where they were and when they might return. Annie didn't work on the basis of getting her own back: it wouldn't have occurred to her that she could show Michael how unkind it was to go AWOL, to prove a point by giving him a taste of his own medicine. This departure, he concluded, was driven by altogether more complex emotions, a potent cocktail of anger, resentment, doubt and fear, along with God knows what other feelings that were exclusively feminine. He'd given her every possible justification for her actions but, perversely, he was comforted by them: at least it levelled the playing field, brought them closer together by her reflection of his own unreasonable behaviour.

In the throbbing emptiness of the house he realised, too, that he needed her more than anything else in the world. Without her he was nothing, drifting hopelessly without an anchor. Did he have to go through all this to understand that? He recalled a master at school who repeatedly told the boys that suffering was essential, hardship a necessary constituent of the growing process. As a surly adolescent Michael had queried the validity of this crusty opinion, but now, with a thicker skin and the benefit of maturity, he saw the truth of it. Get through it, learn from it, don't make the same mistake twice; like a cracked bone that grows back stronger than before, this fracture in their lives would mend. Whilst they might never want to revisit the experience explicitly, it would always be there to prevent them falling into the same trap. That, at least, was how Michael had boiled it down.

None of which stopped him growing more agitated with the current state of affairs. He had come home as the peacemaker, full of apologies and excuses, ready to atone for his sins, all of which had been deflated and devalued by this turn of events. Again he turned to the phone to call her mother, and again he prevaricated. He wasn't sure if Annie wanted him to call, wasn't fully aware of the rules of this game. If she was there, she might refuse to speak to him. If not, he'd set her mother off. He sat on the stairs feeling pathetic. Was this really the first day of the rest of his life? It wasn't going too well and it was only ten o'clock.

When the phone did eventually ring he leapt up from the stairs and ran to answer it. 'Annie?' he cried.

'You're back then,' she replied.

'Oh my God,' he sighed, 'where the hell are you? Are you all right?'

'We're fine. We're with Mum. We're going to stay a few days.'

'But . . . what about . . . I mean, shouldn't Holly be at school?' It was all he could muster.

'I've told the school and there's no problem. She's not going to miss anything vital. Anyway, I think this is more important right now. She's very upset.'

'Do you want me to come down?' he blurted out.

'No.'

He went through his routine in the face of her stony silence. 'I'm fine now, you know. I've been a complete arsehole, I know, and you have every reason in the world to be angry with me. But it's going to be different now, I promise. I'm much better.' He waited, then lowered his voice for greater effect. 'I really have to see you, Annie, you and Holly. I've missed you so much. It's only being apart that's made me realise how much I need you.'

'It isn't just a tap you can turn on and off,' she answered after a moment. 'One minute you can't be with us, the next you can. It doesn't work like that. You have to make up your mind. It's all or nothing. I won't have it any other way.'

'I know that, and we don't need to fight about it. But Annie, I don't think you want to go on like this any more than I do. Come home and we can thrash it all out. We've got to face up to it sooner or later.'

Another pause, another hiatus while she debated with herself. 'How did it go with the police?' she asked, avoiding his pleading.

'No problem. It was strictly routine. He knows damned well I couldn't have been involved.'

'So what happens next?'

'On that front? Nothing. Except . . . well, we have to be fingerprinted. They're doing it to everybody. They have some evidence and they want to eliminate us, that's all.' He found himself rushing this, as if to lessen its significance.

'I didn't mean that,' she said. 'I meant with us.'

'With us?' he repeated, surprised that she would ask him. 'You and Holly come back, and we start to rebuild. It's better than the alternative.'

'The alternative. Yes, I've thought about that, too. It has its appeals, I can tell you.' Even with this remark, Michael could tell she was weakening.

'I don't blame you for that. Part of the problem's been that I haven't been able to live with myself so I don't know how you've managed.'

He could hear Holly saying something to her in the background. 'Listen,' she said, suddenly less intense. 'I've got to go. I need to think. I'll call you, maybe tomorrow. You'll be there, right?' It was an order, not a question.

'I'll be here. But . . . I could come down.'

'No. I'll call you. Bye.'

'Bye, Annie. I love you.' But he was speaking to a dead line.

By five o'clock that evening the supervisor of the BT nuisance-call division had contacted Detective Sergeant Chris Dunbar and had disclosed all the information he needed. It was policy that they would not tell the target: that opened up too many opportunities for recriminations and complications. Dunbar called Skip from his mobile on his way through London.

'We've got him. The trace worked.'

'You're sure? I mean, there's no chance of an error?' Skip sounded mightily relieved but still needed confirmation.

'Not where I'm going. It all fits in.'

'And where is that?'

Dunbar used the old trick. 'Sorry, Mr McMaster, but the line's breaking up and I'm just about to go under a bridge. I'll call you later.'

By rights Dunbar should have left this to Steve and his friends, but he wanted to be there with them when they arrived. He'd arranged it all, and he felt some ownership of the case. He wove his way through the traffic, resisting the temptation to activate the siren. After all, it was only a minor offence, however unpleasant it had been.

He pulled up at the kerb outside the house, nodding at Steve and a couple of uniformed officers as he got out of the car. 'Number twenty-six,' Steve said, pointing at their destination.

'OK,' Dunbar said. 'Nice and easy, no heavy stuff. We just want a chat.'

Steve led the way and, after looking around at the other three to make sure they were ready, he rang on the doorbell. They stood waiting until the front door opened and Jean Retzer looked out at them. Her face was gaunt, skin the colour of wet cement. She stared at each one of them in turn, her head nodding minutely, then, without a word, turned and let them follow her in. She led them to a large, open-plan space which ran the length of the house, and stood in front of the hearth.

'Do you know why we're here?' Dunbar asked, picking up on her resigned air.

'Yes.' Her gaze darted upwards, as if to show them.

'Do you mind if we take a look around?' Steve chipped in.

'It's easier if I tell you,' she replied. 'First door on the right at the top of the stairs.' One of the uniforms reacted immediately and left the room.

'How long have you known?' Dunbar asked.

She shrugged. 'Known? Not long – today, this morning.'

'But suspected, right?'

'You could say that.' She was beaten, this thin woman, defeated by the accretion of so many tragedies. They stood there in silence, the four of them, waiting for it to happen.

'Guv,' a voice shouted from upstairs. 'You'd better come up.' Putting his hand up to show he was in control, Steve moved away.

'Do you want to sit down?' Dunbar said, stepping towards her.

She merely shook her head. 'Will there be a charge?'

'I can't say. Mitigating circumstances, perhaps. Don't worry, we'll go easy on him.'

They heard the footsteps on the stairs as all three came down. Daniel appeared first, his head hung and arms swinging loosely by his side. Steve and the officer were close behind him.

'There's a ton of hardware up there,' Steve said, clearly quite impressed. 'All hooked up to a phone line. The number matches.'

'It was my husband's idea,' Jean said, looking sadly at her boy. 'Daniel's always been keen on that kind of thing, haven't you?' Daniel made no effort to acknowledge this, continuing to stare at the floor. To Dunbar he looked like any other fourteen-year-old kid, with his Reebok sweatshirt, baggy trousers and Adidas trainers, a few nascent spots growing on his nose and neck. How could this boy have done something so vehement, so completely destructive? He could work out the motive quickly enough; the atmosphere in this house was dead, the lingering smell of suicide heavy in the air.

'We'll have to take him down to the station,' Steve said.

'Can I come?' she asked.

'It'd be better if you do.'

It was a sad convoy that trudged from the house to the waiting cars. With a minimum of fuss they carried Daniel and his mother away, while Dunbar waited in his car, collecting his thoughts before carefully tapping in Skip's number on his mobile. One family was falling apart as another began to be repaired. Life was full of ironies like that, but the knowledge didn't make his job any easier.

TWENTY-EIGHT

'In a sense, you have to admire the guy. I mean, he really knew his stuff.' Chris Dunbar shrugged, then curled his lips into his mouth as if he immediately regretted saying this.

Teri was lying on the sofa, a blanket covering her, with Skip perched next to her feet. Dunbar had promised to call in after he'd been briefed on the interview with Daniel, and had arrived first thing that morning. In the background he could hear the phone ringing in Skip's den, but they all ignored it.

'He must have been going through a pretty rough time,' Skip said forgivingly. 'Losing his father like that – it's no wonder he wanted to take it out on someone.' He looked across at Teri who, from her facial expression, didn't seem entirely ready to share his understanding.

'In his defence,' Dunbar answered, 'I don't think he meant you any actual harm. This was just his way of dealing with the grief he felt. He was lashing out randomly, and you two happened to be an easy target. I know that doesn't excuse what he put you through, but it's an explanation.'

'Tell me everything,' Teri said quietly. 'How did he do it?'

'He's a clever young man. He has a very powerful computer in his bedroom, hooked up to the phone system. He spends hours up there, according to his mother, and the bedroom became his operations centre. He had enough information on you to get him started and keep him busy, and the only time he ever left the room, as far as we can make out, is when he delivered that package to your home. He told his mother he was going to visit a friend, set off nice and early and waited until he was sure you were there. He's pretty resourceful. And, as for the phone calls, it's hardly surprising you couldn't tell whether it was a man or a woman. At fourteen his voice is doing some strange things.'

'How did he know so much about us?'

'Mainly because of what his father had told him. They were apparently very close. He knew about the pregnancy because he overheard a conversation you had at his father's funeral. And he copied the death certificate from his father's. Simple, really.'

Skip put his finger up like a schoolboy wanting to ask a question. 'He said once that, whatever I did, however many times I changed the phone number, he'd find us. What did he mean?'

'I can't be sure about this, but I think he might have hacked into the British Telecom database. He certainly knows how to do that kind of thing. He's a very smart boy. Otherwise . . .'

Teri finished the thought for him. 'Otherwise, he was getting help from someone at DataTrak – someone who would know our numbers.'

Dunbar nodded. 'But I think that's a remote possibility. My guess is he was working on his own. That's certainly how it appears from the interviews we've had with him.' He paused, thinking it through and filing the idea for later consideration. 'The other thing you should know is you weren't the only ones. He apparently sent a note to a Charles Turkwood. His father did some work for him after he left DataTrak, and clearly didn't like him and must have mentioned as much to Daniel.'

'I know Turkwood,' Skip said. 'But really, that's taking it too far.'

'Not in the mind of a mixed-up kid,' Dunbar replied.

'And you truly believe that this is the end of it all?' Teri asked.

'Yes, I do. I'm dreadfully sorry it's taken so long to resolve it, but I think you're all clear now.' There was one more line of enquiry Dunbar wanted to pursue, but it didn't need to concern them.

After shooting another look at Teri, Skip spoke. 'What will happen to Daniel?'

'From our point of view, we've already given him the fright of his life, and I imagine his mother will be even harder on him. He didn't expect to get caught, and had no idea of the seriousness of what he'd been doing. But ultimately, that's a question for you. What do you want to happen?'

'We'll discuss that,' Teri said with finality.

'Right,' Skip confirmed. 'We need some time to get through all this.'

'Well, you have my number. Give me a call when you've made your decision.'

Skip wanted this to be finished; he didn't want to linger over questions of recrimination, with all the associated renewal of pain that would entail. Instead he would have liked to proceed by wiping the slate clean, concentrating on the future and how he and Teri would face it together. Their lives blown apart by the loss of the baby, now was not the time for further elongation of what they had suffered. But Teri would have to call the shots on this one, and he was resigned to falling in line with her will.

Later she raised the subject. 'You want to forget it, don't you?'

Skip was cautious. 'It's an option, isn't it? I mean, what good are we going to do by going after him?'

'I don't know,' Teri said wearily. 'I don't really know anything much, truth be told. Everything seems so pointless, like there's nothing worth doing. We could go after him, I guess, but I'm not sure it'd make me feel any better about it.' She was, once again, on the verge of tears, unable to think of anything but her loss and the hollowness inside her.

'You want to think it over? We don't have to decide right now.'

'We do, Skip. We have to exorcise this thing once and for all, and now's as good a time as any. We'll never get over it until we do.' Skip blinked slowly, waiting for her to reach a decision. 'Oh, what the heck, let it go. I can't face any more.'

'We've still got each other, babe. That counts for something.'

'I hope,' she said, and she meant it.

Having called DataTrak only to be told that Pam Shine was away ill, Dunbar made the decision to visit her at home. Professionally and rationally, he had weighed up all the arguments about keeping this last part of his investigation from the McMasters. They didn't need to know, he'd concluded: it was a loose end, an irritation that he'd like to clear up quietly and with minimal fuss. There was probably nothing in it, anyway.

He pulled the car to a halt outside her house. Two cars were parked in the drive – a new Mondeo and an old BMW. It could be any house in any close, nothing to differentiate it or make it stand out. He was being stupid, wasting his time, but he persisted.

Pam opened the front door almost immediately, as if she'd been expecting him. He showed his warrant card and she let him in without any question. She was dressed in baggy jeans – disguising, he thought unkindly, a very fat arse – and a pale blue T-shirt with a logo which said Cats are Purrfect. They went into her neat lounge and she sat down before he did.

'Do you know why I'm here?' he had to ask, so calmly had she dealt with his arrival.

'No idea,' she replied innocently.

'I've been investigating a very nasty case of victimisation, a case that involves your boss, Mr McMaster. He's been getting a lot of unpleasant phone calls and faxes.'

She looked straight at him without her expression changing. 'I know.'

'You know about this?' he said, amazed at how she was admitting the information so casually.

'Well, not the faxes, but I'd taken some calls at work.'

'And what did you do about it?'

'Nothing much. To be honest, I didn't take it very seriously. It was some nutter messing around, and I didn't think it was

232

important enough to worry Skip with. Whoever it was stopped, anyway.'

Dunbar took out his notebook and wrote something in it. 'Can you recall when this was?'

'Not exactly. But it was shortly after Skip arrived in London. And I did tell someone about it.'

'Who?'

'Michael Lensman. I worked for him before Skip came in.'

'Yes, I know Mr Lensman,' he said impatiently. 'So what you're telling me is that you took these abusive calls for Mr McMaster and never said a word to him about them. Isn't that a bit odd?'

She shrugged and tucked her chin into her neck. 'I'm his assistant. That's what I do.'

Dunbar was almost lost for words. 'Do you know Daniel Retzer?'

Pam rolled her eyes upwards. 'Oh, yes. He's one of Jean's boys.'

'Have you spoken to him recently?'

'No. Not since Don's funeral. Why should I have?'

Dunbar exhaled deeply. 'Yesterday we found out that it was Daniel who'd been doing all this. He's admitted it. He says he didn't have any help, but I think he's lying. I think someone at DataTrak gave him the McMasters' new phone numbers, maybe even the old ones too. I think he had inside information. Do you know anything about that?' He was getting too angry and calmed himself with regular breathing through his nose.

'Can't help you there.' A stone wall.

'Mr McMaster told me that you arranged for the new numbers to be issued by BT. Is that correct?'

'Yes. Is there a problem with that?'

'There might be, if you subsequently gave them out to Daniel.'

Pam was unmoved by this accusation. 'But I didn't. They didn't give me the numbers, and I didn't ask for them. Skip was very keen to keep them secret. Said there's been a lot of calls for the old tenants, something like that.'

'But somehow Daniel got hold of them. How do you explain that?'

'I can't. Except . . . well, after Teri's problems, when Skip was working from home, he had to give out his number. Lots of people had it then.'

Dunbar chewed his lip, exasperated by her performance. 'You know, you could have saved a lot of grief if you'd volunteered this information earlier. You obviously know what they've been through. With your help, we could have avoided that.'

'Maybe, maybe not,' she said defiantly. 'In any event, it's not my fault. I did what I thought was right. How was I meant to know it would all end up like this?'

He shook his head in frustration. 'I'm not happy about this, not at all happy. I'm going to go back to the station and think about what you've told me and, in all likelihood, I'm going to be coming back to see you.'

'Suit yourself. I'm not going anywhere.'

'And that reminds me,' he said. 'They told me you were ill. You don't look it to me.'

'Are you a doctor as well, then?'

Dunbar got up and went to the front door. 'You'll be hearing from me,' he said sternly as he stepped out.

'I expect I will,' Pam replied, and there was something in that remark which unnerved him.

From Pam's house Dunbar drove straight to Wimbledon. He called ahead to warn Michael that he was on his way – 'Nothing to worry about, just the final loose ends' – and arrived by five o'clock. Michael was ready for him.

'You needn't worry about the fingerprints, if you haven't already done them,' Dunbar said as they drank tea. 'It's all sorted. We have our man.'

'That must be a great relief. A man, you say – who was it?'

'Daniel Retzer. You know, the younger boy?'

'God, I'd never have believed that in a million years. Just goes to show what can happen to the mind under stress.'

234

'Precisely,' Dunbar said impatiently. 'Look, there's one thing that's bothering me. I've just been to see Pam Shine.'

'Oh,' Michael said with some feeling.

'Do you remember her telling you about some calls she fielded for Mr McMaster? She claims she told you about them.'

Michael reddened. 'God, yes, that's right. She did mention it to me, but I forgot all about it. I told her to talk to Skip. Sorry – is that important?'

'I don't know, to be honest. I'll be blunt with you – I have this feeling that somehow Pam's involved, that she was part of Daniel's plan, but I don't see how.'

'I know Pam pretty well, and I think what you're saying is unlikely. She's a good girl – very diligent, straight as an arrow. It's an unholy alliance if it's true, that's for sure.'

'Maybe, but stranger things happen. Something's not quite right there.'

Michael spoke up reluctantly. 'Look, if I tell you this, I'd like it to go no further.' Dunbar nodded to encourage him. 'Pam's been through a difficult time – haven't we all? But she's recently found out that there's a plan to make her redundant. She came to see me about it in a bit of a lather, and I had to calm her down. I thought I had done. But if you've picked up bad vibes from your visit, that's probably the reason. She loves her job, but she's less than wild about Skip, if you know what I mean.'

'I think I do. That would explain a lot. Don't worry, I'll keep your confidence, and I appreciate you telling me. I'm probably seeing things that aren't there. It's an occupational hazard.' Dunbar laughed at himself. 'I'll see myself out, and thanks again.'

He got back into his car and decided to call it a day. He'd been chasing shadows and he felt distinctly foolish; he had his man, he'd sorted the problem, and it was time to go and have a drink. They could all do without him now.

TWENTY-NINE

Skip was jolted out of sleep by a shout, a single word: 'No!' He turned on his light and looked at Teri, who was lying on her back with her eyes wide open, her hair glistening with sweat.

'Teri?' he said softly. If she'd heard him it didn't register on her face. 'Teri, are you OK?' He put his hand on her shoulder.

She blinked once, lazily, but her expression didn't change. 'Bad dream,' she said, as if part of her were still in it. Her lips barely moved.

Skip supported himself on one elbow and stroked her head. 'It's all gone now,' he said to reassure her.

'Yes, all gone,' she replied distantly.

'Can I get you anything? Shall I make some tea?'

'Tea. Yes, tea.'

She was frightening him, the way she responded without any real interaction. He slipped out of bed, his legs still weak from the shock of being awakened so abruptly, and went downstairs to the kitchen. It was five-thirty in the morning and, unusually, Skip was finding it difficult to shrug off his exhaustion. He could only sleep lightly, all the time conscious of the fragile body next to him, dark thoughts constantly invading to deny him proper rest. He'd never felt this weary. Worrying as that was, he was more concerned about Teri: both her physical and mental condition suggested wounds that would only heal very slowly. He cursed himself for his inability to expedite the process.

He dragged himself through the routine of making herbal tea and set out a little pile of tablets for her on a dish. The tray shook and rattled in his hands as he carried it back up the stairs. When he came into the bedroom Teri hadn't moved at all; she stared at the ceiling with her cracked lips slightly parted.

'Here we are,' he said as he laid the tray on the bed next to her. He placed her mug and pills on the bedside table. 'Come on, let's get you comfortable.' He put one hand behind her damp head and tried to pull her up so that he could rearrange the pillows, but she was a dead weight and gave him no help. He had to hook both his hands under her arms to lift her up.

When she was sitting more or less upright she looked at him with terror in her eyes. It was as if she had never seen him before and had no idea of what he was doing there. Skip tried to ignore it. 'Looks like it's going to be a fine day,' he said breezily. 'We should go out later for a drive or something. What do you say?'

Again, there was no reaction. Skip dropped his head in anguish and frustration and rubbed his hands on his knees. 'I want to go home,' Teri said, her voice fractured and barely audible.

His head jerked up. 'Go home? But you are home.'

'No, real home.'

'You mean back to the States?'

'Yes. Now.' Their eyes met and Skip could see that this was definitive, ineluctable. In a way he was encouraged; at least she was consciously making decisions.

He thought about how to deal with it. 'I guess . . . well, I guess it wouldn't be such a bad idea. You could go stay with your parents, and they could look after you a whole lot better than I can.'

'Today. I can't stay here a moment longer.'

He would do anything, approve any course of action, which would serve to help her recovery, and this was a small price to pay for their peace of mind. 'You sure you're strong enough for the trip?'

'Today, Skip. I have to go.' Teri sat up and got out of bed. 'I'm going to pack a few things. You get on to the airline and book a flight.'

237

Behind her frailty there was a determination which warmed him. He didn't want her to go, and he didn't want to feel relieved that she would, but he knew it was for the best. 'OK,' he agreed. 'As long as you're sure.'

'Totally,' she said firmly, and went off to the bathroom.

By six-fifteen Skip had made all the arrangements, booking a midday flight to Cleveland and calling her parents. Not once had Teri suggested that he go with her, and he'd not had the strength to ask himself. After showering, she had thrown some clothes into an overnight bag and now sat on the bed with a fresh mug of tea. Her face was not made up, the skin almost pellucid.

The silence was threatening and he needed to break it. 'We'll get through this,' he said.

'Will we?' she replied casually, as if it no longer mattered.

'Yes, we will. You'll get your strength back and we'll recover. It's just time, Teri, that's all. You'll see.'

She looked at him disdainfully, then lowered her eyes. 'How much time, Skip? A year, a decade, for ever? It's all bull. I feel crippled, you know? Do cripples ever walk again? Maybe in the Bible, but not in the real world.'

'But what's the point if there's no hope? You must have hope.'

'Why? We'd hoped for this child and it was snatched away from us. What's left to hope for?'

'Us. Our future. That's what it's all about.'

'I don't want to talk about that. I don't even want to think about it. Sorry, but that's how it is.'

Skip was on the verge of saying something when they heard someone at the front door. He shook his head and went downstairs.

Pam was standing on the doorstep. She was wearing jeans, trainers and a leather jacket, and was holding a long canvas bag. Her face was flushed and her eyes were red.

'Oh,' Skip said. 'Gee, this is kind of early for a social call.'

'We need to talk,' Pam said firmly. 'You, me and Teri.'

'Er, this is kind of an inappropriate time. Teri's still pretty weak. Can it wait?'

'Afraid not,' she said as she pushed past him into the house. Skip closed the door and followed her as she found her way into the kitchen. 'Where is she?'

'Upstairs.'

'Let's go and see her.'

'Really, Pam . . .' Skip started to say, but she was already on the stairs before he could stop her. 'Pam,' he called after her as she ascended. 'Wait.'

Pam got to the bedroom door and looked in to see Teri standing by the bed. She walked in, closely followed by Skip. 'Both of you, sit on the bed,' Pam said, menace in her voice.

'Pam, what the heck's going on here?' Skip asked, but he did as she'd said, nodding at Teri to get her to sit down too.

Pam closed the door and leant against it. She raised the canvas bag and unzipped it, never taking her eyes off them. She put her hand in and pulled out a shotgun, dropping the bag to the floor.

'Now that I have your attention,' she said, holding the gun in both hands and aiming it in their direction. She braced herself more firmly against the door.

'Oh God,' Skip said. 'Put that away, Pam. What are you playing at?'

'You two,' she began. 'You two – you've got a lot to answer for.' The weight of the weapon made her arms shake a little.

Skip kept an even tone with her. 'Pam, this isn't good. Put the gun down and we can talk.' He looked at Teri, who appeared almost bored by the scene.

'I just needed to tell you, so you'll understand,' Pam went on. 'You use people up. When they're no use to you any more – or they're too expensive – you throw them away.' She shouted angrily. 'Isn't that right?'

'No, no, that's not right, Pam. I don't know where you're coming from. We haven't harmed anyone. What's this all about?'

'Christ, you're so thick. Do I have to write it down for you? Don Retzer, Michael Lensman, me, all the others you

239

want to fire. Is that enough or should I go on?'

Skip didn't fully understand, but he wasn't about to argue with her. 'I can't operate like this, Pam. Just give me the gun and we can talk over your problems.'

She jerked the gun upwards to show she was still in control. 'Michael and I had something. You didn't know that, did you? We were a team. It was so right, and then you came along and you tore us apart. I can't accept that, Skip. It's unfair. You have to pay – and so does she.' She waved the gun at Teri. The movement worried Skip, and he sought to distract her.

'So what do you propose doing, Pam?' he asked. 'Are you going to shoot us?'

'It's on my mind. Not yet, though. You should suffer first, just like we have. You need to feel it too.' Pam adjusted her position and, seeing his chance, Skip lunged from the end of the bed towards her. She looked up to see him squaring up in front of her.

The shot hit him in the chest and knocked him all the way back so that his calves hit the bed and he flipped backwards, almost somersaulting before he collapsed, blood draining from him on to the duvet. The blast deafened Pam so that she could hear nothing but its echo in her ears. She blinked and turned to face Teri. Teri sat motionless, her face like a mask. They glared at each other. Then Pam inhaled deeply, closed her eyes and pulled the trigger again. Teri was thrown back against the bedhead, and her body slid down slowly, cracking at the waist. Her eyes remained open, never releasing Pam from her stare until her head hit the pillow.

Pam's knees gave way and she fell awkwardly to the floor, letting the gun drop by her side. Though she didn't know it, she was smiling.

THIRTY

'I felt I owed you an explanation,' Dunbar said. 'I'd have come sooner, but things have been rather hectic.'

Michael sat opposite him in the sitting room. A week had passed since Pam Shine had been charged with the murders of Skip and Teri McMaster. Annie and Holly were still away, though Michael was confident they would return soon. The phone calls were longer, less confrontational; the physical distance between them was analgesic. Their lives, he hoped, would return to normality, but a necessarily different brand of normality. He had accepted that, as he knew she would. He was grateful that this scene was not taking place with them in the house; it would have been too painful.

'You don't need to apologise,' Michael said.

'In a way I do. I got it all wrong. I knew there was a link between you and Pam, but I never worked out what it was.'

'Meaning?'

'She was infatuated. She's told us a hundred times about her love for you, almost a kind of worship, and how devastated she was when you were fired. As long as you were there in the office, close to her every day, things were fine. By all accounts she had a happy marriage. He's quite a decent bloke, her husband. He's completely stunned by all this, of course. Didn't have a clue. Home life was completely normal. But Pam had this . . . this thing, and it grew out of all proportion.'

'But why didn't she say anything? I mean, I never got that impression.'

'She wouldn't have wanted to. As long as she said nothing she could pretend that you had a special relationship. She convinced herself that you felt the same about her, and nothing needed to be said. When you left it all began to fall apart, and she had to find someone to blame. The McMasters were in the frame. She didn't need to look any further.'

'But murdering them? That's a little extreme, isn't it?'

'I'd have to agree with that. I'm not entirely sure she meant to do it. She was so confused, so devastated, that all reason left her. But the funny thing is, she hasn't shown any remorse. It's as if she's quite prepared to take her punishment and that nothing else matters now.'

Michael shook his head in disbelief. 'How did she get a gun?'

'A mate of her husband's. He keeps a shotgun in the garage. Of course, it's meant to be locked up but it wasn't. He made it pretty easy for her.'

'And all this was on account of me? That's the thing I find hardest to swallow.'

'I wouldn't torture yourself with that. If it hadn't been you it might have been someone else. She's a very sick woman. This was an obsession, and there's no accounting for the behaviour of the obsessive.' Dunbar paused. 'I should tell you – she's asked to see you.'

Michael grimaced. 'You think I should?'

'Absolutely not. There's no reason to, and it might spark off something else. She needs a lot of specialist help, and I don't think a visit from you would do much good.'

'Thank God for that.'

'You know, she did give the phone numbers to Daniel. She's admitted that, but she claims she didn't have a clue why he wanted them. She says he gave her some plausible story and she didn't see any harm. I'm inclined to believe her.'

'It hardly matters now, does it? Oh, that sounds so callous. Sorry.'

Dunbar raised his eyebrows and smiled. 'Don't worry about it. Everyone's judgement has been screwed up by this one. When I last came to see you – after I'd seen Pam – I knew something was up. I think I told you as much, but you gave me a perfectly reasonable explanation for it all. I left it at that, and I shouldn't have done. Two lives have been lost as a result.'

'I think you're being a bit harsh on yourself. I thought I knew Pam pretty well and I never picked up on any of this. It beggars belief.' Michael wiped his palms on his trousers, as if to rub away all traces of what had happened. 'So what's the next step?'

'Psychiatric evaluation, a lot of technical stuff I don't really understand, and then we see what's left. She's going to go away for a long time.'

Michael spent some time assimilating this. He thought of Pam in the office, always so cheerful and accommodating, her birthday cards and the presents she brought back from her holidays, the way she fussed over his appearance and tried her hardest to ingratiate herself with him. It was another person he was thinking of, not the woman who had coldly blown away two innocent people. What could have driven her to such a point? He recalled their final meeting, when she'd been so distraught, and how she'd miraculously recovered her poise – was that when she had decided? Was his rejection, however softly delivered, the final straw? Could she see no other way out? His ears sang with the touch of guilt.

'I should have known,' he said quietly.

'We all should have known,' Dunbar replied.

'Will you be needing me for anything else? I'm happy to help. I feel a kind of obligation on this one.'

'I hope not. If she pleads guilty, as I'm sure she will, it'll all be over. You won't need to be involved.'

'Well, if I can, I'd like to.'

Michael stood on the doorstep and waved at Dunbar as he drove off, as if he was bidding farewell to a significant part of his life. Relieved, he waited a long time before going back inside.

Annie watched in amazement as Michael loaded the dishwasher after dinner. She sat at the kitchen table, a glass of white wine freshly charged, picking at a bunch of grapes and trying to restrain her unnatural urge to do something. She always felt guilty when she wasn't working.

The house was spotless, with flowers everywhere. He'd made a big effort to mark their return and, against her better judgement, it had made its mark; she felt sorry for him and wanted peace more than anything else. Whatever he'd done, however he'd treated her and Holly, Annie still needed him and had missed his company desperately. Their reunion was stilted and forcibly jolly, both realising that they were starting again and mustn't push things too quickly. The serious talk could wait, if it had to come at all.

Michael tossed a dishcloth into the sink and delivered two cups of coffee to the table, then sat down opposite her. He grinned, conscious of the impression he was making, and took a sip of wine. 'I've missed you,' he said. 'But at least I've had the chance to find out how all these appliances work, so it hasn't been a complete waste of time.'

'Good. No more excuses.'

'No,' he replied wistfully, as if he was reading much more into what she'd said.

'You're a clot, you know that.'

'So I've been told.'

'I cannot understand how you couldn't have noticed what Pam felt about you. God, it was obvious enough to me.'

'Ah, but you're a woman. You've got these famous intuitions and insights that men don't have. I've read *Good Housekeeping* – I know all about it.'

'It beats me why she was so infatuated.'

'Thanks,' he said, and raised his glass to her.

'I suppose there'll be some ramifications at DataTrak from all this,' Annie said, wanting to get the conversation on to more neutral territory.

'I sincerely hope so. When you look at the trail of devastation they've left behind them, something's got to be done. But that's not my concern any more. Let them get on with it.'

'So what is your concern?' she asked in spite of herself.

'Right now, us. Nothing else matters. If one good thing

has come out of all this, it's the fact that I've got my priorities in order. I've finally worked out what's important. I wish there'd been an easier way, but . . .'

'It wasn't your fault,' she said softly. 'We all chipped in. No one knows how these things are going to affect us, and how we're going to react. We all carry some of the blame.'

'Maybe. But I haven't dealt with things very well, and it's left me feeling a little inadequate. I feel as if I've let everybody down, especially you and Holly. I intend to make that up to you.'

'Now you're being silly,' Annie chided. 'We're going to get over this, together. That's the point. And that's what I've learnt. Starting today, now, we're going to pull together, and not against each other.'

'Good plan. I'll vote for that.'

They were silent then, but it was a comfortable silence. They both knew what the other was thinking, and how much there was that should never be disclosed. Already there was a tacit understanding of the boundaries, a sense of how they would go forward without inflicting too much pain on the other. Annie closed her hand on his and squeezed it gently.

'I love you, Michael,' she said.

'And I love you, too.'

'Well then, that's all that matters.'

In her secure hospital room Pam Shine was sitting fully clothed on the bed. She couldn't sleep any more, despite the long hours of evaluation and interviews which had left her drained. Her head was spinning and she needed to think.

Soon they would be back to give her more pills and check on her health, but that didn't worry her. They could fill her up with drugs which were meant to bend her mind, but they were powerless against what she had. They treated her like a moron and that was fine too; what she had done required no further explanation. It was simple and pure, just and logical. Nothing else mattered. She'd told them her story a hundred times and it never changed.

She picked up a pad of paper and a pencil they had given

her. Deliberately she started to write neatly across the page, repeating the same short sentence until her hand cramped:

I love you Michael